THE UNDEAD DAY SEVEN

RR HAYWOOD

RR Haywood

Cover design and artwork by Eduardo Garay Arnaldos

Created with Vellum

The Undead

DAY SEVEN

rrhaywood.com

CHAPTER ONE

Day Seven

Thursday

High above the surface of the Earth, water vapour forms in the troposphere and white clouds expand and quickly cast shadows over the already darkening land. Those clouds form and move with the wind and soon cover the once vibrant city of London.

The already grim-looking streets and buildings appear more despondent, as long shadows form over the bloodstains and the rotting corpses that litter the ground. The abnormally high temperatures of the last week have scorched this normally wet land. Swarms of flies and insects drift around the streets, moving from corpse to corpse, laying eggs. Those eggs soon hatch in the perfect breeding ground, and the corpses look alive as thousands of fat, white maggots writhe and burrow their way through the skin. The first drops of rainfall drop through the warm air to land on the windscreen of the Saxon Armoured Personnel Carrier driving through those grim city streets back to Tower Bridge.

By the time the Saxon enters the Bridge, sheets of rain are covering the surface with spray. Visibility is instantly reduced and the Saxon slows to a stop. One by one, the men climb out from the vehicle and stand under the purifying downpour, letting the water cleanse them from the dirt of battle. Crimson pools form at their feet as the blood is sluiced from their skin and clothes. They hold their heads back, open-mouthed, and drink the cascading, cool water. They wipe their hands, pull fingers through their hair, and then wring their clothes out, to rid themselves of the filth and gore. The three losses they suffered are heavy on their minds and hearts, and their tears blend with the rain as they cry silently. Now they can grieve and mourn those losses. They know more hardship awaits them, and later there will not be time for mourning.

Sarah stands close to the doors of the Saxon, sensing the bond between these men and realising this experience is not hers to share. She watches Howie closely, and can already see the change in her brother. The goofy, playful, sweet-natured man has been replaced by a hardened warrior. She doesn't know how he came to be here or what happened along the way, or why the men follow him, but she saw the reaction Howie had to the dying lad and felt the emotion in all of them as they watched him die.

Sarah held Howie as he wept in the back of the vehicle, and she looked around to see them all with tear-filled eyes; and that small man called Dave ... he stayed by her side throughout the battle back to the Saxon, and the way he moved was extraordinary. It's clear to Sarah that there's a deep connection between her brother and Dave.

Now, standing at the back of the vehicle, arms crossed and sheltering from the rain, she watches them as they stand in silence, letting the rain pour down on them.

'What the fuck happened, Dave?' Howie asks.

'I don't know, Mr. Howie.'

'We were doing so well,' Howie says, shaking his head. 'I know we lost one on the way in, but I thought we'd all be slaughtered – there were so many of them.'

Dave nods as Howie speaks.

'Why did they suddenly stop?'

'I don't know.'

'And what happened to Darren? He just charged them on his own, and I told McKinney to keep an eye on him and stay close ... and now he's dead,' Howie said, holding his hands to his forehead.

'It's not your fault, Mr. Howie, some people just react that way,' Dave replied, with a rare troubled look on his face.

'No, that was something else, mate,' Howie shakes his head. 'It was as if he was possessed or something. I know he'd been feeling rough, but he fought well, he was a brave lad, and to end like that was awful. Poor McKinney, did you know his mother died just a few months ago? He told me, when we were in the hospital. He said he hated hospitals because they reminded him of when his mother was sick. I took him to his death for my own gain; I led them both into it and now they're gone.'

'Something wasn't right with Darren,' Dave says, quietly.

'Yeah, he was sick and we took him into that fight,' Howie snaps back.

'No, I mean something wasn't *right* with him,' Dave replies, his voice trailing off.

'What does that mean?'

'I don't know. He was reckless and taking stupid risks, and he hadn't fought like that before, he kept putting himself at risk and getting away with it.'

'We all put ourselves at risk, it was a monumentally stupid thing to do ...'

'No, they had chances to take him, I took a couple out, but I saw them holding back.'

'What do you mean?' Howie says.

Dave shrugs and shakes his head.

'They could have had him, they had chances, the way he was overextending himself and lunging too far forward.'

'Dave, what are you saying?' Howie asks, concerned at the tone of his friend's voice.

'You said that he was sick ...'

'Yeah, well, we knew he was sick,' Howie says, confused.

'He looked sick and he said he felt sick, then he started going crazy and they were holding back on him.'

'Maybe they were holding back on all of us? I mean, they stopped and moved back, didn't they ... no, they certainly weren't holding back on me.'

'That's what I mean, they took one of Big Chris's men down, and they took McKinney down in seconds, so why not Darren?'

'They did take him ...' Howie starts to say.

'Did they? I didn't see it. I saw him being taken by them, but I didn't see them bite or attack him, they just enveloped him and he was gone ... and when he charged and attacked them, they didn't react, not one of them went for him, but when McKinney got to him they had him instantly.'

'Dave ...' Howie says, shaking his head. 'Spit it out, mate.'

'I don't know, but it's like they didn't want to take him. Think, Mr. Howie. I know you were upset about McKinney, but you saw it, you were the closest to them,' Dave says firmly.

Howie looks down to the water, thinking back to just a short time ago. Darren had become very strange, screaming abuse at the undead and goading them to fight him; he *did* charge at them, and he can't remember Darren being attacked.

He clearly remembers seeing McKinney on the ground with zombies biting into him, and then Howie was there with his axe, knocking them back.

'I didn't see Darren being attacked, but that doesn't mean he wasn't,' Howie says.

'They were both there at the front. Darren was attacking them, and McKinney was trying to stop him, we all saw that, so why kill McKinney and not Darren? I ran to them and couldn't see Darren, he was gone,' Dave says.

'Is this a private conversation?' Big Chris asks as he walks up to them.

'Chris, did you see what happened to Darren?' Howie enquires.

'Those things had him,' Chris answers, confused at the question.

'What did you see, Chris?' Howie questions, staring hard at the big man as Malcolm and Clarence walk over to them.

'Lads, come over here,' Howie calls out to the rest, and they start drifting closer until they're all standing round Howie and Dave in the pouring rain.

Sarah moves closer, watching the group and the serious expression on her brother's face.

'Listen, I'm sorry for what happened back there, both of our groups lost people, and watching McKinney die like that was truly awful.' Howie watches as the recruits' eyes drop down, fresh tears falling.

'I know it's painful, but did anyone see what happened to Smithy?' Howie instantly regrets using the nickname they had all used for Darren.

'He went fucking nuts and got McKinney killed,' Cookey spits out with a flash of anger, and Howie watches a few of them nod in agreement.

'We need to think about this clearly. He was sick right? Then he felt better and then he was laughing and shouting as we fought. I haven't seen him do that before, but you know him better ...'

'No, he never did anything like that before,' Blowers answers.

'Right at the end, when he charged them on his own, what did you see?' Howie presses them.

'Sir, he ran forward screaming, then he started attacking them; they didn't react though. They just stood there and took it, then McKinney tried to pull him back and he got pushed off, then he tried again and Darren knocked him down,' Jamie says. 'Then they went for McKinney and Darren got pulled in.'

The rest of the group all stare at him and he blushes from the sudden attention.

'Jamie ... you saw all of this?' Howie asks.

'Yes, Mr. Howie. They didn't bite him or anything, they just grabbed him and he was gone.'

'Did anyone see Darren getting bitten?' Howie asks the group.

'What's this about, Howie?' Chris asks, with a serious expression.

'Dave says that Darren was fighting recklessly, putting himself at risk, but those things didn't go for him, they were holding back.'

'You think he's one of them?' Malcolm finally voices the unspoken thoughts.

'I don't know, but he was sick, then he went nuts, and they didn't go for him,' Howie shrugs.

'Fuck me ...' Blowers says, reeling from the idea.

'No way,' Tucker adds.

'He stopped firing on that fucking GPMG at the hospital too,' Blowers suddenly adds.

'He did what?' Chris asks, turning on Blowers.

'While you lot were inside, we had a massive contact at the front, Darren was on the GPMG and just froze up. I had to drag him down to take over.'

'But anyone infected just goes down ... I've seen it too many times,' Clarence rumbles.

'It's a possibility, but I don't know how. He hadn't been bitten or scratched ... that I saw,' Howie says.

'So, worst case scenario, he's one of them?' Chris asks.

'We have to consider it,' Dave says firmly. They stand in silence, absorbing the idea and its implications.

'So ... if he *is* one of them, does that mean anything to us?' Cookey asks.

'Yes,' replies Dave.

'He knows our numbers, strengths, where we're heading, the route we took, the access and egress points ...' Chris says.

'So why aren't they attacking?' Blowers asks.

'I don't know, they stopped back there and just let us go,' Howie says.

'Maybe they stopped so Darren would go for them,' Dave adds.

'That would be suggesting it has some form of intelligence,' said Malcolm.

'They knew where we were going, they massed in the exact place we were heading for, and if Darren was one of them, that explains how they knew where we were going,' Howie theorised. 'Which shows a form of intelligence.'

'If they have intelligence, then they pulled back as a tactic – they used strategy to take what they wanted,' Chris says.

'What for? Why would they want Darren?' Tucker asks, trying to keep up.

'If he was the only one infected, then it would have to be him,' Howie says.

'This is fucking ridiculous,' Nick Hewitt suddenly adds. 'They're just fucking, mindless zombies, that's all. They can't plan or make tactics, they were walking off the fucking Bridge, for God's sake.'

'It makes sense – perfect sense,' Sarah cuts in, as they all turn to stare at her.

'Those things were outside before you came, but nowhere near the numbers they are now; they must have known where you were going and flooded the area, ready for you, and, if they knew that lad was infected, then why *not* take him – he's one of theirs,' she continues.

'They came for us at the services, they sent loads after us, and those people said they had gone unnoticed before we arrived, and we already said it was like we were being targeted,' affirms Howie.

'Then they know about *our* place,' Chris adds.

'Your place?' Sarah asks.

'They've rigged up a sort of commune a few miles out, there's about two thousand survivors there,' Howie explains.

'So ... if this Darren knows about the commune, are they safe?' Sarah asks.

'We left them alone and didn't go in for the mass killing, like these boys here,' Chris says.

'We have to accept that they are able to change, we've seen them change at night, and now during the day too ... they can get faster when it suits them,' Howie says.

'Howie,' Sarah says urgently, causing them all to turn and look at her. She is staring at the Bridge. They follow her gaze and look down to see the entire road blocked with undead, a solid and mighty gathering, assembled where the Bridge meets the road.

'Fuck me, they did that quietly,' Chris mutters.

'They're just standing, watching ...' Cookey says. One of them takes a few steps forward and comes to a stop, just over the Bridge line; a symbolic passing of the threshold.

'That's Darren,' Dave says quietly, but loud enough for everyone to hear.

'All the weapons are in the vehicle,' Howie murmurs.

'Dave, are you sure that's Darren?'

'Yes,' Dave replies.

'It is Darren,' Jamie says, with confidence.

'Look at the way they're formed up, perfectly spaced,' Malcolm says, stepping forward to peer through the rain. Darren takes another few steps forward.

'What's he want?' Tucker asks with fear in his voice.

'Fuck it, I'll go and ask him,' Howie says angrily, and starts striding towards Darren as the rest of the group follow in his wake.

'Wait there, I'll go on my own,' Howie calls back, as Dave joins him at his side.

'Okay, Mr. Howie,' Dave says, ignoring him.

'No point asking you again, is there?'

'Not really,' Dave answers. They walk down the Bridge, through the rain, drawing closer to Darren, seeing the perfect lines and spaces between the undead massed before them. All of them have their heads erect as they watch the small, advancing group.

Howie and Dave halt a few steps away from Darren and they all observe one another. Darren looks pale and drawn, his normally ruddy complexion already gone, and the skin pulled tight across his face. He looks almost normal, other than that – apart from the red, bloodshot eyes that stare intently at Howie.

'Mr. Howie ...' Darren says with a sneer, drawing the sound out.

'Nice to see you too, Darren,' Howie replies casually. 'How are you, mate?'

'Great, better than ever,' Darren replies quickly, with a strong voice.

'You don't look it mate, you look rough.'

'No, Mr. Howie,' he replies, drawing the sound of his name out again. 'I feel great, fucking wonderful,' he adds, forcefully.

'Darren, you're infected, mate – but you're still talking ... maybe it's not too late. We've got that doctor back in the commune and all that equipment now. If you're the first that can communicate with them and tell them how it is, they might be able to help,' Howie says.

'Spare me the goody speech, Mr. Howie; I don't need your fucking help. I think I have enough at the moment,' Darren smiles and motions towards the huge horde massed behind him.

'So, what do you want then, mate?' Howie asks.

'You.'

'Me? What for?' Howie replies.

'All of you, I want all of you and especially you,' Darren stares at Howie.

'What for, Darren?' Howie asks.

'I want you to fucking die. I'm going to kill you all slowly and turn you and I'll keep a part of you alive, so you know what's happening when you come back,' Darren says, grinning menacingly.

'Why, Darren?' Howie asks, forcing himself to keep his tone steady, despite the anger rising inside him.

'You have taken so many of my kind down, too many, but the tide has turned, Mr. Howie, oh yes. I've got an army now, and not just a bunch of fucking idiots chasing you 'round the country.'

'Your kind? Darren, listen to yourself, you were part of this just a couple of hours ago, you killed them, just as we did. They took our lives and our families and everything we loved, they are evil, Darren, and you don't have to be part of them. Come back with us, mate.'

'No, I am not with you or your ragtag bunch of misfits. I killed them because I followed you. They only kill them because of you. Just because they took your parents, oh, poor Howie lost his parents and now they're zombies, poor Howie is all alone so he decides to kill every living thing to try and rescue his whore sister,' Darren laughs as he shouts.

'His fucking whore sister, dirty fucking sister. He killed everything and risked the lives of everyone to rescue his dirty, fucking cunt of a sister just because his parents died.'

An icy hand grips Howie inside but he remains motionless, watching Darren shout and laugh as he starts to walk back and forth between Howie and the massed zombie mob behind him.

'Oh look, here come Howie's heroes, a shambling fucking mess, look at them,' Darren laughs, as Howie turns to see the rest of the group walking down to stand behind Howie and Dave.

'Oh no, Howie's heroes have come to get me, oh no, someone save me, maybe your dirty, cunt, whore, slut, sister will come and rescue you, Howie,' Darren screams out.

Howie remains still, and despite the growing rage inside of him, he keeps his face neutral. The rest pick up on Howie's lack of reaction and remain quiet.

'Oh ... hi Jamie,' Darren waves at the quiet lad. 'Have you fucked Dave up the arse yet? You know you want to ... oh, and there's Tucker the fat fucker. Hey Tucker, how many pies have you eaten yet, you fat, roly-poly cunt. Ha! That's fucking funny – Tucker the fat fucker,' Darren throws his head back and laughs.

Then he suddenly turns back to the undead and shouts:

'LAUGH!' and thousands of undead voices start laughing hard.

Darren spins back to face Howie and the group, smiling as the forced laughter erupts from behind him. He slowly raises his hand and clicks his fingers; the laughing stops instantly.

'Oh, and there's Nick – thick cunt who can't read or write ... can you, Nick? You never got past 'Spot Goes To The Beach' did you mate? Still playing with the *Join the Dots* Books, eh, Nick?'

'Yes, Darren,' Nick replies quietly.

'Yes, Darren,' Darren mimics Nick, in a high-pitched voice.

'And then there's Blowers and Cookey, what a pair of utter cunts, fucking playing at soldiers ... yes, Mr. Howie, and no, Mr. Howie, and can I suck your cock, Mr. Howie?' Darren shouts as he walks back and forth, spittle flying from his mouth. Then he stops and stares directly at Dave.

'Hello, Dave,' Darren says with a mock friendly tone. 'How are you Dave?'

Dave remains void of expression, his cold, hard eyes staring directly at Darren.

'Oh ... are we playing the staring game, Dave? Okay mate, let's do that.' Darren takes a step forward and stares hard into Dave's eyes.

Dave doesn't flinch, he doesn't move a muscle, and no hint of emotion escapes his cold eyes.

'You are a fucking little runt,' Darren explodes in fury as Dave stares back without moving.

'You just want to fuck Howie up the arse – you fucking fag. You want to do a reach around with Howie while his dirty cunt sister licks your arse.' Darren turns and starts thrusting his pelvis back and forth, while stretching one arm out.

'That's fucking brilliant,' Howie bursts out laughing, as Darren spins around to face him. Howie starts applauding him, while laughing.

'Very good mate, have you finished?' Howie asks.

'Don't fucking laugh at me, you cunt. I've got an army and I will not be laughed at!' Darren screams and clicks his fingers.

The massive horde all take a step forward, perfectly in time, and stamp their feet down, which booms out in the quiet air.

'Very impressive, mate,' Howie smiles. 'Can you make them dance too?'

'I don't think you should be mocking me, Mr. Howie,' Darren says through gritted teeth.

'What do you think, Dave, should we be taking Darren seriously?' Howie asks.

'No, Mr. Howie, I don't think we should,' Dave replies.

'But he has got such a big army behind him though, what do you think, lads? Should we be taking Darren and his army seriously?' Howie calls out behind him.

'I think they look a bit gay,' Cookey replies.

'You'd know,' Blowers replies, quick as a flash. 'Have they set off your gaydar?'

'Blowers, it's time you stopped hiding behind the gay jokes and came out, mate,' Cookey retorts.

'You want to hide behind *me,* that's for sure,' Blowers replies, to a few sniggers, and Howie smiles inside.

'Oi ... Tucker, have you got any *mince* pies, I think Blowers wants one,' Cookey says, laughing.

'Hey Darren, do you get to choose the ones you want to bum?' Nick shouts out to more sniggers, and Howie watches Darren's face grow darker.

'Chris, did you ever see such an impressive army, mate?' Howie asks, drawing the big man into the conversation.

'Oh no, they're the biggest and bestest I ever did see,' Chris replies, scathingly.

'And the uniform is the best we've seen yet,' Malcolm adds. Darren takes a sudden step forward with his fists clenched; the group drops the laughing and takes a step towards him, which, in turn, makes the massive horde take another step forward.

Howie and Darren lock eyes, both breathing hard and staring with fixed intent.

'You come for me, Darren. I've killed many of them and I won't stop. I'll fucking slaughter every single one of them that I can find, so you come for me and see what happens, mate,' Howie says, quietly.

'Oh, I will, Mr. Howie, and I'll turn every person I can find and ... along the way, I will leave this land ravaged and destroyed,' Darren snarls back at him. They stand with eyes locked and Howie visualises ripping his throat out there and then.

Night hits and, as one, the undead look to the sky and howl into the air; thousands of voices filling the night sky, sending shivers down the spines of all the men that watch them. They start to back away but Howie stands his ground for a few more seconds, watching a slow smile form across Darren's face. Then Howie leans forward and stares hard at his former friend.

'Roar,' Howie says simply, and walks away, showing his back to the horde and praying they don't cut him down.

'Am I the only one that wants to fucking leg it?' Cookey says, as they all walk steadily back to the Saxon.

'No, I certainly do,' Big Chris adds.

'So why are we walking then?' Tucker asks.

'Don't give them the satisfaction,' Clarence rumbles.

'FUCKING RUN!' Howie shouts as he sprints past them, causing them all to break out and start running. Howie dives into the back of the Saxon and clambers through to the driver's seat as the rest climb into the rear.

'They're fucking running at us,' Blowers shouts as he pulls the rear doors closed with a slam.

Howie starts the engine and pulls away with a jerk, sending them all lurching backwards, and Sarah falls into the laps of the men. Soon, she gets her balance and stands back up, suddenly becoming aware of the big men in the confined space and the very wet t-shirt that she is wearing.

'Err, does anyone have a spare top?' Sarah asks sweetly; a dozen tough men start scrabbling about quickly in the tight confines.

'Here you go, Miss,' Clarence speaks first, holding out a dry top to Sarah as the others all stare daggers at him.

'Is that my top?' Nick asks, recognising the clothing.

'I don't know, is it?' the massive man stares innocently back at Nick.

'Er ... maybe not,' Nick adds quickly, looking up at Clarence.

'Chris, does that truck driver still have one of the radios?' Howie shouts back.

'Yes, but they're only short range things, do you think they'll go for the commune?' Chris shouts.

'I'm sure of it – is that GPMG working now?' Howie yells.

'I'll get on it,' Dave replies, and climbs up to start working as the Saxon speeds up through the dark city streets.

No street lights come on, none of the shops are illuminated, and there is no warm light spilling from houses or apartment blocks any more. The rain clouds cover the night sky and cast the streets into absolute darkness.

The powerful headlights shine out like beacons in the darkness, and the zombies surge towards them like moths. The solid-plated front of the Saxon hardly rocks as they plough through body after body. The zombies bare their teeth as they lunge to the front of the vehicle.

'Should we be shooting them down from the back doors?' Tucker asks.

'No, we're going too fast, and it's not worth it for dropping just a few of them. We need to get back as soon as possible,' Chris says, with worry clearly in his voice.

'How secure is it, Chris? Will it withstand a mass attack?' Howie shouts back.

'No, we can hold against a few of them at a time but we've only been going a few days; a big push would get them through easily.'

'Can we make it more secure?' Howie asks.

'If they're coming for us with large numbers, we'll have to bug out. We can't repel 'em, and we don't have time to secure it more,' Chris shouts back.

'How soon can they make ready to leave then?' Howie asks.

'It'll take hours. We don't have enough vehicles, and we've got kids and sick people too.'

'I don't think we'll have hours, Chris, they move fast at night and *he* knows where it is now, he can send them in to attack it.'

Chris looks to Malcolm and his men; they have families and friends at the commune. Fighting huge hordes of the undead in hand-to-hand combat is one thing, but now there is a direct threat against the people he offered safety and security to.

'Are those Forts big enough for all of us?' Malcolm calls out.

'I don't know, it depends how many have already gone there, and how full they are. They are big though, especially the main one,' Howie replies.

'Is there anywhere else we can go, easy to defend and hold many people?' Clarence asks.

'Probably loads of places, but I don't know of them,' Howie shouts back.

'We need to make a decision, Chris – we'll have to move out as soon as we get back,' Malcolm says.

'Okay, we'll go for the Forts. Women and children into whatever vehicles we can find, there's still space in the truck we can use,' Chris says.

'They've probably started to unload it already,' Clarence joins in.

'We'll have to take essential equipment only and use the rest of the space for people. We've also got the trucks that we used as barriers across the access roads,' Chris says, thinking as he goes along.

'Right, Malcolm, I want you to arrange the vehicles, get those trucks ready and lined up on the exit road. Clarence, I want you to sort the hospital out, don't take any shit from Doc Roberts, and make sure he only takes essential items,' Chris barks out.

'Got it,' Clarence nods.

'Howie, can we use the Saxon at the rear access road to cover, if we get the GPMG working again,' Chris asks.

'I'll get it working,' Dave calls down.

'Okay, Saxon at the rear with Nick on the GPMG, Jamie as sniper. Blowers, Cookey and Sarah, I want you with the vehicles to help load the people up, they will be scared and confused, so be nice, but get them moving,' Howie calls out to nods and yells of affirmation.

'Chris, do you have a stores area?' Howie asks.

'Yes,' he replies.

'One of our blokes excels in that area, can you make use of him to help organise?'

'Yes, definitely,' Chris shouts back.

'Tucker, that's you.'

'On it,' Tucker shouts back.

'Dave, me and you will stick with Chris to work from a central point – we stay put, so everyone knows where we are so they can come to us, that okay with everyone?'

Sarah watches as the men and lads all shout out in acknowledgment, then she looks at Chris, a naturally big man with a dark beard and very white teeth – he has an air of natural leadership about him. He and the older men are clearly ex-soldiers; when they took their tops off in the rain she saw the scars on their bodies: bullet holes and knife slashes, long healed but still very visible. Clarence is a huge man-mountain with muscles on top of muscles, but with a kind face. Then she looks to her brother. Less than a week ago he was working nights in a supermarket. Always a kind man, fun loving and very caring, but now there is a hardness to him and these men respond to him and listen to what he's saying. Her brother is giving orders in a manner that just makes them want to follow him.

She had watched as he stayed at the front fighting towards her, and then went back again, swinging that axe with a look of pure fury and hatred on his face – and these battle-hardened men and young lads are following him.

She can see the difference in him, the way he uses humour and kind words, but then gives an order that leaves no doubt it will be followed, and the thing is, it all makes sense. He shows respect to Big Chris, knowing that the big man is the leader of his group – but Sarah suspects that even if he hadn't shown that respect, they would have still accepted what he said. Life has changed, the whole world has changed, and her brother has changed the most.

He walked alone towards a huge horde of undead back on the Bridge; maybe he did feel fear, but he faced it and walked towards it. She knows he came for her and now that he has saved her, he could turn tail and run far away, but even now he's accepted the responsibility of trying to save those other people. They are nothing to him, and these young lads don't hold any loyalty to them, or Howie. But they accept what he says without question.

She feels an immense sense of pride in her brother; she felt pride in him before, just for being a good person. But now ... now he shines with a glowing light. He is amazing.

'He's a good man,' a rich voice intones, and she snaps out of her reverie to see Clarence smiling at her.

'What?'

'Your brother, he's a good man, a natural leader,' he repeats.

'Yeah, I guess he is,' she smiles back at him.

'HOLD ON TIGHT,' Howie yells, as the Saxon slams into a horde gathered in the road; the impact at such high speed sends the Saxon rocking on its suspension, causing them all to slide and fall in the back.

A huge hand shoots out and grabs Sarah round the waist to prevent her falling back.

'Thanks ... again,' Sarah says to Clarence.

'THERE'S MORE,' Howie bellows, and the Saxon rocks and jolts as it slams into body after body, pulverising them instantly from the raw power of the impact. The Saxon careers through the streets as Howie negotiates the bends and turns. Zombies launch themselves into the oncoming vehicle, screaming as they run and lunge forward, only to be splatted against the front like flies.

'BIG GROUP,' Howie yells, as the lights pick up an oncoming horde running full tilt at the Saxon. Howie pushes his foot down hard, and the big engines roar out into the night as the vehicle surges forward. Howie grips the wheel and growls deep in his throat.

'BRACE,' he screams as they impact.

A horde of undead zombies play chicken with an armour-plated military vehicle. The result is devastation, with bodies exploding as they strike the corners, and skulls imploding on the solid metal being driven into them at speed.

'They really don't like us anymore,' Howie shouts back, as they continually slam into the living corpses.

'Have we done something to upset them?' Cookey asks.

'They got fed up with you touching them,' Blowers says, to loud groans from everyone else. He smiles around at them. 'What?'

'Please don't start that again,' Tucker whines.

'Hey, don't tell me, tell Cookey – I'm only saying what I see,' Blowers replies.

'Blowers, you are homophobic and I find it offensive,' Cookey says in a serious tone, causing a few of the others to burst out laughing.

'Homophobic! Me?' Blowers says back at him.

'You are homophobic and you offend me and you could offend some of these new people with those nasty comments,' Cookey says, retaining his serious tone, to more laughs.

'Who am I going to offend?' Blowers laughs back at him.

'Me,' a rich, deep voice says from behind him.

Blowers turns to stare up at Clarence, who, in turn, stares back down with a very serious expression.

'You?' Blowers asks. 'You're not gay,' he adds.

'Aren't I?'

'Err ... are you?' Blowers asks, looking up at the huge man.

Clarence stares back in silence, a silence that is only broken by the thumps and bangs as the Saxon hits more zombies.

'Err ... I'm really sorry, I didn't mean anything, I ... was just ... um ...' Blowers stammers, unaware of Big Chris, Malcolm, and the other men all smiling behind him.

Blowers keeps going for several seconds, stuttering and stammering his words, while staring up at the imposing face of Clarence.

Clarence suddenly bursts out laughing, like a braying donkey with his deep voice, and they all erupt as Blowers glares around at them.

'Piss off, I knew he wasn't gay,' Blowers shouts out.

'You shit yourself mate,' Cookey says, wiping tears from his eyes; even Sarah laughs at Clarence's deep braying.

'Never seen you nervous before, Blowers,' Nick laughs at him.

'Yeah, very funny, very funny,' Blowers mutters and starts laughing himself.

The Saxon drives through the night until it reaches the road leading to the rear of the commune. Within seconds of arriving in the area, the undead suddenly stop attacking them, standing still, but leaning forward to scream and bare their teeth as the vehicle roars past them.

'Why are they holding back?' Sarah asks, leaning forward to look through the windscreen.

'We're right near the commune, they must be waiting to gather more numbers before attacking,' Howie shouts back. 'There's no other reason I can think off.'

'The entrance is in sight, Chris, are we safe to go straight in?' Howie yells.

'Yes, they'll recognise the vehicle,' he shouts back.

'GPMG is sorted,' Dave says, as he drops back down. 'I've cleaned it the best I can, too.'

'Right, if they're starting to mass, we need to move very quickly. Nick, get on that GPMG, you're with Jamie here, the rest need to get moving,' Howie shouts as the vehicle pulls up in front of the truck parked across the road.

Big Chris jumps out of the back and shouts for the truck to be moved, as he strides forward. Within seconds, the gap opens and the Saxon pulls through.

'We'll leave it here, Curtis, you stay with them, mate, they might need a driver for it,' Howie says as they all get out and start moving off to their allocated positions. Chris is surrounded by people coming to greet them. He silences them all by holding his hands up in the air.

'We will be attacked very soon,' he says loudly and simply. 'We have to get everyone out and we need to do it now, get those trucks turned 'round and every vehicle we have down to the front.' Chris turns to a few of his men.

'I want you to start sweeping down. Do it quickly but thoroughly, get everyone you can find to help you, get them all to the front ready to get on the vehicles. Women and children first, no stopping to get toys or clothes. We will be overrun very soon and we must move quickly. Do it now,' Chris urges, as they start sprinting away.

He turns back to the guards still standing by the access point:

'You lads, you heard what I said, we've got the Saxon here and a couple of lads with it, but I need you to stay and hold this area. Take this radio and keep me updated if you get contact, got it?'

They nod back and turn to stare out; Nick climbs up through the look-out position and turns the machine gun around to face back down the road. Jamie and Curtis sit inside the back of the vehicle, facing down the road with their rifles aimed and ready. Howie, Dave, and Big Chris start striding down the main road as his men move quickly ahead of him, darting in and out of the buildings. All down the wide main street, people start running about with panicked looks, grabbing at children and pulling them along; as soon as Chris comes into view, they aim straight for him.

'I'm sorry, I don't have time for this, get ready and get down to the front,' Chris repeats over and again, his voice staying calm. The truck they used to transport equipment from the hospital in Canary Wharf back to the commune is resting in the main road. The rear doors are open wide and half the equipment has already been carried into the makeshift hospital. Howie looks over at the building as they pass and sees Doctor Roberts with his shaggy eyebrows peering out at them.

'Chris, what's going on?' Doc Roberts walks swiftly towards them, his long white coat flapping out behind him.

'Doc, we're going to be overrun very soon, get loaded with whatever you can grab and get down the front,' Chris calls back.

'Right,' the doctor calls out, without breaking stride, a man used to processing information very quickly and reacting without panic. He turns to stride back inside the hospital, barking orders to people as he goes.

They reach the pub on the corner, amidst scenes of bedlam: people shouting and torches flashing, as men run back and forth. The refugees scurry towards the assembly point, all of them clearly terrified; children scream and cry as desperate parents cajole and snap at them to move faster and keep up. Armed men and women run through the masses towards Chris, taking instructions, and are told where to position themselves. Howie assists where he can, diverting questions from terrified residents and urging them to move quickly. The truck from the rear entrance point drives slowly past them, followed by more vehicles taken from the commune's hastily gathered collection.

'I think you'll be needing these.' A woman appears, carrying a tray with three steaming mugs of coffee, a small pot of sugar next to them on the tray. She puts the tray down on one of the wooden bench seats outside the pub, and Howie sees Chris smile for the first time since they got back.

'Thanks love, are you ready to go?' Chris asks gently, drawing the woman into his arms.

'I'll be ready when you are,' she replies, smiling up at him.

'I suppose there's no point in asking you to get down the front, is there?'

'I suppose you know the answer to that,' she replies quickly, but still with the smile.

'How was it out there?' she adds.

'Bloody awful,' he replies.

A man marches towards Chris. Howie steps out to intercept him, trying to give the big man a moment of privacy.

'Hi, can I help you?' Howie asks, in his best supermarket manager's voice.

'I want to know what's going on. We were told we were safe here ...'

'*CONTACT AT REAR ENTRANCE,*' Dave's and Chris's radios boom out.

'*Chris to rear entrance, what have you got there?*'

'*Lots of zombies, they are staring at us from the end of the road, looks like they are getting ready. Permission to engage.*'

CHAPTER TWO

The infection has mutated far beyond anything it was ever designed or cultured to be. Up until now, each host has been completely consumed by the virus working *into every cell of the body. This method worked well, but it had limitations that the infection was only too aware off. But now the mutation has become extreme. Darren has ceased being a human and has been completely infected, but rather than destroying every part of Darren, the infection worked to* integrate *with him – keeping memories, skills, and a lifetime of learning, and allowing Darren access to anything that will help the cause while denying any sense of guilt or remorse. The greatest advancement by the infection has been the ability to strictly control the flow of memories and instincts, but, more than this, it is the mastering of the chemical hormones that control these bodies.*

These chemicals excreted throughout the human system control every emotion and every possible feeling that can be experienced. The infection has learnt that these bodies can be controlled by using electrical impulses to the muscles, and they can be given a primary function of seeking new hosts. But those hormones and chemicals make the difference between a human and a deeply feeling person. Every pocket of resistance around the world suddenly finds themselves facing a disciplined and organised army of undead. Hordes gather at the entry points, and, rather than attacking prematurely, they wait in silence and with patience, concentrating on the resistors who have killed the most hosts, for they must be stopped.

In London, Darren walks with a fast pace through the streets towards the commune, at the head of a huge trailing army of zombies – each of them walking with purpose and a fixed stare. The infection floods them with chemicals that make them aggressive and angry. They growl and roar as they stalk through the streets, fighting the ever-increasing urge to break free and race forward to take the resistors down. The zombies ahead of them hold and wait for the head of the army to pass, roaring out with loyalty as Darren walks by them. He doesn't flinch, but stares ahead with a determined glare on his face, fixed on images of Howie dying painfully and that whore sister of his being ripped apart, and Dave being slowly tortured and begging for his life with his dying breath.

Darren also conjures up images of Blowers and Cookey being made to humiliate and degrade themselves with disgusting sex acts before they too become killed and are turned into his loyal subjects; Jamie Reese having his eyes gouged out; Tucker being force-fed human flesh. One by one, he thinks through his former comrades and dreams of ways of torturing and killing them slowly. But the one that matters the most is Howie, and Darren will not stop until he can slaughter his sister in front of him, slaughter every one of them in front of him, and then slowly turn Howie. The infection inside him revels in the power and the sudden organisation using this host has brought, and it knows the resistors' time is now very limited. Darren sends the undead to the access points of the commune and holds them in position; he has learnt that a coordinated and focussed attack on many points will be far harder to repel. Learning the skills of survival, strategy, and tactics from Dave, he now puts those to use and holds the undead army in the shadows. Darren knows that the increasing numbers standing just close enough to be seen will send fear and dread through the people in the commune. They will be panicked, and make mistakes – and be far harder to control.

Not like his loyal subjects, who are easy to control and bend to his will. But those people, those feeble people, will panic and scream in fear, which will only make his zombie warriors fight harder to get at them.

The infection has also learnt that the more speed he applies to the hosts, the less power and strength they have. Even at night, if the infection can hold them at a steady pace, rather than an all-out, reckless charge, they will have greater energy for the killing and the taking of more hosts.

CHAPTER THREE

Big Chris, Howie, and Dave stand outside the pub, receiving a constant flow of intelligence from the eyes and ears placed all around the perimeter. The undead are massing at nearly every access point, but they hold and wait. This knowledge spreads like wildfire through the area, and people start running and screaming in panic, fearing they will be attacked at any minute.

'That fucker knows what he's doing,' Howie says bitterly. 'Maybe we should open up on them, start cutting the numbers down.'

'I think we should, better than waiting for them to go for us,' Chris says.

'No, we'll keep loading the people up – if they attack now and break through, we'll get overrun. Every minute they hold off buys us time,' Dave says firmly.

'Chris to all units and access points, do not engage until they attack, do not prompt them to attack, hold positions and wait.'

'I'm going down the front to see how they're getting on,' Howie says, feeling frustrated. He walks off with Dave stepping beside him.

'Mate, this is nuts,' Howie says, shaking his head.

'It is.'

'Fucking Darren, did you see him back there? He was fucking demented and twisted up, poor lad.'

'Do you feel sorry for him?' Dave asks.

'Sort off, don't get me wrong though, I'll fucking kill him the first chance I'll get, but still ...'

'Still what?'

'You know, we knew him, he was one of us and that doesn't just go away.'

'Oh, yes, of course,' Dave replies.

'Dave, have you ever had anything like this happen before?' Howie asks.

'You mean having the world end from a zombie outbreak, fighting across the country in an Armoured Personnel Carrier training vehicle in order to rescue a woman, and then fighting back out, while one of my men gets turned into one of the aforementioned zombies, no ... I haven't.' Quite a long speech from Dave; Howie's influence was wearing off on him.

'Funny fucker, I meant have you ever had one of yours turn against you,' Howie laughs.

'Yes, it does happen. Blokes get paid off, or offered other things to go rogue,' Dave replies.

'What did you do?'

'I killed them,' Dave says.

'Makes sense,' Howie nods, as they reach the end of the row of vehicles and sees Blowers and Cookey urging people into a line and then sending them forward to the vehicles as they pull forward.

'How's it going, lads?' Howie asks, as he walks up.

'Bloody nightmare, Mr. Howie, everyone's going crazy. We got them in a line here and send them forward to Sarah at the vehicles; she's helping them get loaded and shouting when the next one is ready,' Blowers replies.

'We got loads into the first truck, if we can get them down here, we'll shift them a lot quicker,' Cookey adds, as he waves the approaching people into the line.

'MOVE OVER TO THE LINE PLEASE, WE WILL GET YOU AWAY VERY SOON,' he yells out.

'Howie to Chris, we need the trucks down front, we've got too many people here waiting for vehicles,' Howie says into the radio.

'Chris to any units listening, get those trucks down to the front as a priority,' his voice returns on the radio.

'Clarence to Chris, I'm on it now. Doc Roberts has got half his truck filled, I'll get them down to you now,' Clarence's deep voice booms out. Within minutes, the huge bald man is walking down the road ahead of two trucks. He steps aside and waves them towards the front of the vehicle line. Sarah steps out of the vehicles and stands in front of the first truck, waving her arms high to stop it.

'HOLD IT THERE, BLOWERS AND COOKEY, GET THOSE PEOPLE INTO THE BACK OF THIS ONE FIRST,' she yells out with a calm and confident voice.

'GOT IT,' Blowers shouts back.

'Your sister takes after you then, Mr. Howie,' Blowers says with a smile.

'She's bossier than me, mate, she'll be running the show within an hour,' Howie laughs back.

'OKAY, LISTEN UP PEOPLE. WE NEED TO GET YOU INTO THE TRUCK. WOMEN AND CHILDREN FIRST, STAY CALM,' Cookey shouts out as the crowd start surging towards the rear.

Howie walks around to see Clarence and Sarah at the back doors of the truck, helping people up, a constant surge against them as the panicked people try to clamber in.

'MOVE BACK AND WAIT,' Clarence shouts out to no effect, and Howie nods at Dave.

'YOU WILL WAIT AND MOVE CALMLY,' Dave's voice booms out into the air, silencing the entire area as everyone turns to look.

'Cheers Dave,' Clarence rumbles with a smile as he and Sarah return to helping lift people up into the back.

Questions are thrown at them, and children scream as they are pushed up into the darkness of the back of the truck. The first vehicle gets filled and Sarah rushes to the front, to wave it on, while Clarence waves the next one in.

The rear doors are already open with Doctor Roberts standing there, still in his white lab coat.

'My staff are already in here; we'll stand across the back to protect the equipment,' Doc Roberts says, not so much a question as a statement.

'We're doing well,' Sarah calls out. 'Considering how many people are here and the lack of time.'

'*Chris to all units, the access points are reporting mass numbers now, get them people out, do it now.*' The urgency in his voice is clear. '*I'm sending more vehicles down now.*'

On cue, headlights appear down the road, and the sound of diesel engines of vans and small delivery trucks fill the air. The group waves them down and sends the people into the back of them. The waiting crowd has thinned down considerably, which makes it easier to manage the loading.

Latecomers run down to the area to join the people cramming into vehicles. A small truck then appears and pulls up next to Howie and Sarah; Tucker's face peers out from the passenger window.

'Supply vehicle, Mr. Howie,' Tucker says.

'Bloody hell, mate, that was quick,' Howie answers, impressed.

'They were well organised, well sort of, they are now anyway,' he laughs. 'Is it okay if I stay with this vehicle, they will need an armed escort.'

'Good idea mate, get in the middle somewhere. Do not be the first or last vehicle in the convoy,' Howie yells as the vehicle rolls forward. There are many vehicles stretching back into the main street, loaded with refugees; headlights shine into the night, casting deep shadows and making the guards cover their eyes as they look up and down. A deep roar splits the air from all around them – deep and guttural and truly terrifying.

'Here they come,' Howie calls out as the hairs on the back of his neck stand up.

The roaring ends as the sound of gunfire erupts from all the access points at the same time. Small arms automatic weapons spitting out, alongside the distinctive sound of the GPMG, at the far end.

'FORM A LINE ACROSS HERE,' Howie bellows out, pointing at armed men and indicating a section of road back from the refugees who are still waiting to get loaded.

Men and women run into position and stand across the road, facing out with grim faces and shaky hands.

Cookey and Blowers run in the middle. Now experienced and hardened from the battles they have faced, they stand still, calmly. Both of them feel the exhilaration and excitement that comes the minutes before the fighting starts. Without speaking, they take magazines from their bags and lay them down face up on the road in front of them, checking their rifles and assuming a kneeling position.

The experienced ex-soldiers and police officers look down to see their actions and quickly copy them.

Within minutes, there is a line of armed men and women stretched out, kneeling in front of spare magazines, weapons ready.

'Cookey,' Blowers says.

'Yes, mate,' he answers.

'Don't try and bum them this time.'

'Ah, that's not fair,' Cookey says.

'Well, maybe just one, then.'

'Okay mate, just one, I promise.'

'Thanks mate,' Blowers replies, as the rest of the men and women look at them, seeing them joking with easy banter, even knowing what they are about to face.

Howie looks at them with an immense sense of pride.

'Clarence, you and Sarah keep loading those vehicles, we've got seconds now,' Howie shouts back at them from position behind the line, Dave standing at his side.

'Rear access point to all units, we are getting overrun. We are

pulling back. We will move slowly down the main road. There are fucking thousands of them.'

'Chris to all units, start pulling back towards the vehicle form-up point, staggered fall back, keep them suppressed.'

'Malcolm to Chris, we are running out of room in the vehicle form-up point, we need to start pulling out, but once we start we are not stopping.'

'Chris to Malcolm, Roger that. Chris to Clarence, are we loaded and ready?'

'Clarence to Chris, we are not loaded, but we are almost there. Clarence to Malcolm, start rolling out slowly, keep it slow – we'll throw them in as you move past.'

'Malcolm to Clarence, Roger that – we are starting to roll out now, I need guards to the front.'

'Chris to units, get guards to the front in support of Malcolm on point position.'

'Clarence to Chris, I cannot spare any guards from my position, can you take them from the access points.'

' Chris to Clarence, that's a negative, they are doing a fighting withdrawal, they are swamped.'

'Howie to Chris, we can send every third person from our line and move them to the front, that gives you about four guards, is that enough?'

'Malcolm to Howie, Roger that, just send two. We will work on speed and momentum. Get that Saxon to the front when you can.'

'Howie to Malcolm, Roger that. Two guards on way to you now.'

'Chris to rear access point Saxon, did you copy the last from Malcolm?'

'Rear access Saxon to Chris, Roger that, fighting retreat down the road and then we move to point position.'

'Blowers, get two from the line and send them to the front in support of Malcolm until the Saxon can take point,' Howie shouts out, as Blowers jumps up and motions to two people within the line.

They are both much older than the nineteen year-old Territorial

Army recruit, but they accept his orders without question and sprint down towards the front of the vehicles. Howie stands watching back down the road, then turns to see Clarence and Sarah pushing people into the backs of vans and small trucks and shouting at the drivers to move on. The fleet starts to move slowly, being held by Malcolm at the front.

'MOVE,' Clarence's voice booms out, as he starts picking people up to push them into vehicles, Sarah lacks the physical strength but her strong character and force of personality achieves the same aim and she shouts, bellows, and urges them into the vehicles.

'HERE THEY COME,' Blowers shouts from the line.

Howie spins around to see the Saxon slowly rolling towards them, the GPMG firing constantly from the top.

'WE HOLD THIS LINE!' Howie shouts out.

'LET THE SAXON THROUGH AND WE HOLD THIS LINE UNTIL THOSE PEOPLE ARE LOADED. WE WILL NOT FAIL. WE WILL HOLD.'

'YES SIR,' Blowers and Cookey chorus back.

'DO YOU HEAR ME? WE HOLD THIS LINE.'

'YES SIR,' voices from the line shout back at him, as Howie feels the adrenalin start to surge through his system.

He spins back to look at Clarence. They make eye contact and Howie raises two fingers to his own eyes and then points at Sarah. *You watch her for me.* Clarence nods once and goes back to pushing people into the vehicles.

'WE ARE NOT SCARED. WE DO NOT FEEL FEAR. WE ARE GOOD AND THEY ARE EVIL AND WE WILL NOT FAIL. WE WILL HOLD THIS LINE!' Howie roars out. The Saxon draws close and flashes the headlights; Cookey and Blowers move to the side and create a gap for the Saxon to pull through.

Once the back of the vehicle passes the line, they close up and form a kneeling position. Howie and Dave run to the line and take up positions between Blowers and Cookey, kneeling down and looking up to the solid wall of undead zombies marching towards them.

'FUCKING HAVE IT,' Howie roars and opens up with his assault rifle.

The GPMG pauses as Nick bellows, 'MAGAZINE.'

The line opens up as every weapon starts firing; bright muzzle flashes light the dark sky and the oncoming horde starts dropping. Bullets rip through the zombies, tearing them apart. They drop many and keep killing as they get closer and closer.

'MAGAZINE,' Blowers shouts and, within seconds, he has expelled one and snatched one from the ground, rammed it home, slammed the bolt back and opens up.

'WE ARE COMING IN,' Chris shouts down the radio, as Howie sees groups of men and women running into the main road from the side junctions, firing behind them.

'CEASE FIRE,' Howie shouts, and the line all drop their weapons, but Howie can see the reduction in fire rate stops the killing and every step of the zombie army brings them closer and closer.

'WE ADVANCE ON ME.' Howie stands and pauses for a second to allow the men and women to grab the magazines in front of them.

Howie paces forward with deliberate steps, watching as the line walks with him.

The guards from the access points run down the road with Big Chris leading them, turning to fire back as the side junctions suddenly become stacked with zombies marching out to meet the main horde.

'HOLD,' Howie shouts, and they all drop down again as the access point guards stream past them.

'FIRE,' Howie roars and they again open up on the horde, giving the retreating access point guards a few seconds to move back to the Saxon.

'PULL BACK,' Chris shouts out and, as one, the line stands to start stepping backwards, each man and woman firing as they go.

Voices shout 'MAGAZINE' as they eject and ram new ones

home. The fire rate is devastating, and the front ranks of the zombie army are torn down under the deadly hail of bullets.

'HOLD,' Howie shouts as they reach the back of the Saxon.

'ARE YOU READY NICK?' Howie shouts behind him.

'YES,' Nick shouts down as the GPMG opens up.

One heavy calibre machine gun and two lines of men and women firing automatic weapons slaughter the oncoming zombies. They are shredded as they walk and the massive fire rate devastates them.

'ATTACK FROM THE REAR,' Dave's voice booms out and Howie spins to see zombies surging into the vehicle area.

'CHRIS, GET THOSE VEHICLES MOVING NOW,' Howie screams as he leans into the Saxon and draws his axe out. He pauses and grabs the other double-bladed axe and starts running towards Clarence, who is fighting them with his bare hands.

The huge man grabs them as they swarm at him, throwing them aside as he roars and screams with violence.

Dave is at Howie's side, his knives drawn; Cookey and Blowers run on the other side of Howie, bayonets in hand.

Howie looks ahead and watches Sarah pushing the last few people into the backs of vehicles. They run faster, seeing more of the zombies going towards Sarah as she pushes the last one into the vehicle and slams the rear doors closed.

'SARAH, GO WITH THE VEHICLE,' Howie bellows out; she turns back to see four undead striding towards her, and she backs into the vehicle, becoming trapped against the closed doors. The zombies spread out in a line only a few steps away from her.

Howie screams and sprints with all his strength.

A deep roar drowns every other noise as Clarence picks a zombie up and throws him high into the air, then charges the line of four undead with his shoulder dropped down. The man mountain powers into the first one and drives through the rest, scooping them up on the way. Clarence bowls them over so they are underneath him, then his arms pull back and start piling in massive punches to the zombie heads beneath him.

Clarence roars and those fists lift up and drive down again and again as he pulverises the skulls. They don't stand a chance, and the big man kills them all, then stands up to run back to Sarah. He lifts Sarah by her waist and opens the rear door of the van, pushes her in, then takes a small black item from his back pocket and presses it into her hand before slamming the door closed.

'MOVE NOW!' Clarence slams his hand on the side of the vehicle, causing it to rock on its suspension, and the vehicle pulls away with squealing tyres.

Finally he looks back at Howie, and they nod once to each other as Howie hands him the axe. They turn to face out towards the oncoming zombies, both holding their axes with faces drawn with intensity. Howie launches forward and starts driving them down, swinging the blades through their heads and necks. Brains burst apart and blood pours out from necks as Dave whips through them, slicing them apart.

Jamie comes running in with his knives held the same way as Dave; he drops down and starts slicing into the backs of legs, cutting through tendons and ligaments. Zombies drop down from the deadly wounds to writhe on the floor, only to be stamped on by Clarence's huge boots. The vehicles slowly pull away as the men fight amongst them, battling to keep the zombies away from the vehicles and the people within them. The last vehicle leaves the compound, a row of bright red lights reflecting off the wet ground, and headlights dimming as they draw away into the inky night. The small group backs away towards the line behind them, keeping pace with each other and fighting out as the zombies come at them sporadically.

Howie slashes out, swinging the axe in a vicious uppercut and driving the blade straight through the thrusting chin of an undead male, bursting his face apart in a spray of blood, bone, and teeth.

They reach the Saxon and Howie looks out to see the carpet of slaughtered undead.

'They're pulling back,' Chris shouts over as the group take position around the Saxon.

'I'm not surprised, you've bloody killed 'em all,' Howie shouts back, to see Chris give a big grin, his white teeth gleaming in stark contrast to his dark beard.

'The Saxon can't fit us all in, we need more vehicles,' Howie shouts; his voice is drowned out by the weapons firing all around him. He walks around to stand near Chris and repeats his concern.

'There's a couple of things we might be able to use at the end of the barricade; we left the keys in the glove boxes of the ones we might need,' Chris replies.

'But they're all piled up, they'll be fucked,' Howie says.

'No, there's some right at the beginning, I know which ones, we'll have to work our way down there,' Chris says. 'There's not so many of them now,' he adds, looking up the road.

Howie looks up to see small groups still advancing, but nothing like the volume that were coming just a few minutes ago.

'CEASE FIRE,' Chris calls out. The ones closest to him hear and respond immediately, but the GPMG keeps going and the ones further down the line do not hear.

'CEASE FIRE,' Dave bellows; the firing stops immediately as they all turn to look at him.

'KEEP THE GPMG GOING AND MOVE 'ROUND THE SAXON TO MOVE DOWN THE ROAD,' Chris orders as they start re-grouping.

'Curtis, are you okay to keep driving, mate?' Howie shouts over.

'Yes, Mr. Howie,' Curtis responds, and clambers into the back and through to the driver's seat. They start grouping around the Saxon, as Nick aims the fire into the last few groups of zombies struggling over the fallen and mashed-up bodies on the road ahead of them.

The GPMG falls silent after a short time, as Nick calls out the all clear.

'MOVE OUT, STAY CLOSE TO THE VEHICLE,' Howie shouts, and the Saxon starts moving with the armed men and women standing shoulder-to-shoulder around the vehicle.

They inch down, sacrificing speed for the ability to stay to together as one unit.

'CONTACT,' someone shouts from driver's side of the Saxon, and weapons fire as the zombies are cut down.

'TO THE REAR,' Jamie shouts, and more weapons open up as zombies continue to push out from the darkened buildings and run into the road towards the vehicle.

'KEEP GOING, YOU'RE DOING WELL,' Chris shouts out, and slowly they move step-by-step down the road.

The constant contacts keep them busy as they fire into zombies pushing in from the sides and the rear, and then, as they near the section where the truck was used to block the road, they start coming from the front.

'NICK, FOCUS ON THE FRONT, WE NEED TO KEEP OUR ROUTE CLEAR' Howie shouts out. Nick spins around to face the road ahead, his face grim from the constant use of the machine gun.

The recruits and guards shout out directions as they spot zombies flitting through the shadows.

The contacts suddenly cease and a silence descends, only broken by the low rumble of the heavy diesel engine of the Armoured Personnel Carrier.

'Why have they stopped?' Nick shouts out, spinning around to get a full view.

'I can't see them anywhere,' he adds.

'They're still there,' Jamie calls out. 'They're keeping pace with us in the shadows.'

'Dave, can you see them?' Howie asks.

'Yes,' Dave replies. A small child walks slowly out from the shadows towards the passenger side of the Saxon; she wears a long white nightgown, and her flowing blond hair gleams in the moonlight. She shows no sign of injury.

She stops just ahead of the vehicle and holds her arms out, offering an embrace.

'Come here, darling,' one of the male guards shouts out, and rushes forward; the girl looks normal and terrified as she holds her arms out and glances around behind her.

'DON'T!' Howie yells; the guard scoops the girl up and starts running back with her, but he screams as the girl sinks her teeth into his neck, savagely tearing the soft flesh apart with a violent gnashing.

Her face is instantly soaked as the artery is opened and the hot red liquid spurts out. Two more guards rush forward; one of them grabs the girl and starts pulling her away. She wraps her arms around the first guard's head, clinging on, as she devours the flesh with frenzied biting. A small horde of zombies then rush out from the shadows, taking advantage of the distance the guards have created between themselves and the Saxon.

They are on the guards instantly, pulling them to the floor and sinking teeth into the flesh. Screams erupts as more guards rush forward to beat them away.

'STOP,' Chris shouts, as they are set upon by more zombies surging out of the darkness.

'CUT THEM DOWN,' Dave booms out, and opens up with his assault rifle, firing indiscriminately into the melee of fighting bodies.

More guards scream out as they see their comrades being cut down by Dave. More zombies rush in, flying into the frenzied attack; their screams rip the air apart. One of the guards lunges at Dave, desperately trying to stop him from shooting down his mates. Blowers steps in and pushes him away. The guard staggers but lashes out with his fist, knocking Blowers back. Cookey strides forward and slams the stock of his rifle into the guard's face, dropping him instantly. Clarence grabs the back of his collar and drags him around to the back of the vehicle and launches the unconscious form into the rear.

'NICK...' Howie shouts out.

Nick grimaces and slowly shakes his head as he aims down to the struggling mass of bodies. Some of the attacked guards are clearly still alive.

'Fuck it,' Nick mutters and squeezes the trigger. The GPMG

roars as it fires solid rounds into the mass of bodies, cutting them down instantly.

Sobs sound out from the guards as the zombies and their friends are killed by the firing.

'KEEP IT TOGETHER,' Howie shouts. 'STAY WITH THE VEHICLE.'

Shots sound out from the driver's side as the zombies show more intelligence by attacking that side with force while the resistors are focussed on the passenger side. Nick spins around to see a mass of undead coming from the shadows at full pelt.

He opens fire, trying to shout a warning at the same time.

The zombies impact within seconds and more guards are taken down as their assault weapons become useless in the close quarters combat. The brawling bodies are right at the side of the vehicle, and Nick pushes the machine gun over, but can't get the angle to fire down. Dave runs around the back of the vehicle, throwing his assault rifle into the rear as he passes the open door, then draws his knives from the back of his waistband.

Within short steps he reaches the scrabbling line.

The first guard is pinned against the side of the vehicle with zombies savaging her face. She screams and thrashes, but the body weight is too great.

Dave steps behind them and draws a knife across each of their throats. Hot, infected blood bursts out into the female guard's face. Dave slips one of the knives between the gap between the zombies' bodies and pushes the sharp tip into her chest, pushing down until the blade cuts through her heart, killing her instantly. Dave twists the handle with a violent motion and pulls the blade out before spinning around to drive the two blades into the neck of a lunging undead female, then steps back as the zombie falls beside him. He works along the side of the still moving Saxon, cutting down zombies and injured guards alike. At the last one, he spins through the air, slicing the throats open of the remaining zombies as his blade comes to rest millimetres away from the throat of the last guard.

They keep walking sideways, keeping pace with the vehicle, as the guard tries to push himself backwards into the solid metal side of the Saxon.

'ARE YOU BITTEN?' Dave roars into his face, terrifying him even more.

'No, no, they didn't get me,' he stammers back.

'I AM WATCHING YOU,' Dave says and promptly pulls away. 'THIS SIDE IS UNGUARDED,' he bellows out.

Howie comes around the side from the front and looks back at the fallen bodies of the guards and zombies, as the Saxon slowly advances down the narrow lane of the stacked vehicles.

'Fuck me ...' he mutters, taking in the now unguarded side of the vehicle, apart from Dave and one shaking guard who keeps glancing at Dave with a terrified expression.

'Are they all gone?' Howie asks.

'Yes, Mr. Howie,' Dave answers, as he stalks next to the vehicle, his knives upturned against his forearms.

'LOAD UP NOW,' Howie shouts out, as Chris appears from the rear of the vehicle.

'What the fuck ...' Chris's mouth drops as he looks back at the fallen bodies.

'We need to load up and go,' Howie shouts down, aware they will now fit in the vehicle as so many of the guards have been taken down.

Chris nods back in silent agreement.

They load up one by one, covering each other as they work back down the side of the vehicle and into the rear doors of the moving Saxon. Howie is the last to load and pulls the doors closed.

'ALL IN,' he shouts.

'Catch up with the convoy, Curtis! Someone take over from Nick, give him a break,' he adds, sinking down onto one of the side benches in exhaustion.

The Saxon increases in speed as Curtis works to catch up with the fleet; the vastly reduced numbers are exhausted from the sustained battle. The remaining few guards weep and sob at the loss of their fallen friends. Howie looks up to Blowers and Cookey, both sitting forward with their heads down. Nick is slumped, leaning back with his eyes closed.

Jamie and Dave are both sitting straight, eyes open and staring ahead out of the windscreen. Howie ticks them off in his mind as he goes, the mother hen counting the brood: Curtis driving, Tucker with the supply vehicle, and Sarah in the back of the last vehicle. He looks over at Clarence, the big man taking up the space of two people with his enormous frame, leaning back with his eyes closed. Howie remembers him saving Sarah and offers a silent prayer of thanks that he was in the position to react so quickly. Other than Dave, none of them would have been able to take so many down with their bare hands and walk away, unscathed. Finally, he looks to Big Chris. They lock eyes: two leaders who have suffered losses and taken the responsibility of so many lives, and have fought to keep those people safe. One a former soldier and criminal, the other a supermarket manager. Something passes between them – a meeting of minds, an unspoken contract that they will do anything to ensure the survival of the people that have trusted them with their lives.

CHAPTER FOUR

Sarah stands with her head resting against the inside of the door. The last image as the doors were slammed was of Clarence staring hard at her and a scene of utter carnage behind him, and of Howie sprinting towards her, carrying two axes. She realises that she is holding something in her hand. The inside of the van is pitch black, and she feels around the object; it feels like a knife handle but there is no blade. Her fingertips brush against a small button on the side. She looks back up to the door as she realises what he gave to her. She quickly tucks the item into her back pocket as she turns around. The motion of the vehicle and the gentle sway as it turns increases her sense of fear; any notion of space and dimension disappear and she stretches her arms to press her hands against the insides of the vehicle.

She feels the heat from the bodies pressed tightly into the back of the van, and sweat starts to forms on her face. Then she feels something small pressing into her and reaches down with a hand to feel a small head with long hair.

'Hey, it's okay,' Sarah says softly, as the small body flinches away from her hand.

A tiny hand reaches up to touch hers, fingertips brushing gently, then gripping tightly.

'Mummy?' a small voice says.

'No, I'm Sarah, where is your mummy?' she asks.

'I don't know,' the child whimpers.

'Hey everyone, there's a small child here missing her mummy,' Sarah calls out to the darkness.

'Who is it?' a female voice answers from somewhere near the front.

'What's your name, sweetie?' Sarah asks the small child.

'Patricia,' the small voice replies.

'Her name's Patricia,' Sarah calls out.

'What's her mum's name?' the same female voice answers.

'What's your mum's name, sweetie?' Sarah asks.

'Jane.'

'Her mother's called Jane,' Sarah says.

'I don't know her, does anyone else?' the female voice calls out, to no reply.

'What about your daddy, what's his name?' Sarah asks Patricia.

'I don't know,' Patricia whimpers, her voice small and weak.

'Come here, Angel,' Sarah says, as she drops down low and draws the small girl into her body; the child throws her arms round Sarah's shoulders, squeezing tightly.

'I wanna go home,' Patricia says quietly.

'I know sweetie, but we'll be okay, it won't be dark for long,' Sarah replies, rubbing the girl's back.

'Is there a light in here?' The female voice from the front calls out.

Sarah listens to the rustle of hands feeling alongside the sides and roof of the van, scrabbling about in the pitch dark.

A feeble light switches on from the front.

'Hey, look over there,' Sarah says softly. The girl turns slowly to see the very soft yellow light illuminating the many faces packed into the van, all of them women.

A few of them smile down at the girl hugging Sarah.

'See, we're not in the dark anymore, and soon we'll be able to get out, we just have to wait,' Sarah assures the girl.

'Will those things get us?' Patricia asks with fear in her small voice.

'No sweetie, they won't get us,' Sarah says, as Patricia pushes into her shoulder to cover her face.

'Do you promise?' Patricia asks.

'I promise, I know the men looking after us and they're very, very brave. They won't let anything happen to us,' Sarah says.

'Will they stop those things?' Patricia asks.

'Yes, they will stop them and they will keep us all safe, I promise. They're big and strong and brave, and we're in here and those things can't get us in here.'

'How do you know them?' one of the women asks.

'My brother is one of them,' Sarah replies.

'One of the guards?' Another asks.

'No, Howie is with the Army vehicle, he's in charge of them,' Sarah replies with pride.

'HOWIEEEEEEEE,' a woman screeches out from the far corner of the vehicle; heads turn at the sudden noise as the voice screeches again:

'HOWIEEEEEEEEE.'

A commotion breaks out as another woman screams.

'She's biting her, she's one of them!' a voice shouts out.

Sarah catches a glimpse of an old woman sinking her teeth into the neck of a younger woman and blood pumping out.

The packed bodies try to push away, as others try to push in to stop the attack.

'GET HER OFF!' Sarah screams out, as a hand reaches out to grasp the hair on the back of the head of the old woman, pulling her away with a violent yank.

The attacked woman drops to the floor, as women start pummelling into the freshly turned zombie and she goes down in the packed confines, the women screaming with fear. Feet start stamping down, desperately trying to kill the old woman.

'SHE GOT ME,' one of the women screams out as her ankle is bitten into.

She drops down to beat her away until more boots and shoes can stamp down on the old woman's head and neck.

'IS SHE DOWN?' Sarah calls out.

'Yeah, where's the other one that she bit?' another voice shouts in panic.

'She's on the ground, she's not moving,' someone answers.

'Kill her, she'll come back as one of them,' the first voice shouts. In the dim light, Sarah makes out women pushing and scrabbling to get away from the fallen woman, some of the braver ones fighting to get to her, none of them able to move much because of the small space. The woman with the bitten ankle screams and sobs as she clutches her ankle.

'I've been bitten, I've been bitten,' she repeats over and again. Sarah pulls the girl closer, her hands going around her chest in a protective embrace.

'Go behind me, sweetie,' Sarah whispers in her ear and pushes the girl around.

Another scream pierces the air as the savaged woman rises up and lunges with bloodshot eyes, sinking her teeth into the closest leg.

Hands start beating at her as the van erupts in panic.

The air is filled with screams, and the van rocks from the pushing and pulling as the women fights to get away. More of them fall down from vicious bites, as zombie teeth tear flesh apart. Women start slipping over as the wooden base of the van becomes slick with the spilled blood; more women are bitten and go down onto the ground.

Sarah watches as the bodies fight and writhe on the ground. She slips her hand around and draws the handle from her back pocket, feeling for the small button. She holds it down at her side with her finger pressed gently on the button.

The driver of the van hears the screams and bangs clearly; his hands grip the steering wheel as pure terror grows inside him.

He leans forward to stare at the red light of the vehicle in front. He knows he's the last in the fleet, and if he stops now he will be left behind, defenceless in the dark streets of London, surrounded by the undead.

The bangs and screams increase as he drives, and hot tears start spilling down his face. He beats his hands against the steering wheel, imagining the scenes breaking out just inches behind him.

Instinctively, he reaches for the radio and presses the on switch; static fills the air. The driver finds a CD in the cubby-hole of the dashboard and tries to force it into the CD slot, his hands shaking.

The CD refuses to budge and it takes minutes for him to realise there is already a CD in the player. He throws the CD down onto the floor, frantically pressing buttons, as the screams and bangs get louder from the rear. The driver finally presses the right button and loud rock music bursts out of the speakers; he twists the volume knob until the sound is so loud it comes out distorted. He looks up to see he has drifted off to the side in his panic to fill the van with noise. He overreacts and yanks the steering wheel hard; the van swerves over and then back again as he fights to get control.

Sarah watches as the biggest bitch fight in the world breaks out in front of her, then she lowers down to speak into the girl's ear:

'Put your hands over your eyes, sweetie, and keep them there.' The girl does as she is asked and pushes her small hands over her tightly closed eyes.

'I'll be right back, I promise,' Sarah whispers, while watching the unfolding mess in front of her.

Half the women in the van are bitten and the rest are fighting like troopers to protect themselves, falling and tripping over the bodies wrestling on the floor.

An infected woman stumbles backwards, having been thrust by a large built woman at the front. The zombie stumbles into Sarah, who reaches around to grip her around the neck, squeezing tightly. She presses the small button on the handle, a shiny blade sliding out instantly, and Sarah digs this into the throat of the woman, while gripping hard. Blood pumps out, covering her hand and arm. She pushes the body away just as the large woman sends another one her way. Sarah steps forward and grabs the zombie, pulling her head forward as she sticks the knife deep into her throat, then twists the handle left to right and back again, tearing a ragged hole in her windpipe. Loud rock music booms out from the front, drowning out the screams, grunts, and groans of the women trying to kill each other.

Sarah drops the woman down and lunges for the next one as the van swerves violently, causing all the women to fly into one side, landing in a crumpled heap, with Sarah at the bottom of the pile.

Pinned to the floor by bloodied bodies, she thrashes her legs, frantically trying to prevent any of the undead from biting her ankles. The bodies fight and writhe about as Sarah struggles for breath under the heavy weight; the van swerves again as the bodies slide across the slick floor to ram into the other side. Sarah is now free and rises up to see red, bloodshot eyes pushing towards her.

She yells as she sticks the blade into the throat, missing and stabbing the woman through the cheek instead. She pulls the small handle back and lashes out again and again, swiping the blade back and forth across the throat. Another one pushes her head out of the mess of limbs and Sarah rams her foot into the face, feeling bones crunch underfoot.

She tries to roll away as the van swerves again, and they slide back across the floor to pin Sarah against the side.

Once more trapped under the bodies, she fights to draw her legs into the foetal position, hoping the press of bodies will protect her. She feels the blade sinking into the back of another woman pressing into her, with no idea if she is stabbing a zombie or another survivor. She tries to pull the knife away, but her arm is pinned into position as the body writhes on the blade. Another swerve sends them back across the floor, and Sarah loses grip on the knife as they slam into the other side. She crabs backwards as a body drops down on her, blood pouring from a deep bite wound to her neck. Sarah cranes her neck, trying to keep her face away from the blood, and she rolls hard to displace the body, pushing it aside as she gets back to her feet.

Another zombie comes from the right and Sarah quickly ducks down and moves behind to wrap her arms round her neck. Sarah squeezes with all her might as the body staggers forward, arms flailing. A woman in front of them turns around to bite into the mass of bodies and Sarah sees the knife sticking out of her back. She reaches out to grab the handle as the zombie pulls away; Sarah squeezes hard and pulls her upper body backwards, forcing the zombie to fall down. Sarah slams her booted feet down again and again on the face, just as the one with the knife stuck in her turns to Sarah with bloodied teeth bared.

Sarah slams her fist into the side of its face, snapping the head away, then sidesteps and finally gets a grip on the knife. She pulls it out and forces the blade into the side of the zombie's neck, sawing and hacking away until a large, ragged hole forms in the soft flesh. She turns to see an undead lunge at Patricia, still cowering in the corner with her hands over her eyes. Sarah dives forward onto the floor and grabs the ankles, pulling them back as hard as she can. The zombie slams down face forward into the floor as Sarah clambers over its back to grab the head and slam it down again and again into the hard flooring.

Remembering the knife in her hand, she repeatedly stabs into the rib cage, breaking bones and puncturing the lungs. The body eventually goes still, as Sarah rolls off to find another one bearing down on her.

She lifts her feet up and takes the weight of the zombie body on its chest. Her boots push into the zombie's breasts as she tries to force it away. The zombie is heavy, fighting forward, and Sarah feels her legs starting to buckle; she rolls to the side as the body falls down, just missing her.

She slams her arm down and forces the blade into the back of the neck before the zombie can roll or turn towards her. Sarah keeps fighting and knifing the zombies down, as they are bitten and turned, one by one. She fights out with desperation, until she is side by side with the large built woman from earlier. The large woman wraps her arms around a zombie, pinning her against the side of the van.

'STAB HER,' the woman yells, as Sarah lunges forward with the knife to slice open the undead's throat.

They back away as the body slides down onto the already crowded floor. The large woman thrusts her arm out to grab the hair of a zombie about to bite Sarah from the other side, yelling a warning as she fights to pull the undead woman away. Sarah sticks the small blade deep into the exposed neck. They keep going until the last one drops down onto the top of the gory pile of corpses, both of them soaked with blood and filth.

They back away until they are both standing protectively in front of Patricia. Sarah hands the other woman the knife and drops down so she is eye level with the little girl.

'Sweetie, I want you to turn 'round and face the other way now.'

'Can I take my hands away?' Patricia answers.

'Yes, but only when you've turned 'round.'

'Did those things get in here?' Patricia asks. 'You promised they wouldn't.'

Sarah looks up to exchange a glance with the other woman.

'Just turn for me, Patricia, there's none of them in here now, it's safe,' Sarah says, as she turns the girl around.

'I'm Mary,' the large built woman says when Sarah stands up. 'Nice to meet you, do you want your knife back?'

'Yes, if you don't mind,' Sarah replies. 'Nice to meet you too, Mary,'

'You're better with it than me, I'll grab 'em and you stab 'em,' the large woman jokes.

'Deal,' Sarah replies, as they stare down at the bodies piled in front of them.

CHAPTER FIVE

'There they are,' Curtis says to Howie, who is now in the passenger seat.

'Nice one mate, just need to get to the front now,' Howie replies.

The taillights disappear around a bend in the road, but soon come into view again as the Saxon speeds up.

Curtis drives up close behind the last van, the one containing Sarah, Mary, Patricia, and the pile of zombie bodies.

They flash headlights to alert the driver they are going around, as Curtis pulls out to start overtaking them. One by one, they drive past the fleet of vehicles, Howie giving a wave or a thumbs up to the drivers while wondering how they will feel when they find out most of their guards have been wiped out.

'Which Fort are we heading for?' Chris calls out from the back.

'There's quite a few of them, but I reckon we should go for Fort Spitbank; it's the biggest one that I know of and it's been maintained,' Howie shouts back.

'Have you been there before?' Chris asks.

'Yeah, but years ago, we went with school and then a couple of times later. It's huge and the rear wall goes straight onto the sea; from memory it had open flat land all around it too.'

'Let's just hope it's not full then,' Chris says. The Saxon weaves its way past the fleet of vans, cars, and trucks, until it eventually reaches the front; a long convoy, snaking out of London into the pitch black of the countryside. Howie checks and re-checks the map, planning ahead and making sure they stick to major roads so the big trucks can fit through.

'Malcolm to Chris, we are being flashed by headlights from behind; there must be an issue. Can we find a safe area to pull up?'

'Chris to Malcolm and all units, Roger that. I know this road, there is a section ahead with high concrete walls on both sides. We will stop there.'

'About a mile or so further, Howie, you'll see big walls on both sides, we want to stop there,' Chris shouts forward.

'Got it mate. Curtis, make sure you keep to the middle lane so we have equal distance on both sides,' Howie says.

'Okay, Mr. Howie.' Within a few minutes, the Saxon is slowing down as they enter into a very long, straight section of the motorway. High concrete walls create a tunnel effect from the headlights and the dark sky.

'Who's on the GPMG?' Howie asks.

'Jamie,' Blowers answers.

'Right, I want us out, down the sides, keeping watch, and Curtis, I want you to drive forward a short distance so you Jamie can get a good view of the sides. Everyone ready? Good, everyone out then,' Howie shouts as he jumps down and runs back to meet Chris.

They stride down the left flank of the convoy, pausing as Malcolm jumps out from the front vehicle to meet them.

'What's up?' Chris asks him.

'I don't know, we were getting constant flashes from behind,' Malcolm replies. They walk to the next vehicle and shout up to the driver. He leans out of the open window with a cigarette hanging out his mouth.

'Everything all right?' Howie calls up.

'We're fine, we were getting flashed from behind, so I passed it on.' They walk to the next vehicle to find Tucker climbing down from the passenger door and stretching out.

'That looked a bit nasty back there, Mr. Howie,' Tucker says.

'It was, mate, was it you flashing?'

'Nope, came from behind,' Tucker replies. They walk down the fleet of vehicles, with each driver giving the same response. With only a few vehicles left in the fleet Howie looks back to see the driver of the last vehicle running towards them, waving his arms in the air.

'That's Sarah's vehicle,' Howie yells, as he starts running forward, Big Chris and Dave sprinting beside him.

'They were screaming and banging, I didn't know what to do, I didn't want to get left behind,' the driver sobs as they run past him.

Howie twists around the back of the van and wrenches the rear doors open to see Sarah standing, facing him, covered in blood. A small knife is held tightly in her right hand; her left hand grips the fingers of a small girl who is also holding hands with a large-built woman. The three of them drip with blood and gore.

'Sarah ...What the fuck?' Howie stammers, as he jolts forward, picking the girl up to pass back to Chris. As Sarah and Mary step down, Howie's mouth drops open as he looks at the utter scene of carnage in the back of the van. Dead bodies are strewn about and piled up, thick pools of blood shimmering on the floor and smeared up the sides; dead eyes, both human and zombie, stare blankly; dead mouths gape accusingly at him.

'What happened?' Howie says to the women.

'One of them turned and it just sort of exploded from there,' Sarah replies calmly.

'This is Mary – Mary, this is my brother, Howie.' Howie stands speechless as Mary calmly says *hello*.

Dave then steps forward to peer into the back of the van. He gazes at Mary and Sarah, then down at the small knife, then finally back to the bodies.

He looks at Howie and nods, clearly impressed at the work completed.

'Who is the girl?' Howie eventually asks when his brain catches up with the sight before him.

'Patricia, she lost her mum,' Sarah replies, still in a calm voice.

Mary steps forward to take the child from Chris, who is also standing with his mouth hanging open.

'We'll come with you,' Sarah says flatly.

'We don't have a lot of room ...' Chris starts to say.

'She said we're coming with you.' Mary glares at Chris.

'Yeah, fine, no problem,' Chris replies quickly, holding his hands up.

The vehicles move off again, the Saxon in the lead, with Sarah and Mary sitting in the hastily vacated seats, using wet wipes to clean themselves and Patricia of the blood and filth.

Hardened and battle-experienced men watch them with keen interest. They work with purpose, chatting with the small child as though nothing had happened.

Before the women arrived, Chris had got to the vehicle ahead of them and quickly whispered what they had seen inside the van. Clarence had moved quickly to Sarah on seeing the state she was in, asking her again and again if she was okay.

'You can have your knife back now,' she offered, as the huge man fussed around her.

'No, you keep it, in fact ...' Clarence said, as he unbuckled his belt and removed one of the large sheath knives from it before handing it to Sarah. 'You'd better have a bigger one.'

'How does it go on,' Sarah said, taking the big knife and pulling it from the sheath to admire the weapon.

'Here, let me,' Clarence said, as he unbuckled Sarah's belt and pulled it free from the loops, then, suddenly realising what he was doing, he looked down to see her smiling at him.

'Oh, sorry, I didn't mean to ...' He blushed bright red, to Sarah's delight.

'What didn't you mean to do?' she asked mischievously.

'Err ... undo your belt,' he stammered.

'But you *did* undo my belt,' she replied.

'Yeah but, you know ...'

'I know what?'

'I ...err, well, didn't mean it like that.'

'Like what?' she asked innocently, and laughed as he went even redder.

'I'm only joking, thank you for the knife,' she said, touching him on his massive forearm as his face split apart with a huge grin.

Howie had taken over the driving, seeing Curtis looking tired and drawn, and suggested he get some rest in the back.

'Did you see those bodies?' Howie asked Dave as they continued driving.

'Yes, Mr. Howie, I was there,' Dave replies.

'Oh, not this again. I meant ... did you see how many there were?'

'Yes. I was there.'

'Do you do this on purpose?'

'Do what?'

'Answer each question literally.'

'How do I answer that?'

'What?'

'You asked me if I answer each question literally, so in order to give you an answer, I would have to be literal – which would then suggest that I do, in fact, answer each question literally.'

'You never cease to amaze me, Dave.'

'Thanks, Mr. Howie.'

The crowded Saxon settles into near silence as they travel towards the coast. The exhausted survivors try to sleep in whatever space they can find.

Patricia dozes fitfully, snuggled into Mary in one rear corner while Sarah rests in the other.

The others find space where they can. Clarence and Chris both remain standing near the front, leaning in towards Howie and Dave and chatting in muted tones.

'Have you seen any yet?' Chris asks.

'Nope, not one, fuck knows where they've all gone,' Howie replies.

'Can't be a good thing,' Chris says.

'Darren knew all along we would be heading for the Forts, but I don't think I ever said which one,' Howie says.

'So there's no doubt they're going to be coming for us then,' Chris says.

'He'll come – it just depends how long it takes him, and we haven't seen any for a long time, so I reckon they're massing again,' Howie says.

'Or waiting for him to pass through, so they can join in,' Chris says.

'Jesus, there'll be thousands of them if he collects them all on the way,' says Clarence.

'More than that,' Chris says.

'I was wondering if he would try to use vehicles, he's obviously got control over the rest of them somehow ...' Howie says.

'Yeah, and if he can tap into their memories and knowledge, then it wouldn't be hard to get the keys for the vehicles and move down here quickly,' Chris interrupts.

'He'll come on foot,' Dave says in his normal flat tone.

'How do you know?' Howie asks.

'They've been going for a week now with no sign of slowing down. They're decaying, but still moving. I haven't seen any of them eat or drink, so they don't need sustenance, which also means time is not relevant to them. He held them outside the commune until he thought there were sufficient numbers, but he held himself back away from harm – which shows he has awareness for his own safety. They also massed in Canary Wharf when we went for your sister, so the biggest single tactic deployed by them is high numbers. Logistics for any army on the move is difficult at the best of times, and will be even harder using vehicles ...'

'Not if they have collective intelligence,' Howie cuts in. 'And it does look like they have. Darren snapped his fingers and they all started laughing, then he made them take a step forward perfectly in time. With that kind of power and control they could find it easy.'

'I don't think they will,' Dave replies. 'That would mean having every one of them have access to a vehicle and be ready in the right place at the right time to slip in with the main fleet. Even if they share intelligence, that is an extremely hard thing to organise. A forced march is the best way for them to pick them up as they go.'

'So, if they have a collective intelligence or consciousness, then they would know the route they are taking and would just have to wait at those points,' Chris says.

'Yes,' Dave responds.

'So why not get vehicles and wait at those points?' Howie asks.

'Their motor skills have got better, but during the day they shuffle and become slow, and are not able to control their own bodies that well. We saw them increase speed during the day, but that made them weaker. Darren will have no choice but to keep them moving at a set pace that can cover ground but will conserve energy to prevent them weakening,' Dave explains clearly.

'Okay, so how long will it take to walk that distance?' Howie asks.

'They can go as the crow flies, in a straight line, so that would be about fifty miles or so,' Clarence says.

'If they shuffle along like they do during the day, then a couple of days at least; if they move fast the entire time – it could be as little as sixteen to twenty hours – but we know that weakens them. But if they have enough ... err ... people, I guess, then they might not worry about being weaker,' says Chris.

'People,' Howie laughs.

'Yeah, I know, I don't like the other word though,' Chris replies.

'What? Zombies?' Howie asks.

'Yeah, it seems like a movie or something when I use that word,' laughs Chris.

'What do you think, Dave?' Howie asks.

'About the word zombies? It doesn't bother me.'

'No,' Howie laughs again. 'About the speed they'll move at.'

'Oh, sorry. I don't think time is an issue for them, so they will do what all big organisations do.'

'Which is?' Clarence asks, after a lengthy pause.

'They will work out the best speed to make the best distance using the least amount of fuel, like airlines do, or shipping companies,' Dave replies.

'Sounds ridiculous when you say it like that,' Howie says. 'But I guess that's about right though.'

'Well, we have no answer to the question then, we don't know when they'll turn up,' says Chris.

'In short, nope,' Howie replies.

'Brilliant. We have a huge army of dead people marching through the country specifically looking for us, and we're heading for a hundred and fifty year old Fort, somewhere on the coast, with a handful of men able to fight ... I like those odds,' Chris laughs.

'Stuff 'em,' Clarence says in his deep voice.

'Stuff 'em? What kind of an insult is that?' Chris laughs, looking at the huge man mountain.

'Well, there are ladies and a child present and I didn't want to be a potty mouth,' the deep voice rumbles, as the rest burst out laughing.

'Potty mouth!? That's even worse,' Howie says, laughing. 'I just watched you take four of them down with your bare hands ...'

'Yeah, well, there's no need for foul language in the presence of ladies,' Clarence replies defensively.

'I think your sister has an admirer, Howie,' Chris says, wiping tears of laughter from his eyes.

'No, just hang on,' Clarence tries to interrupt, going red in the face.

'Oh really, you fancy my sister, do you?' Howie asks, pretending to be offended.

'No one said anything about me fancying your sister, Mr. Howie,' Clarence says.

'Oh, he's *Mr.* Howie now, is he? Trying to win him over are you?' Chris laughs again as Howie bends forward, trying to stop laughing so loud.

'No, he *is* Mr. Howie, everyone calls him that,' Clarence says in a more defensive tone.

'So ... you don't fancy Sarah, then?' Chris asks, unable to stop goading him.

'No, of course I don't,' Chris replies, going even redder.

'Where's your knife then?' Chris asks innocently.

'My what?' Clarence replies, his voice going higher as Howie starts to laugh harder.

'Your knife, I gave you that knife years ago, after you broke that cheap thing you had.'

'Well ... err ... well, she only had that little knife.'

'That little knife that you gave her, and now you've given her your big knife, what's next? The axe?' Chris says, between laughing.

'Oh, just fuck off,' Clarence finally snaps, his voice louder.

'Language please, there's a child back here, keep that potty mouth for later,' Mary calls out, as Howie and Chris burst out laughing even more. Even Dave chuckles, as Clarence drops his head into his hands, groaning.

'What's so funny?' Sarah asks, clambering over the legs of sleeping forms to get to the front.

'We were just talking about Clarence,' Chris replies, still chuckling.

'Oh, what about?' Sarah asks, stretching.

'Chris ...' Clarence growls, his face bright red, and tries to turn away from Sarah.

'Just about the knife he gave you,' Howie cuts in, tears streaming down his face.

'Oh, that was sweet, thank you again, Clarence. You'll have to show me how to use it though, it's very big,' Sarah replies, smiling at him.

'Howie, are you all right?' she asks, as Howie's body heaves with laughing, bent forward enough to be almost biting the steering wheel.

'Fine, I'm fine,' Howie whimpers.

'Clarence was just saying how he wants to show you some moves,' Chris says innocently.

'That's great, thank you, Clarence,' Sarah says, placing her hand on his shoulder.

'It's no problem,' Clarence replies.

'Are you okay? Your face is very red,' Sarah says with concern. 'Are you coming down with something?' She presses the back of her hand to his forehead.

'No, no, I'm just very hot in here,' Clarence replies, very softly.

'Okay, well, I'll leave you boys to it and try to get some more rest,' Sarah says, as she clambers back down the Saxon.

'Okay, we'll be quieter now, Sarah,' Chris smiles, as she goes, then looks down at Clarence bent over resting his head on the back of the seat, his face now beetroot-coloured, but his forehead tingling from where she touched him.

'Poor Clarence, are you okay?' Chris says in a sweet voice, and puts his hand on Clarence's face.

'Fuck off, you wanker,' Clarence whispers.

'Oh, poor Clarence, come here you big teddy bear and give me a cuddly wuddly,' Chris laughs, as he tries to wrap his arms round Clarence's huge shoulders.

'I said fuck off, Chris,' Clarence whispers, as he starts laughing, trying to squirm out of the manly embrace.

'So, how do you feel, Howie, about Clarence showing your sister some moves with the knife?' Chris asks.

'Me? I'm fine with it mate, you carry on,' Howie replies, still chuckling.

'Really?' Clarence looks over at him, as Chris laughs again. 'You don't mind, then?'

'No mate, but Dave's the one with the knife skills, maybe he should do it,' Howie says. 'What do you think, Dave?'

'I think your sister would like Clarence to do it,' Dave replies, showing a rare ability to pick up on a social situation.

'Cheers, Dave,' Clarence says softly.

From the motorway, the convoy takes a slip off to pass quickly through rural villages as the night sky starts to lift. The lush landscape of rolling hills, wooded copses, and cultivated fields soon becomes flat, open heath land, the first signs they are nearing the coast. The Saxon leads the vehicles through an industrial zone with large hanger-style buildings, signed for marine engineering. Expensive looking powerboats and luxurious yachts loom high on giant stands dotted about the area.

'This is the road in to the Fort,' Howie reports back to the rest. 'As far as I can remember, this is the only road in.'

The convoy drives through the industrial units and into a country lane bordered with high hedges. Within a few minutes, they enter a housing estate, full of large, detached houses. The road passes through the middle of the estate, which abruptly ends with lines of dwellings stretching out on both sides, bordering open heath land.

Howie explains that the landscape changed abruptly, one hundred and fifty years ago when the Fort was constructed, to allow the defenders a wide view of the entire area. Thickets of trees and undulating hillocks had been flattened, and now the area remains wide open.

Lights shining in the distance are the only sign of the Fort ahead of them.

'Can you slow down please, Mr. Howie,' Dave asks quickly.

'Do you see something?' Howie replies as he slows the vehicle down, causing a long line of red brake lights to shine out behind him.

Dave looks to the rows of buildings stretched out on both sides, then out to the flat land, the sky getting lighter with each passing minute.

'Is the Fort down there, where the lights are?' Dave asks, pointing down the road, away from the estate.

'Yep, you can see it clearly during the day,' Howie replies.

'Okay, thanks Mr. Howie,' Dave says, apparently satisfied.

'Chris, can you hear me?' Howie calls out.

Chris lumbers back to the front and leans forward. 'What's up?' he asks.

'Chris, when we get there, we need to make sure we are isolated if we discuss anything ...' Howie whispers just loud enough for Chris and Dave to hear.

'We don't know how long Darren was infected before he turned, and we don't know anything about the people here,' Howie adds, as they both nod, understanding.

'How do we know none of us are infected?' Dave asks.

'Well, I know I'm not,' Howie replies quickly.

'Darren would have said that too,' Dave says.

'True, so how can we be sure?' Howie asks.

'Check for bites and scratches, any open wounds?' Chris says quietly.

'How about we get Doc Roberts to check us over, to be sure?' Howie suggests.

'Sounds good, I'm okay with that,' Chris replies.

'Dave, that all right with you?' Howie whispers.

'Yes, Mr. Howie,' Dave nods.

They drive forward on the straight road as night transforms to morning. The rain clouds of the previous day have now drifted away, leaving a beautifully clear sky. The flat grassland suddenly rises into steep embankments that stretch out to both sides with the road cutting through the middle of them.

Once past the grass banks, they see another stretch of flat grassland, then another high, steep embankment which drops down into a wide ditch on the reverse side. The ditch is cut deep into the earth and is at least ten feet in width, with sheer sides.

'So we've got the first high bank, flat land, then another high bank dropping down into a deep ditch, then more flat land,' Chris voices his thoughts out loud as he takes the scene in.

'It looks like the banks stretch out to both sides of the spit; so does the ditch. Is that an outer wall or just the main wall?' he asks Howie.

'Err ... I think it's an outer wall,' Howie replies, trying to remember. 'From memory, the rear of the Fort has a high wall that drops down straight into the sea. The land was dug out, so the sea is very deep straight away, with no beach – I think there's a rear access point though,' he explains.

'The rear wall runs the length of the rear section and then curves back 'round with the natural lay of the spit. The front section here isn't a straight wall. It has two sections that jut out, one on each side where the wall starts coming back inland, and then there's the long, straight bit we can see here,' Howie finishes.

'We'll need a good look around, as soon as possible,' Dave says.

'Ah ... you mean we need an advanced recce reconnaissance pathfinder,' Howie jokes.

Dave smiles back at him, remembering the previous conversation of a few days ago.

'Hello, we've got company.' Chris point up to the high walls to see heads moving about, peeking over and then dropping back down.

Howie brings the Saxon to a halt a few metres back from the gates.

'I'll go and say hello,' he says, opening the door and dropping down to stretch his arms out and arch his back.

'Ah ... that feels nice,' he mutters, Dave jumps down and walks around to join him at the front.

'Well, we made it, mate,' Howie says, as they walk towards the gates.

'We did, Mr. Howie, and we got your sister,' Dave replies.

'It's all good in the hood, mate – apart from the zombie army coming to eat us.'

They stop a few feet back from the gates, looking at a single door cut into the solid metal plates. A small hatch opens from the inside and a pinched face looks out.

'Are you bitten?' a high-pitched, female voice calls out.

'Oh yes, we are bitten all over and completely infected,' Howie smiles broadly. 'I'd recognise that voice anywhere, hello Debbie.'

'You have to strip off again,' the voice laughs back from the hatch.

'Now stop being a pervert and trying to look at Dave being naked and let us in, we're gasping for a brew,' Howie says, laughing. The single door swings inwards and Sergeant Debbie Hopewell walks out, looking neat and tidy and still wearing her all-black police uniform.

'Hello, Mr. Howie,' Debbie smiles as she reaches them, genuine pleasure on her face.

They hug briefly.

'It's good to see you Debbie, I somehow knew you'd be at the front gate,' Howie says.

'Well, we can't just have anyone at the main entry point now, can we,' Debbie says, turning to Dave and giving him an awkward hug, which makes him blush bright red.

'Let me guess, you had a meeting and got it submitted in triplicate and posted the rota on some wall – somewhere,' Howie jokes.

'Oh yes, there must be order, Howie,' Debbie smiles back.

'Hello 'ello, there's a couple of ugly faces I wouldn't forget in a hurry,' a loud voice booms out into the quiet morning air.

'Ted! Hello mate, it's good to see you,' Howie calls out, as he steps forward to shake hands with the former policeman.

'You too, Mr. Howie ... hello Dave, you've kept him alive then,' Ted says, looking at Dave, but nodding towards Howie.

'Hello Ted,' Dave leans forward to shake his hand but stops midway.

'Did you wash your hands this time?' he jokes.

'Bloody hell, someone's taught him a sense of humour,' Ted says, as they shake hands.

'So, you made it down here okay, then?' Howie asks them both.

'Easy run really, we just kept going, despite young Tom whining that he needed to pee,' Ted replies.

'You should have seen the state of the place though,' Debbie cuts in.

'Absolute bedlam, people arriving every few minutes, there was no order, no rationing, no lists, nothing. It's taken days to get things shipshape,' she adds.

'Well, we've got a couple of thousand tired, scared, hungry and thirsty people crammed into these vehicles,' Howie says, turning back to look at the vehicles and seeing Chris, Clarence, and Sarah walking towards them.

'We'd better get them inside then, they'll have to come in on foot, we don't have the room for the vehicles,' Debbie responds in a business-like fashion.

'Ted, Debbie, this is Chris, Clarence, and my sister Sarah. Chris had set up a safe area in London, but it got overrun last night as we left,' Howie introduces them, as they shake hands with polite greetings.

'Right, we need to get the people out and filing in here,' Howie says. 'No room for the vehicles though, have you set up a vehicle area?' he asks.

'Not inside, I made them take the vehicles out and put them into the estate,' Debbie replies. 'We have kept a few for patrolling and gathering supplies though,' she adds.

'Okay, how do you want this done?' Howie asks.

'We're recording the names, date of birth, and last address of everyone entering and then allocating them a specific place inside the compound. We also record any specific skills such as butchery or carpentry, that kind of thing,' Debbie replies.

'We've got doctors, nurses, and some hospital equipment with us,' Chris adds.

'Brilliant, we're desperate for medical personnel. Right, I suggest you get them out of the vehicles and line up in front of the gates. I'll get some people out to distribute water while they wait,' Debbie says. They depart from the brief meeting, as Debbie and Ted head back inside to prepare for the incoming refugees.

Howie and his small group walk back to the Saxon, and Howie calls the recruits and guards over. Chris calls out on the radio for all guards to make their way to the front. Within a few minutes, the small force are all assembled in front of Howie and Chris – Doctor Roberts and a few of the medical team stand to one side.

'Right, they've got enough room for everyone, but we have to line them up for details to be taken. We need a perimeter set up and Curtis, I want you to take the Saxon and go to the rear; keep sweeping back and forth across that area. Nick, I want you on the GPMG. Blowers and Cookey, you're both at the gates being nice to people again. Sarah, would you mind going with them?' Howie asks.

'No problem, I'll take Mary with me,' Sarah replies.

'Be on the lookout for anyone with cuts, bites, or any open wounds,' Howie continues.

'What if we see any?' a voice asks.

'They need to be isolated, but do it quietly with no fuss and do not create panic,' Chris cuts in. 'Doc, can you set something up inside to check people over as they enter?'

'Yes,' Doc Roberts replies curtly, and moves off with his team.

'Jamie, I want you up high somewhere with the sniper rifle,' Howie says to the quiet lad as Jamie looks about.

'Go in and get up on the inside of the outer wall,' Dave says to him.

'Right, spread out, stay sharp, and get those people out,' Howie calls out as they depart. Jamie runs back to the Saxon and draws the sniper rifle from the protective bag. He loops the bag over his shoulder and starts jogging towards the gate.

'Tucker, we'll get that supplies vehicle up front for unloading. Can you get inside and see what the situation with supplies is like. I would imagine Sergeant Hopewell would have a tight grip on it,' Howie asks him.

'Okay, Mr. Howie, I'm on it now,' Tucker replies and starts striding after Jamie to the gate. Doc Roberts and his team walk past, carrying armfuls of equipment and soon disappear into the gate too.

'Mr. Howie!' a voice calls out.

Howie turns to see Tom Jenkins and Steven Taylor walking towards him, both of them with huge smiles.

'Hello Tom, hi Steven, good to see you lads again,' Howie smiles as they shake hands with genuine warmth.

'I knew you'd make it,' Tom says excitedly, looking back at the armed guards. 'Wow, you got more soldiers with you, are they SF too?'

'Err, no. Some of them are ex-soldiers, police officers, like you, and some Army recruits we ... sort of found,' Howie says.

'Wow, and you're in charge of them all,' Tom looks at Howie with awe.

'Well ... I wouldn't say that ...' Howie starts.

'Yes, Mr. Howie is in charge, with that man over there,' Dave says flatly, pointing at Big Chris.

The vehicles are slowly unloaded; scared and terrified survivors drop down from the trucks and squint in the bright sunlight, or slowly emerge from cars to stretch wearily.

Howie watches as Sarah and Clarence work their way back along the fleet, telling the people to move down to the gates where Blowers and Cookey are standing, smiling and joking with their assault rifles strapped to their shoulders. Howie, Chris, and Dave stand near the front, watching the Saxon drive off with Nick waving at them from the top, smiling as they go back down to the rear.

'They're good lads, those recruits,' Chris says.

'Very good, considering what they've been through,' Howie replies. 'Bloody brave, too.'

'We need to start thinking about defence,' Chris says, turning to look at Howie.

'No time like the present then,' Howie replies, as they make their way over and finally step through into Fort Spitbank.

They step into the shadow of the gate and pause for a few seconds to allow their eyes to adjust. The outer wall behind them stretches off in both directions, with a gap wide enough for a few vehicles to drive abreast before the inner wall looms up.

'Bloody big walls,' Chris mutters.

'Good job really, we should just close the door and hide,' Howie replies, to see Chris smiling back at him.

'Well, we could, but where would the fun be in that?' says Chris.

'Hello gentlemen,' a voice calls out from behind them.

They turn to see an old man walking towards them, wearing a blue jumper marked with the *English Heritage* badge. A cravat is tucked into the front of the v-neck jumper; grey roots show in his thinning, dyed ginger hair.

'Hi,' Howie responds as the man draws closer; they shake hands and Howie watches as the man turns to Chris and Dave in turn, Dave quickly wiping his hand immediately after the shaking.

'So, which one of you is Mr. Howie?' the man asks, looking at them each in turn.

'Err, that'll be me,' Howie says.

'Name's Hastings, Roger Hastings, as in the famous battle,' the man smiles at Howie.

'Oh, err, nice to meet you, Mr. Hastings,' Howie replies.

'Oh now, call me Roger,' the man beams back at him.

'How did you know my name?' Howie asks.

'There's been some talk of you in here – quite some talk of Mr. Howie and Dave rampaging round the country killing off the heathen undead.' Roger talks quickly, with an effeminate voice.

'Oh, err, really? Well ...' Howie stutters, unsure of how to respond.

'I think there's quite a few of the people you've met already in here. I keep hearing stories of the famous Mr. Howie and Dave and here you are in the flesh,' Roger speaks, waving his hand as he talks.

'Now Roger, they've only just arrived, so take it easy with them,' Ted calls out, walking over to them.

'Howie, this is Roger Hastings, he was the principal guide here for the guided tours. Apparently he's been here since the place was first built,' Ted adds, smiling at Howie.

'Oh, stop it, Ted, you big brute,' Roger simpers, smacking a limp hand on Ted's old but still solid shoulder.

'Excuse me for interrupting, but your doctor has set up an initial screening room, just off to the right, inside the inner wall; the people are getting processed fairly quickly and we should have them all inside quite soon. Debbie has got a few of her team getting details as they come through,' Ted says.

'Thanks Ted, appreciate the update. How many people are already here?' Howie asks.

'You'll have to ask Debbie for the official figures, but with your lot coming in, I'd say that puts us to maybe seven thousand,' Ted replies.

'Seven thousand?! In here? Bloody hell,' Howie exclaims, looking at Chris who looks equally stunned.

'Word spread quickly; people met up on roads and told each other about it and well, they just kept coming. It slowed right down yesterday and the day before, but, obviously now we've got a lot more coming in,' Ted shrugs his shoulders.

'Listen, I need to get back and help Debbie before young Tom and Steven drive her mad. I'll leave you in the capable hands of Roger for the full experience,' Ted winks at them as he turns away.

'Thanks Ted,' Howie calls out.

Ted waves back at them.

'Are you all ready?' Roger asks, hand on hip and head cocked to one side.

Howie glances at Chris, then looks to Dave, who is staring wide-eyed at Roger.

'Err, yeah I guess so,' Howie says.

'Okay boys, follow me please,' Roger says as he starts to walk towards the inner wall.

They follow behind, exchanging glances and shrugging shoulders.

Stepping away from the gated section of the outer wall, they walk through a large gap in the inner wall and enter the Fort proper. The sight that greets them is staggering and they stop to take in the view. Ahead of them lies the interior of the Fort: open land with the thick, inner wall running around the entire perimeter. The wide open grassed area of the Fort is thick with tents and marquees. Some wooden structures have been hastily erected amongst them. Tents of all sizes and shapes have been placed into the grounds. At first it looks to be a mess of canvas and modern tents, but Howie quickly realises there has been order in the layout.

'Right, gents.' Roger drops the effeminate speech as he launches into full tour guide mode. 'Initially we were using the buildings built into the Fort walls. As you can see, there are doors and gated entrances built into the inner wall. Within those doors and gated entrances are many rooms and tunnels. They were originally designed for ammunition storage, food and supplies, also barracks, sergeants and officers' quarters; there were hundreds of soldiers based here. They had to live and work within the Fort, so everything they needed was within these walls. There is even a fresh water well here.'

'Does it still work?' Chris cuts in quickly.

'Oh yes, we've been using it constantly. They knew what they were doing back in those days, the site was very carefully chosen – they would have needed fresh water in the event of a siege, which they fully expected,' Roger continued.

'Anyway, we were using the buildings and rooms within the Fort walls as accommodation, until we started getting more and more people arriving. Some of those people were surveyors and architects, so we were able to start designating the grounds to be used. We have sectioned off small areas, to the best of our ability, so we can keep walkways and avenues running between them.'

'It looks impressive,' Howie comments.

'It took some doing, but Sergeant Hopewell was very good at getting the right people into the right roles. We were cooking from a central point, but as the population grew, we had to separate that into several smaller cooking points. Each person or group that arrives only gets entry on the basis that they hand over their supplies, to make sure the distribution is fair.'

'Has anyone refused?' Howie asks.

'A few got upset, which is understandable, but we were able to convince them to leave the supplies outside and step in to see it was a good set up and they were not going to be robbed. Most of them are just glad to get somewhere safe.'

'I can imagine, so have you got many supplies then? A population this size will need a lot of food,' Howie says.

'Well, as soon as we got some organisation in here, we started sending out armed foraging patrols. They were tasked to gather supplies and avoid contact at all costs. They have been bringing back tents, sleeping bags, wet weather clothing, bedding, food, medicine, and anything that will help us. They've been raiding every outdoor and camping shop for miles. In terms of food, we are okay, not brilliant, but with careful rationing we have been able to make sure everyone at least gets something,' Roger explains as they walk into the grounds and stroll down the wide central path.

People scurry about, or sit looking forlorn outside of tents. They all stare at Dave, Howie, and Chris as they walk through, and Dave picks up on some nudges and whispers.

'Are the Fort buildings in use now?' Chris asks.

'Sergeant Hopewell uses one as admin offices, and there is a larger section of rooms built into the south side that have been taken over as a hospital. The rooms are the biggest, cleanest, and most recently repaired. In fact, most of the rooms and sections built into the south side are being used; we have the supplies section in there and the armoury.'

'The armoury?' Dave asks immediately, upon hearing his favourite word.

'Yes, we have sourced some items: shotguns, rifles, and quite a lot of ammunition. It's where we stored the black powder for special events,' Roger explains.

'Black powder?' Dave asks again.

'The Fort has retained some of the original cannon and armaments, which one of the historical societies still use for events and public displays.'

'How much black power do you have?' Dave asks, staring hard at Roger.

'Quite a lot,' Roger replies.

After a brief pause, while Dave soaks in that information, Roger continues. 'So that's the south side. Over towards the east section we have the visitors centre, gift shop, and café. We are using that as a meeting place and information point.'

'This is great, Roger, really very good and well organised,' Howie says, genuinely impressed.

'We're not even at the start yet,' Roger replies, immediately back in his camp voice as they enter the visitors centre.

There is a quiet calm inside the building, and Howie recognises the young lady sitting behind the reception desk, speaking to a few people.

'Hello Terri,' Howie calls out to the female police officer that he met in the police station.

'Mr. Howie, wow, I heard you arrived,' Terri smiles sweetly, rushing around the desk and running to hug Howie.

Howie responds, slightly embarrassed, as the pretty blonde girl squeezes him tightly.

'Err, so how have you been?' Howie asks, unsure of what to say after the display of affection. He had thought of Terri Trixey as stuck up and prudish when they had first met.

'Well, apart from Tom and Steven being a pain in the arse, we've been very well,' Terri smiles back at him, finally releasing him from the hug.

'Hello Dave, lovely to see you too.' Terri turns on Dave, stepping forward to embrace him. Howie holds his laugh in at the look of pure terror on Dave's face as he squirms uncomfortably.

'Terri, this is Chris,' Howie introduces them. 'Chris, this is Terri

Trixey, she's a police officer from Portsmouth.' They shake hands formally, then Terri immediately turns back to Howie.

'I heard you brought loads of people with you?' Terri asks.

'Yeah, Chris was in charge of a sort of commune in London that got overrun, so we managed to get them out and down here ... listen, we need to have a look 'round with Roger, can I catch up with you in a bit?'

'Yes, of course, come back for a coffee as soon as you've finished,' Terri smiles at him.

'Err, right, yes of course, a coffee sounds nice,' Howie says.

'She seemed nice,' Chris smiles at Howie as they step away. 'Going for a coffee later then?' he jokes, putting emphasis on the word coffee.

'Piss off Chris, you did that with Clarence and my sister, don't bloody start on me,' Howie laughs at the big man.

'Right gents, up here please,' Roger cuts in, back to business.

He leads them up a flight of metal stairs, across a small landing area and then up onto the top of the inner wall.

'The Fort was commissioned in the 1850's and completed in 1858. The Fort was designed primarily as a motor battery with over fifty mortar placements, which could be angled to fire both out to sea and inland. The smaller sections we will see are for the mortar placements. These are primarily on the south and north walls. The larger sections are for the RMLs, which means ...'

'Rifled Muzzle-Loaded guns,' both Dave and Chris say, in unison.

'Very impressive,' Roger responds quickly. 'These forts, especially the larger ones like this, used new techniques and equipment that had never been deployed before. Those small metal rails that loop in the half circle around this section were used for the loading of the cartridges.' Roger keeps the information flowing, as they slowly walk round the walls to the south side.

'The ground at the rear of the south wall was dug away, so the sea comes straight up to the side of the wall – it gets a bit shallower when the tide goes out and, over the years, the sediment and mud has built back up – but it's still pretty deep down there.'

'How deep?' Chris asks.

'At high tide it's well over head height, at low tide it's probably chest height,' Roger admits.

'We'll have to have look-outs posted at the rear then,' Howie says.

'Why? Are you expecting trouble?' Roger asks.

Chris gives Howie a warning look.

'We'll talk later mate, let's keep going,' Howie replies.

'As you wish,' Roger says.

'After the threat of French invasion finished, the Fort was used as public grounds and then re-commissioned for the First World War. By 1920 it had passed back into public control. Then the Fort was re-commissioned in 1939 for the outbreak of the Second World War – during this time, the Fort was taken over by the Navy and re-named HMS Spitbank. It was mainly used as an anti-aircraft site, but there were also radar installations and, due to the close proximity of the sea, it was used for the designing and testing of landing craft. Then, in the early 1950's it again passed into public hands. *English Heritage* acquired the site during the late 1980's. By that time, most of the interior had fallen into disrepair. Work conducted by *English Heritage* and the historical societies brought it back to the present glory you see today.'

'You said that you had cannon,' Dave says, once Roger finished speaking.

'Yes we do, two on the south wall and two on the north wall, they are not the originals – but the type they would have used in that era,' Roger replies.

'And they can be fired?' Dave asks.

'Yes, they can, but only by members of the historical society – but none of them made it here and I don't think anyone else has the knowledge,' Roger says.

'I can work it out,' Dave says.

'Cannon are very difficult to use,' Roger says with a concerned expression.

'I wouldn't worry – Dave likes blowing things up, did you know he once blew up a cow?' Howie says lightly.

'A cow?' Roger asks, aghast.

'Oh yes, you should hear some of the stories Dave has told me, incredible really,' Howie says, looking about nonchalantly.

'Oh really, sounds fascinating,' Roger says, back in the camp voice. They reach the north wall and stand looking out. The view takes in the vista of the flat land stretched out in front of them. From the other side it appeared that the outer wall was higher, but the design was well thought out and the inner wall is raised slightly higher to allow a clear view, but with the ability to drop down to a lower section. Two sections of the front wall jut out, with large, flat platforms situated on top of the inner wall. A huge cannon rests on each buttress, the wide dark mouth facing out to the flat lands.

'Big cannon,' Howie remarks.

Dave examines the cannon closely, feeling along the surface and peering at the rear end. Finally he stands back up and nods.

'Roger, I apologise for being rude, but can you give us a few minutes, please,' Howie asks.

'Why, yes, of course, call me when you're ready.' Roger walks off a respectable distance and turns to face the other direction.

'They'll come from that direction for sure,' Howie remarks, looking out to the houses in the distance.

'And I wouldn't be surprised if they come 'round the back, too,' he adds.

'If the tide is low enough,' Chris says.

'But that's only a matter of six hours or so.'

'Priorities ... we need to make everyone aware of what's happening, we don't tell them details of how we plan to deal with it, just what the threat is. We know Darren was turned for a while before we knew about it, so we have to assume any of these could be turned too.

I think we'll tell everyone what the threat is, then we make secretive arrangements.' Howie says.

'It's actually an old tactic,' Chris explains. 'In old days, when kings suspected a traitor, they would give each general a set task; some of them would be fake tasks and some real. All of the generals were told not to discuss their tasks with any of the others.'

'Can we do that?' Howie asks.

'No reason why not,' Chris replies.

'Right, so we've got a massive zombie army coming for us, what do we do?' Howie asks, staring out over the walls.

'Thin the numbers down before they get here,' Dave replies. 'And we keep thinning the numbers down until we can either meet them equally in battle, or they leave.'

'I don't think they will leave, and the numbers will be huge by the time they get here. We need scouts out there, so we get notice of when they arrive. We should gather all the weapons in and see which ones will be best; make sure ammunition is distributed evenly. Dave, these cannon can be fired, but I guess they don't actually fire cannon balls, can we use something else?' Howie asks.

'Grapeshot, lots of little metal things that will spread out, like a shotgun,' Dave replies.

'Good, how about the GPMG, can we get that up here to fire down? Or is it better on the vehicle?'

'There's a long slope over there, we should be able to get the Saxon up here,' Chris replies, looking back towards the south wall. Howie turns to see a long, wide, grassed slope leading up from ground level to the top of the inner wall.

'Perfect, we can get the Saxon up here with Jamie sniping, see if he can take Darren out early in the game,' Howie says.

'If we organise quickly we can dig pits, use spikes and caltrops. If there is enough black powder we could rig something up in the housing estate, too,' Dave says.

'Caltrops?' Howie asks.

'Sharp metal spikes hidden in the ground that pierce the feet; it won't kill them, but it will cause horrible injury and slow them down,' Chris replies, for Dave.

'I like it, and the spikes?' Howie asks, again.

'Put them in the ditch and cover them with something, or dig pits and cover them up,' Chris explains. 'They're called Punji sticks.'

'Punji sticks? Sounds nice,' Howie says. 'Oh, like the sharpened bamboo canes?'

'Yeah, wood or metal will do it.'

'We've got a lot to do and not much time to do it in, if you're both happy we'll get everyone together, tell 'em what's happening and sort who can do what, according to skills and materials we have available. Once we've done that we'll set up in one of those rooms and use runners to tell them what we want done,' Howie says, the confidence and natural leadership showing in his voice.

'Agreed,' Chris responds, and Dave nods firmly.

'Roger, thanks for that mate. We need to get everyone together, how can we do that?' Howie calls out.

'Everyone? That's a lot of people,' Roger replies in a business-like manner, rather than camp.

'Yep, I know, but it's very important. The Saxon has a loud speaker on it, can we get that inside and everyone gathered 'round, somehow?'

'Right, yes of course. Leave it with me, I'll get some people on it now,' Roger replies quickly, before scampering off back down to ground level.

'It's gonna be a big fight,' Howie says, after a pause.

'It will be, Mr. Howie,' Dave replies.

'How many of these fights have you had so far?' Chris asks.

'A few,' Howie replies quickly.

Chris looks to Howie and Dave to see the dark looks on their faces.

'There's gonna be a whole lot of them,' Chris says softly.

'Fuck 'em, we'll win,' Howie says, in a firm voice.

CHAPTER SIX

I stare out at the flatlands and look to the housing line in the distance; Dave is by my side, Chris a few steps away.

I hear noise behind me, and turn to see Clarence and Malcolm climb up to stand with us. No words are spoken. We look to the view before us and each of us thinks of what is to come. After a few minutes, I hear more noise behind me; Blowers and Cookey are coming to tell me they have been relieved by some of the Fort's guards. They are joined by Tucker, chasing after them noisily to try and catch up. They sense the mood and join us looking out, spread out in a line. I almost don't hear the stealthy Jamie until he is standing at the end of the line, sniper rifle hanging from his shoulder. We stare at what we know is coming our way. What we know is coming to wipe us out. The hatred they have for us, *for me,* is incredible, and thoughts pass through my head that maybe if I offered myself to them they would leave the rest alone. But I know that isn't true; they won't stop until every last one of us is taken and turned. Can I do this? Can I fight these things again? Maybe we should turn and run, but the sea is behind us and there is nowhere to run to. We could take boats and ships and sail away, but more of them will be there to meet us, wherever we go. We don't have boats or ships for several thousand people. Running is useless. Even if we used every vehicle we could find, they will seek us out. We need food, water, warmth, and rest. They need nothing.

Injuries hurt us, blood loss makes us weak. Nothing less than death stops them. My head spins. I feel like I'm drowning. I'm in too deep and I can't go anywhere or do anything else now. I dragged Dave across the country to get Sarah, and I picked those lads up on the way. Why did they follow me? I'm not a leader, not a soldier. I can't do this. Self-doubt and fear grow in me. I had Sarah to fight for before, I had something to keep me going, but she is safe now, and without that driving motivation I don't know if I can do this again. The cost is too much. If I fail, then they all fail, they all die. I think of McKinney. Poor McKinney, he followed me and I let him down. He died because of my mistakes. I taunted them and fuelled my revenge by killing too many. The loss of my parents provoked me and I went after them. Poor McKinney followed me and did what I asked and I watched him die, I held his sweet face and he knew he was dying. I feel sick, weak, and pathetic. But then I look to my left and to my right, and I see those men and boys staring out, the fixed eyes, the set expressions. No words are spoken. No words are needed. I look behind me to the people going about mundane tasks in the Fort: washing clothes, playing with children, and walking between the tents. Smoke drifts up lazily from the cooking points.

The people look like normal people, trying to make sense of their worlds torn apart and destroyed. They are not safe, Sarah is not safe. None of us are safe. The Fort won't protect us forever. At some point they will get through, and then we will all be taken.

The men beside me look resolute and ready, but I feel anything but that. I don't feel ready for this. We turn and start walking back down the slope. Each step feels heavy and wrong. I feel fake. These battle-hardened men keep looking at me like I have the answers. These are soldiers that have fought in proper wars; they were trained and taught tactics and strategies. I am a supermarket manager; I don't belong here on this slope with these men. I belong down there with the other survivors. Who am I to take this on and show the way? Who am I to think I could even breathe the same air as these professionals?

As we stride down, the people of the Fort stop and watch us. The sounds of the camp all cease, conversation stills into silence, and children stop playing. The new arrivals lining up for checking and details all stand and watch. We are higher than them; we stride like warriors. They know we have fought and will fight again, but they don't know what's coming. They look up and I see many faces looking directly at me. Don't look at me, I am nothing. I shouldn't be here, let alone out in front with these men following me. I can't do this.

Chris can lead, he's a proper leader and he should take this from now. Not me.

We keep walking and I notice Dave glancing at me, but I feel ashamed and I can't look back at him. The others walk in silence behind us. We get to the bottom and then have to walk through the camp to get to the front area. I can't help but look to the people standing, watching me as I pass. Their faces look drained and old. Their skin is taut and tight from the lack of food and sleep. Dirty children with unwashed faces stand and stare at the heroes as they pass. The heroes led by a phoney, a fake, a nothing.

I can feel my leg swinging with each step. I am aware of each step and the thousands of eyes standing in silence to watch me. I understand that Roger has spread the word that we need to speak to them all, but suddenly I am not the man to do it. The pressure of so many lives depending on me is too much. Just Dave and I running round quiet streets was one thing; nothing can touch Dave and there was no risk to him, so there was no pressure. All I had to do was get to London and get Sarah, but I made the recruits think I was something special, that I could lead them. I made them believe in me. We reach the Saxon and I see Curtis Graves standing by the open driver's door; he nods at me as I get closer and respectfully moves out of the way, showing deference to the leader, showing that he was in my place but now that I am back, he will stand aside.

I am a joke and none of these men should show respect to me. I turn to see the thousands of Fort occupants walking towards us, crowding around the Saxon to hear what we have to say. My stomach flips and I feel sick; my throat is instantly dry. There are thousands of eyes all watching me, waiting for me to speak, and more are coming. The new arrivals move away from the line. I recognise some of their faces from the night before. I see Sarah pushing through the crowd to stand by the side of Clarence. Clarence is a man-mountain. He looks the part, big and tough. He should do this; he has a deep voice and looks hardened from years of fighting. Chris is a big man too and looks like a leader. But they both look to me; Chris has shown deference too. He could step forward and do this and these people would listen to him and believe in him. Why has he stepped back? Why is he doing this? Can't he see I'm a fake and out of my depth? Leaning into the Saxon to draw the handheld microphone feels like swimming through mud. My hand reaches out through treacle to switch the microphone on, as Nick drops down from the look-out hole on position with the GPMG.

'You should climb up top, Mr. Howie, so they can all see you,' Nick smiles at me, as he clambers out of the rear doors. I pull the cord and realise it is very long, long enough for me to climb up on the top. I wish it wasn't. I wish I could sit in here, hide away and close my eyes and they would all go away. But instead, I persist in continuing my farce and I clamber out onto the front of the Saxon and then up onto the top. I stand up straight and my legs feel like they will buckle as I look out at the thousands of faces all staring at me. The whole fucking lot of them are staring at me, watching and waiting for the promised speech, the news they have been told I will deliver.

I lift the microphone to my mouth. My thumb hovers above the button. I look down. Dave is looking out to the crowd. Everyone else is watching me: Cookey and Blowers, Tucker, Sarah standing next to Clarence, Chris and Malcolm with arms folded and legs apart.

Jamie, Curtis, and Nick stand together. They are closer to the Saxon than the rest, separating themselves from the main. I hesitate, as my thumb starts to depress the button. I freeze. I can't speak. I look at Sarah and I see a proud look on her face. Her brother is standing on top of a military vehicle addressing a crowd of thousands. Why can't she see I'm a fake, she must see I have frozen. What do I say? What do I tell them?

There is a massive army of undead zombies coming to eat you, but don't worry, I'm here, and even though I have no training or skills I will protect you.

Fuck off. Get off Howie, get down and let a real warrior do this, I scream at myself, as I feel the panic rising within me. I scan the crowd as the fear threatens to consume me: faces old and young are waiting patiently. It feels that I look at each and every face in that crowd and they see me for what I am. I look down and see Dave staring at me.

His eyes lock on mine. He knows I am freezing, he can see right through me. Our eyes lock and something passes between us. A warrior born to fight staring at me hard, passing a message. His gaze is intense, so intense. He nods at me, just once, and that's enough. I look back up at the crowd and press the button down; my voice booms out, strong and confident:

'There is an army of thousands of those things coming for us. Tens of thousands, maybe more. They are coming, and they won't stop until every last one of us is dead and turned into one of them.'

Concerned expressions abound. This isn't why they came here; this isn't what they were expecting.

'They are coming and nothing will stop them from getting here. The Army has gone, the police are gone. There is no government, and no one is coming to save us. Behind you is the sea and there is nowhere left to run. This Fort is strong, but they will get through and they will kill every last one of us.' Fear and panic grips them, and tears start streaming down faces as parents clutch their children close.

'We have all lost loved ones. Just in one week we have lost everything we knew. Our friends and families have been taken from us – and now they will come and try to kill us. The way of life we had is gone and will never come back. All that remains is what we have here and now; this is it. There is no rescue party coming, no fighter jets or warplanes that will wipe them out. This isn't a nightmare that will end; this *will* happen.' I wait and let those words sink in; they need to know how bad this is.

'We are few, compared to the size of them; we are tiny. But there is one thing we have that they don't. We have life. We have life within us, and if you want that life to continue, then we have to fight.

'One week ago, I was the same as you, living normally and working towards the future. But in that one week I have changed. I decided not to just wait and let them come for me. I fought back. I met Dave and then together we fought back and, since then, we haven't stopped killing them. These brave young men you see in front of me, they joined Dave and me, and together we fought back and we took them down. We took them down for killing our families and taking away our loved ones. We did not run away and hide. We went to them and we fought and ... we are still here. We learnt that if we stand together we can survive.

'We went to London and our small group joined with Chris. Then, together, we fought against thousands of them. One small group of men took the fight to them and we walked away from it. We lost men, but only a few, and for each one of ours they took, we took down many of theirs. We showed them we are not scared and we do not fear them. Our small group took hand weapons and attacked them. They are dead already and they don't feel pain. Blood loss doesn't hurt them like it hurts us. If we bleed we get weak, they don't. The only way to kill them is by a massive loss of blood or by taking out the head and the brain. We learnt that, so we adapted and we took them down.' I can feel my voice rising.

'Now we are here, with you, and this is clear; if we hide, they will find us. If we run they will catch us. If we stand still and let them, they will take us. So what else can we do? I'll tell you what I want, I want to show them we will not hide, and we will not run, and we will not stand still. We will fight. We will take as many of them down as we can. We may lose, but to the last man, we will fight back. They are undead. They are evil. They do not have the right to walk amongst us or take our air. They have taken everything from us, but this place, this place here, this is ours, and they will not take it from us without a fight. These men in front of you have stood on the line and survived. On this occasion, we got beaten back, but many times before, we took ground from them; not only surviving but winning.

'When they come we will be ready. We will prepare and do whatever it takes to make ready. Not one person here will sleep or rest until we are ready. There is no choice in this. Every man, woman, and child must be prepared to fight. There is no hiding away and letting the bigger boys fight for you. We will meet them and we will fight them and the last one standing will go down fighting!' I roar out at the crowd.

Chris smiles and turns to stare out at them; Clarence follows his lead, and I see all of them turn to face the crowd. I see defiance creeping in, firm looks, as expressions harden. Men cross their arms and women lift their heads to stand proud.

'We have the right to be here and they do not. This will be hard. Harder than anything you can imagine, but we will work and prepare and then we will meet them and show them no fear, for we shall stand proud. What do we need to do this? We need tools, weapons, we need to know who can make things, fix things: engineers and mechanics. We need foraging parties to go out and bring us the things we need to prepare, we need you to listen to the instructions we give, and accept those instructions without argument. We need you to work and toil and then, at the end of that, we will need warriors, fighters, brawlers and scrappers, and, most importantly ... we're gonna need buckets of coffee to keep us awake.'

I get a few smiles and nods from this.

'We can do this, we few here at the front have shown that we can fight back. We did not roll over and accept it. We are humans and, throughout history, we have fought with each other. But now, at this time and at this place, all differences are set aside and we stand together and we fight together and if needs be, we will die together, but they will know that we did not weaken and we did not run.'

I see the change in them; faces look ready, men look to one another with pride on their faces, and women stand straight and true, ready to fight to protect their own.

'Stand with us and show those things that we are not to be touched.' I nod once, firm and strong, and start to clamber down, to an explosion of cheering.

'Thanks Dave,' Howie says quietly, after jumping down from the Saxon and sidling over to the small, quiet man.

'What for, Mr. Howie?'

'You know very well what for,' Howie smiles at him.

'I don't know what you're talking about,' Dave replies.

'Okay mate, thanks anyway,' Howie says again, still smiling at the glint in Dave's eye.

There is a sudden excitement and air of action within the group. Howie's words have stirred them, motivated them, and, given the opportunity, they would charge out of the Fort now and attack the zombie army with just forks and spoons.

'Good speech, Howie,' Chris calls out over the noise from the thousands of voices, all speaking at the same time.

'Thanks, mate,' Howie replies.

'Seriously, I've heard some corkers before, normally from some officer who will be safe in the base when we charge out, but that was good. You told them the truth and then got them going,' Chris says, closer now, but still having to raise his voice.

'Yeah,' Howie says, feeling just a little embarrassed.

'Honestly Howie, it was good. Typical British spirit that was,' Malcolm joins in.

'Well I had to tell them something,' Howie says. 'And the microphone is still there, mate, you can have a go, if you want.'

'No no, honestly it was good stuff,' Malcolm laughs.

'Hey Howie, that was great.' Sarah appears at his side, still accompanied by the giant Clarence.

'Thanks, Sis,' Howie replies, uncomfortable with all the praise that is being heaped on him. 'Right, we need somewhere private to work,' he says to Chris and Dave; they both nod in return and Chris strides off to find Roger.

'Why the secrecy?' Sarah asks, concerned.

'That lad, Darren, he was turned for some time before we knew; any one of these could be the same, so we can't risk everyone knowing exactly what we are doing.'

'Oh, that makes sense ...' Sarah looks around, staring at the many faces.

'It's possible, there's too many here to check everyone, and Darren wasn't bitten or scratched that we knew about,' Howie says. 'So, for safety's sake, we have to assume any of them could be.' He looks around at the crowd. Their faces suddenly look sinister; plots being hatched and plans being made.

'Howie, Roger has a room for us that we can work from. You ready?' Chris calls out, walking towards him.

'Yes, mate, I'm ready. Who are we taking with us?'

'I was thinking you, me, and Dave definitely – I would like Malcolm and Clarence too, if you're okay with it. Any of yours?' Chris answers.

'Blowers is good, but then we'd have to ask Cookey too, that pair are joined at the hip. I think we'll get them initially, then stick them on the door to prevent anyone else walking in, that sound okay?'

'Hmmm, maybe we should just go with you, Dave, and me then,' Chris rubs his bearded chin.

'I know what you mean, but Malcolm and Clarence are good, experienced blokes – it would be good to have their input,' Howie replies.

'What if they're infected though?' Chris asks.

'True, any of them could be. Fuck it, any of us could be, for that matter,' Howie says.

'Okay, so we get Doc Roberts in with us initially, he checks us over first, then a visual check on each other and we crack on?' Chris suggests.

'Yep, sounds good to me. We need everyone to meet over at the south wall, so we can talk quietly,' Howie replies.

'You go, I'll round them up and send them on,' Sarah says.

'Thanks, Sarah – are you sure you don't mind doing that?' Howie asks.

'No it's okay, I'll get Clarence to stand over them, while I smile sweetly,' Sarah laughs, leading the big man away with her hand on one of his meaty arms and his face going bright red again.

It takes many minutes to walk to the south side of the Fort and the rooms set aside by Roger. Survivors stop to shake hands with Howie and Chris at every few steps, patting them on the back and calling out as they pass. At first Howie tries to move on quickly, but after the first few people, he gets a mischievous glint in his eye.

'Hey, don't just thank me, Dave and Chris here did as much as me,' Howie replies, then watches as the people move on to offer handshakes to Chris and Dave.

Chris takes it in his stride, smiling good-naturedly and making comments, while looking them in the eye – inspiring confidence and looking every inch the warrior leader. Dave, on the other hand, looks aghast at the many hands being thrust in front of him, knowing that to refuse would cause offence, but clearly hating the idea of touching so many people.

'Don't forget to smile, Dave,' Howie calls out, as they work their way through the crowd.

Dave glares back as he frantically wipes his hand on the back of his trousers between each handshake.

Howie and Chris both laugh as they watch Dave trying to smile, the corners of his mouth turning up and showing teeth, which looks very strange on the normally impassive face. Eventually, they break through to the far side, as Dave pulls a bottle of anti-bacterial spray from his pocket and starts cleaning his hands.

'Sorry Dave, I couldn't resist it, your face was a picture,' Howie laughs, as Dave offers him the spray bottle.

'It's okay, Mr. Howie,' Dave says, vigorously rubbing his hands.

'Is it here?' Chris asks, looking at the south wall looming above them. Several doors set into the wall are spread along the ground floor.

'I don't know, where's Roger?' Howie replies.

'Coo-eee gentlemen, over here,' Roger calls out, leaning out of a doorway further up and waving an arm at them. They walk up and enter the door; the room is big and square with a solid-looking old table in the middle. Large, rolled-up sheets of paper lie on the top of the table. Howie looks up to see a single electric bulb hanging down.

'You've got power?' Howie asks, as Roger turns the switch on.

'These rooms have a dedicated generator supplying power, you can't turn all the lights on at the same time, but it will mean you can work privately with the door closed, if you need to,' Roger replies. 'Through that door are more rooms; some of them have old camp beds and chairs, if you need to rest – let me know if you need anything.'

'This is great, thank you Roger, where will you be?' Howie says.

'Just a few doors down, that's where Sergeant Hopewell is working from and the hospital is further down,' Roger replies. 'Oh, there's more of you,' he adds, backing away from the door as the recruits and more of Chris's men start piling in. They chat quietly as they wait for everyone to arrive.

'Nick, can you nip down a few doors and see if Sergeant Hopewell and Ted are there, please mate,' Howie asks.

'No worries, Mr. Howie,' Nick calls out, disappearing out of the door.

Howie looks amongst the group crowded into the room. The recruits are chatting to each other and now mingling more with Chris's men and women left from the commune. Howie thinks of the losses they took last night and the image of McKinney flashes back into his mind. 'We can grieve later,' he mutters.

'Did you say something, Howie?' Chris asks.

'No mate, just talking to myself,' Howie replies.

'First sign of madness,' Chris smiles, as he looks back to the room.

'Don't even joke about that,' Howie laughs.

'What are those on the table, Dave?' Dave has unrolled some of the large sheets and is bent over, studying them.

'Maps and plans of the Fort and surrounding areas,' Dave replies.

'Hello, what's all this then,' Ted booms out, as he strides confidently into the room, followed by Sergeant Hopewell and Terri, who immediately smiles at Howie.

'You never came back for that coffee,' Terri admonishes him.

'Hi Terri, err, well, kind of been busy,' Howie replies, feeling Chris and a few of the others watching him.

'That's okay, I heard your speech. It was amazing,' Terri says, staring with big blue eyes directly at Howie, her pink lips revealing perfect white teeth as she smiles again.

'Oh, yeah, err, thanks Terri.' Howie feels himself starting to blush.

'Hi, I'm Sarah, Howie's sister,' Sarah steps forward, becoming aware of her brother's discomfort; they start chatting as Howie discreetly steps over to Chris.

'I don't know you very well, Howie, but I've not seen you nervous before,' Chris says quietly.

'I always get nervous around pretty girls,' Howie whispers back, as Chris throws his head back, laughing loudly and drawing attention from the whole room.

'I've seen you charge into thousands of those things,' Chris says, still unable to use the word zombies. 'And then give a rousing *gung ho* speech to thousands of people, and you get nervous 'round one pretty girl?

'Shush, keep your voice down, oh, bollocks, I think she heard you,' Howie mutters, seeing Terri staring over at him.

'I think we're all here,' Malcolm says, as Doc Roberts enters the room with his white lab coat flapping open.

'Thank fuck for that,' Howie mutters again, grateful for the reprieve. 'Can someone close the door? Thanks. Right, most of us know what's coming our way, and these people will be looking to us for confidence and reassurance. I know we're all tired and have had enough, but without us they don't stand a chance. The plan is that a few of us will be working from here and sending out instructions for what's needed.'

'And we expect you to see them through,' Chris steps in.

'From now on, only those with a reason are to go up onto the walls, and I expect each of you to try and make sure that happens. We know that people can be infected and either not know it or hide it very well, so we will be taking every precaution to prevent all of our plans from becoming known. If you are given a task, please do not question it or discuss it with anyone else.'

'Debbie, we will need a list of skills, and we are going to need runners too, people that can run out and pass messages, or find the people we need,' Howie says.

'Okay, I've got more lists than you will ever need and I'm only a few doors down. Also, we've got a pool of bored, older kids that need something to do; we can use them as runners. I'll organise that and have them nearby,' Debbie replies.

'Good, we also need guards on the gate. I don't want to tell the people out there what they can and can't do, but for now, we need to restrict who goes in and out,' Chris continues, after Sergeant Hopewell finishes. 'There's some rooms back there to relax in, or outside, but stay close and wait for further instructions. Has anyone got any questions?'

'Weapons, sir, we've got some, the people out there have some too, and I think there's probably some more knocking about ... are we going to centralise them and work out who has what?' one of Chris's men shouts out from the back.

'Good point, we'll cover it and make sure they are distributed to the right people and in the right place,' Chris answers.

'We're going to need sleep, we've been going all day yesterday and all night – if we work through the night and then fight tomorrow, we'll be dropping like flies,' a man says from the front, half-dressed in a police uniform.

'Try to sleep when you can, rest when you can, but, ultimately, tough shit. If they come and we're not prepared, we'll die, simple as that,' Howie replies quickly, and without humour.

An awkward silence follows, with the armed men and women looking down at their feet, avoiding Howie's intense stare.

'But ... Mr. Howie, we're exhausted, we've been fighting and going for a long time, we can't keep going like this,' the man whines, rubbing his forehead.

'Okay mate, I'll tell you what, why don't you fuck off and get some sleep then, go and sleep and feel sorry for yourself and whine that no one is giving you a suitable rest period. Even better, we'll send someone to the massive zombie army and ask them nicely to please wait so we can all have a nice sleep.' Howie's voice rises as he speaks, and the darkness spreads across his face quickly. '*I'm sorry, zombie army, but we're tired and you're pushing us too hard.* Get this, mate, we are all going to die and become brain-eating zombies if we don't do whatever it takes.'

'Yeah, I get that, but listen, there's only so much we can take before we just drop ...' the man carries on, oblivious to the whining tone of his own voice.

'MAN UP AND DEAL WITH IT, OR DIE,' Dave's voice booms out, suddenly causing everyone to jolt backwards; the man goes to speak again, but Dave steps forward with lightning speed and stands nose-to-nose with him.

'WHAT? DO YOU HAVE SOMETHING ELSE TO SAY?' Dave roars at him.

'... no, nothing,' the man replies, avoiding Dave glaring at him and staring down at his own feet.

'DO YOU WANT TO DIE?' Dave bellows.

'No.'

'DO YOU WANT TO LIVE?'

'Yes,' the man replies quietly.

'MOANING AND WHINING IS MORE INFECTIOUS THAN THOSE THINGS OUT THERE. IF I HEAR YOU MOANING AGAIN, ME AND YOU WILL HAVE AN ISSUE. IS THAT CLEAR?'

'Yes,' he mutters. 'I'm sorry, I didn't mean to whine, I lost some good mates back there and I'm in shock, but you're right and I apologise to you and everyone else in here,' the man says, turning back to face the room with a look of shame.

Another one of Chris's men steps forward and rests his hand on the man's shoulder, nodding gently at him.

'Debbie, can you get on to those lists and have the runners ready ... Tucker, would you mind arranging for some food and cleaning supplies to be brought over?' Howie asks, breaking the silence.

'Yes, of course ... err ... is there anything else?' Debbie asks.

'No, that's it – get some rest while you can, but stay close,' Howie says.

The door opens and Debbie files out first, followed by Ted.

Howie turns to see Terri coming back into the door; the sunlight catches her golden hair, framing her soft skin, and casting an angelic halo about her. Howie finds his breath catching in his throat as she smiles at him. *She is beautiful*, he thinks, staring at her with an open mouth.

'You'll catch flies,' she says quietly.

'What? Eh?' Howie says quickly, snapping back to reality.

'Sarge said for me to stay close and act as your liaison officer,' Terri says. 'Are you okay, Howie?'

'Yep,' he replies, too quickly.

'Now, I wouldn't do this for anyone else, as I'm not a bloody secretary, but I'm going to get you some strong coffee and stay here while you drink it, got it?' she says, seriously.

'That sounds lovely, Terri ... we need to speak to Doc Roberts for a few minutes, anyway,' Howie replies.

'Did someone say something about coffee?' Chris calls out, looking up from the maps on the table.

'I'll come with you,' Sarah interrupts, knowing what the men need to do.

They leave the room and Howie calls out for Blowers, asking him to prevent anyone coming in from the back rooms for a few minutes.

Blowers nods once and turns to face the other way, standing with his arms folded and blocking the door.

'Doc, shall we?' Chris asks.

'Shall we what, Chris? You asked me to come here, but I don't know why?' Doctor Roberts snaps back in his usual, clipped tones.

'Doctor, we need to make sure, as best we can, that none of us three are infected. Darren, one of my lads, was infected for a while before he turned, and we can't risk any of us three turning, while we are planning ...' Howie explains, as the doctor holds a hand up to stop him talking.

'Right, got it, I understand, gentlemen. You are going to be planning the defence from here, and if one of you is infected, then you could potentially let the other side know about the plans, is that it?'

'Yes,' Howie and Chris say in unison.

'There is no sure way of checking without blood tests, but we don't have time for that. There are some tell-tale signs we have learnt: an increase in body temperature and increased heart rate. I'll do the best I can and check you visually. Strip off,' the doctor commands.

Howie and Chris shrug at each other and start to slowly peel their clothes off. Dave doesn't hesitate and is stripped naked within a minute. Doctor Roberts starts with Dave, checking his temperature first, and then listening to his heart rate. He examines his eyes closely, shining a bright light into the pupils, then into his ears. After that, the doctor conducts a very close visual check, examining each inch of skin to check for scratches or open wounds.

'Turn 'round,' the doctor orders, and starts checking Dave from behind, first his back, then down to his buttocks and then his legs.

'Bend over,' the doctor commands, shining a torch into Dave's backside.

'I can see that light shining out your mouth, Dave,' Chris jokes.

'Clean and healthy, as far as I can tell ... Chris, you are next ...' The doctor drops down onto his knees to examine Chris's legs and, after a few minutes, the doctor pauses and stares over at Dave – Howie and Chris realise the same thing and both stare over at him.

'You can get dressed now, Dave,' the doctor says quietly, as the door opens and Terri steps in, holding a large, metal flask.

'Oh, my God,' Terri fumbles with the heavy flask, staring at the three naked men standing behind the table.

Howie and Chris both quickly cover their privates as Dave spins around to face the other way.

'Err, I'll leave this here,' Terri says, flustered, as she walks further into the room and places the flask on the table, glancing at Howie as she does so.

'We're just being examined by the doctor,' Howie says feebly.

'All at the same time?' Terri says quickly, then sees the doctor crouching down, examining one of Chris's kneecaps.

'Oh, hi, Doc', she says, and smiles at Howie trying to cover his bits with both hands. 'I'll leave you to it.' She smiles and walks out, as Chris bursts out laughing.

'That wasn't funny,' Howie groans, to the sound of Blowers stifling laughter from the doorway.

'I think she enjoyed it,' Chris laughs.

'Stop laughing and stand still please, now turn round and bend over,' the doctor orders, oblivious to the interruption.

CHAPTER SEVEN

'They have to approach from the front, the Fort is built onto this spit,' Chris says, running his finger around the outline of the land on the map. 'They cannot attack from the sides or rear in any great numbers, so at least we know to expect a frontal attack.'

The three of them pore over maps, drinking strong coffee, after being left with explicit instructions from Doctor Roberts to report any changes in body temperature and to watch each other closely.

'Okay, so we know which way they are coming. We've got a large, open, flat land in front of us with two big banks, one of which drops down into a type of dry moat. Before that, we've got the housing estate,' Howie continues, describing the area.

'If I can use that black powder I should be able to rig up some traps within the housing estate,' Dave cuts in.

'What sort of thing?' Howie asks. 'I don't think we've got any cows to blow up.'

'I'll have to have a look 'round and see what's there first, but the amount of numbers they're bringing means they will have to funnel through the estate,' Dave replies.

'Cows?' Chris asks, puzzled.

'Dave once blew up a cow to take out an enemy target,' Howie explains.

'Oh, was that you? We heard about that,' Chris says.

'And a refinery too,' Howie adds.

'You did the refinery? We were on standby for that, Christ that went up, didn't it – you should definitely rig the estate then,' Chris says.

'How many will you need?' Howie asks.

'Just one other. Jamie?' Dave replies.

'Yeah, good idea, how about you take a few more and place them for spotters, put them out as far as you can,' Howie says.

'Okay, Mr. Howie, we'll take a couple of vehicles and use one of them as the furthest obs point – do they have any spare radios here?'

'Check with Debbie, those radios that we used yesterday ... will they reach into the estate from here?' Howie asks.

'Not likely,' Chris replies, shaking his head.

'Dave, see if you can source some more, we will need constant radio contact with you, and make sure you can get back quickly if it goes bent,' Howie says.

'Okay, Mr. Howie,' Dave replies, gathering his backpack and assault rifle, before heading out the door to find Jamie who is sitting patiently in the sun.

'You're with me,' Dave says to him.

'Okay,' Jamie replies, instantly on his feet and ready.

Howie walks into the back room to find several of the recruits and Chris's guards dozing quietly.

'Blowers, can you get Cookey, Nick, and Curtis to come in, please mate,' Howie asks, keeping his voice low.

'On it, Mr. Howie,' Blowers replies, instantly awake and alert.

Within minutes, he rounds the others up and leads them back into the room with Howie and Chris.

'Lads, between the four of you I want to make sure the top of the walls stay clear from anyone else. Curtis, I want you to get the Saxon up onto the inner north wall; the slope is wide enough to drive up.

Position it so that the GPMG can fire down onto the flat lands. Nick and Curtis, you take the Saxon and swap round between manning the GPMG and making sure no one else goes up on the wall. Blowers and Cookey, I want you both on the front gate, making sure no one goes outside. Blowers, find a couple of Chris's guards and get them positioned at some of the access points up onto the walls, to politely discourage anyone from going up. Got it?' Howie asks.

'Yes, sir.' Howie gets a chorus of replies as they ready themselves and move out of the room.

'So that's Dave and Jamie taking care of the estate and putting spotters out, and then the walls and look-outs taken care of. What's next?' Howie turns to Chris.

'Weapons,' Chris replies, and steps out of the door to call Malcolm inside.

'Malcolm, find Roger and get a suitable place to work from. Get an inventory of all the weapons we have and ammunition. Do it as quickly as you can, also try and find out if there are any gunsmiths anywhere near here that we can raid or make use of,' Chris says to him.

Malcolm nods back and is gone within seconds. Chris disappears into the back room and drags two chairs over to the table, placing one on each side.

Howie pours more coffee and they sit down, examining the maps closely, while drinking the strong java.

'I remember reading historical novels about cannon firing grapeshot ...' Howie says. 'If Dave can get those cannon working, we can use them from the tops of the wall.'

'Good idea: chains, nuts and bolts, anything will do for them,' Chris replies, leaning forward to look closely at him. 'Listen, we can go for a siege situation and pick them off bit by bit, maybe we don't have to go out and meet them face to face, Howie.'

'It won't work, Chris, if we bed in and one of these thousands of survivors in here turns, all it would take is for them to infect a couple, those couple get a few each and, within minutes, we're attacked from inside and outside with nowhere to go. I honestly think we should do what we can to reduce their numbers and pick them off, but then we end it, once and for all,' Howie replies, staring back at him.

'I do agree with you and I think it's the right thing to do, but I want to be sure we know what we're getting into.'

'I know, mate; I think we need to choose our ground. We can use the estate and flat lands to lay traps and pick them off; the banks and the deep ditch we can use too. That open land between the ditch and the outer wall, that should be our ground,' Howie says, indicating the area on the map.

Chris nods, looking down at the area Howie traces with his fingers.

'It gives us some cover from the cannon firing overhead, plus we get to use the banks and ditches to slow them. It's a big enough area.'

'There it is then, our ground,' Howie says quietly. They both stare down at the map, just marks on paper showing the outline of the Fort walls and the positions of the embankments and ditch.

'Who'd have thought it. One hundred and fifty years ago this was built to protect us from the French, and now it's being used again to stop a zombie army,' Howie chuckles.

'I hate that word,' Chris mutters with distaste.

'We could dig some ditches along the edge of the flatlands, by the estate, then put the spikes down in the longer grass and then something after the first bank ...' Howie says.

'If we put vehicles on this side of the first bank they wouldn't be seen, until they're coming down the sides,' Chris cuts in.

'Okay, so a load of vehicles set to explode, then they go up the second bank and they've got the deep ditch. Fuck it, let's fill it with petrol and blow the shit out of 'em,' Howie laughs.

'Why not? As long as we're far back enough, it's a good idea,' Chris replies, seriously.

A knock at the door interrupts them and Terri walks in.

'You're dressed, then?' she asks, lightly.

'Dave asked me to give you this. He's got one and said to tell you the spotters have them too.'

'Ah that's great, how many more have we got?' Howie asks.

'I don't know, Malcolm came in and took all the radios into one of the other rooms further down,' she replies.

'Okay, Terri, have we got any diggers or plant machinery here?' Howie asks, taking the radio.

'I'll find out, the sergeant has lists of everything,' Terri answers, before smiling at Howie again and heading for the door.

'That coffee was really nice, by the way,' Howie calls out; she turns and smiles back again before closing the door behind her.

'*Howie to Dave,*' he speaks into the radio, holding the big side-button down.

'*Dave receiving, go ahead, Howie.*'

'*Radio check, receiving you loud and clear.*'

'*Dave to Howie, Roger loud and clear this end, out.*'

'Right, let's go and find Malcolm and see what he's got,' Howie says.

They step out into the bright sunlight to find guards lazing about, stretched out in the warm sun, leaning against the wall, or chatting to each other and the survivors.

Howie and Chris stroll down until they reach Sergeant Hopewell's office; they see her sitting at a desk and looking up at Terri.

'Hi, Mr. Howie.' Howie turns to see Tom and Steven walking towards him from the main camp area.

'Hey mate, everything all right?' Howie replies.

'Yeah, the sergeant's got us patrolling the camp to show a presence – everyone keeps asking us when the fighting starts, or if they can have weapons,' Steven answers.

'Steven, Mr. Howie was asking me, not you,' Tom says petulantly.

'No, he wasn't, he was asking both of us,' Steven fires back.

'I'm the policeman, you're just a community officer, so leave the serious stuff to us.'

'No, Tom, you *were* a police officer, but Mr. Howie said there isn't a police force anymore, so if there isn't one, how can you be a police officer? Ha, we're both the same now.'

'No, I've been trained more than you,' Tom says defensively.

'Trained in what? How to take a statement? Custody procedures? That doesn't really help us now, does it?'

'I've got more unarmed defence training than you, Steven.'

'No, you didn't, we both got the same, you just got taught how to use your baton and pepper spray – I know, because we partnered up for the training, you bloody idiot.'

'Lads, listen, I think it's probably fair to say that you're both the same now, but you're both very valued and it's good you're going 'round the camp and letting people know you are there,' Howie says, diplomatically.

'Ha, fuck you, Tom Jenkins,' Steven shouts, triumphantly, as Tom stares at him in horror.

'I'll leave you to it, lads,' Howie chuckles and steps into the office. Terri and Sergeant Hopewell both stare out, shaking their heads.

'They'll never bloody change that pair,' the sergeant mutters.

'They seem good lads, though,' Howie laughs.

'Did you find out about the diggers or plant machinery, Terri? Oh, hi Sarah, I didn't see you there.'

'My job was mainly administration, so I thought I'd put myself to good use; besides, Patricia here was feeling a little lost, so I said she could stay with me,' Sarah replies, indicating the girl sitting further in the room, drawing on some paper.

'Where's the other woman that was with you? Mary, wasn't it?' Howie asks.

'She's getting cleaned up, then is coming over here,' Sarah says.

Howie turns back to see Terri standing at a desk loaded with thick piles of paper.

'Bloody hell, that's a lot of lists,' Howie says.

'Language, Howie,' Sarah warns.

'Sorry, err, so ... about the diggers?'

'Right, so we have compiled a list of all the people within the Fort: name, date of birth, and last known address. We added work skills and any former military training or firearms experience, pistol or rifle clubs – that kind of thing. We have divided and subdivided the interior of the Fort into sections and allocated people into those sections, so we know roughly the area they should be in. We also appointed a contact person within each section that we can go to them and find out where the section residents are. The idea is that each resident of each section reports to the section contact where they will be, in case they are needed,' Terri explains.

'We have also listed every vehicle in the area, and if they are usable or if we have access to them with keys. We categorised each vehicle into commercial or non-commercial, with a reference to how much fuel the vehicle has, and, of course, which fuel type. So, in answer to your question ...' Terri pulls a clipboard from the pile and starts flicking through the lists.

'You've listed the people that have military experience or firearms knowledge?' Howie asks.

'Yes,' Terri answers, without looking up.

'Can you get that list to Malcolm, he's setting up an armoury here, somewhere – I don't suppose you recorded what kind of firearms they have previously used, have you?' Chris asks.

'Of course we have,' Terri replies, still not looking up. 'We'll get that to him straight away. Ah here it is, yes we have access to three diggers and a cross-reference to the people that can operate them.' Terri looks up and smiles, her blue eyes twinkling.

'Wow, that's great,' Howie says, amazed at the volume of work they've undertaken already. 'Can you get those digger drivers to us, as soon as possible.'

'Of course, *Mr. Howie*,' Terri says mock demurely, as she steps outside.

'Can I have three runners in here please?' Terri calls out.

Within seconds, three slim, teenage boys run into the room, almost standing to attention in front of Terri, who runs her finger down the list of vehicles and then starts flicking through the pages of names of the Fort occupants.

'I need you to find George Kimberly from Section 2, Martin Aylesbury from Section 7, and Mark Donovan from Section 18. Bring them back here, as soon as possible, thank you.' Terri looks up with a stern face, nodding at the boys to get moving.

They run into the thick crowds and weave through the tents and structures.

'That's brilliant,' Howie says, watching the lads sprint away.

'Is there any kind of blacksmiths here or workshops?'

'There's workshops, quite well equipped too, from what Ted told me,' Sergeant Hopewell replies.

'Terri, can you also find engineers, mechanics, and metal workers, and send them up to us?' Howie asks.

'Of course, leave it with me, I'll get more of those runners out,' she replies, examining her lists.

'Those runners are great,' Howie says, admiringly.

'Oh, those boys all like our Terri here, especially when she smiles at them,' Debbie says, without looking up from the papers in front of her.

'I bet they do,' Howie says, then instantly blushes as he realises what he said. 'I mean, err, I'm sure they ... do ... shall we go and see Malcolm then?' he says, turning to Chris, who is smiling broadly and leaning against the wall.

'Or we could stay here and watch you trying to pull your foot out of your mouth,' Chris replies.

'Very funny, thanks for the list, Terri, err ... we'll be off then,' Howie says, turning to see Sarah leaning back in her chair, watching him with amusement.

Howie steps out, rubbing his face, groaning softly to himself. Chris comes out, shaking his head silently. They walk down a few steps to find an armed guard outside a set of solid-looking metal gates that lead into a tunnel.

'Is Malcolm in here?' Chris asks the guard.

'Yes, Chris, down there to the right.' the guard opens the gate to admit Howie and Chris.

They enter the short tunnel and turn right into a large room. Natural light trickles in from barred windows set into the wall. Long workbenches run down one side, and weapons of all types are stacked up next to boxes of ammunition. Malcolm and Clarence work their way through the weapons, checking and clearing.

'Hi Chris, we've got quite a lot here really,' Malcolm says, straight to the point.

'We've got some decent rifles, which will be good on the walls for longer range; we've separated the assault rifles, though some of them are only 9 millimetre, no good for longer range. There's loads of shotguns, too.'

'How about ammunition?' Chris asks.

'You can never have enough rounds,' Malcolm replies. 'We've got quite a lot, but it'll soon go if we get into a period of sustained firing.'

'Did you find out if there are any gunsmiths nearby?' Chris asks, picking up one of the rifles from the bench.

'There's a few actually, all in a ten mile radius,' Malcolm replies.

'Clarence, can you get some people together and a couple of vehicles – vans would be good – we're going to need a foraging party. See Sergeant Hopewell next door, I bet she's got a list of them somewhere,' Chris says to the huge man.

'Got it,' Clarence rumbles, putting down an assault rifle.

'What else do we need?'

'Any kind of weapon you can get: guns, knives, swords, axes – anything we can use. Also, we'll need nuts, bolts, and short chains, to make grapeshot for the cannon.' Chris explains.

'Clarence, try and get some more arrows too,' Malcolm calls out.

'Arrows?' Chris asks, looking about.

'There's quite a few competition level archers in here, have you seen the range and power on modern bows?' Malcolm replies, indicating the end of the bench and the modern bows racked up next to a pile of arrows.

'Fair enough, get whatever you can, Clarence,' Chris says.

'On it,' Clarence replies and steps out of the room.

Back in their planning room, Howie and Chris sit down and go over what they've already set in motion, discussing the finite details. There is a knock at the door.

'Come in,' shouts Howie.

'Hi, we were asked to come here?' A middle-aged man enters, followed by two younger men.

'Hi, thanks for coming. Excuse me asking, but who are you?' Howie stands, holding his hand out to the closest one.

'I'm George,' the first man answers; the other two introduce themselves as Martin and Mark.

'Ah, you must be the digger drivers then,' Howie asks.

'Yeah, we are, not just diggers, but anything like that really,' George answers.

'Do you know each other?' Chris says, watching the men closely.

'I've known Martin for years, we worked together before, err, before this – we only met Mark here, though.'

'When did you arrive?' Howie asks.

'Saturday afternoon. We heard the broadcast and came straight here; me and Martin didn't have far to come, we live near each other too, well we *lived* near each other ...'

'Mark, when did you arrive here?' Chris takes over the questions.

'Sunday morning, sir,' Mark answers, in a polite tone.

'I apologise if this is an insensitive question, but did you come with your families?' Chris asks.

'I've got my wife and son with me, sir,' Mark says.

'We've got our wives and children here too,' George adds.

'Have any of you been bitten, scratched, or had any direct contact with those ...'

'He means the zombies, have you had any contact with the zombies?' Howie finishes off for Chris.

'No, sir, I saw them, but we hid in the house and then got down here quickly; they were in the street when we left, but it was daytime and they were slow,' Mark says first. Howie looks to George and Martin.

'Well, we had a spot of bother getting out of our road; there was a couple of them in the way ...' George says, nervously.

'What did you do?' Chris asks.

Martin and George look at each other, then back at Chris.

'We, err, well we run them over with the van,' George says, after a pause.

'You were all in one van and you ran them over? Did you make contact with them physically, get any blood on you or get cut, bitten, or scratched, or did any of your families?' Chris says, staring hard at them.

'No, sir, nothing like that, the van got blood on it, but none of us did,' George says, as Martin nods in agreement.

Chris looks to Howie, nodding once.

'Okay, sorry about the questions, but we had to be sure none of you were infected or ran the risk of being infected. We have a task for you, but before we say anything about it, would you all be willing to have a full medical examination?' Howie asks.

They each nod and reply that they would agree to the exam.

After the men are thoroughly examined by the doctor, Chris starts to explain.

'Okay, gentlemen, we need some trenches dug into the ground near the housing line, but we want to do it so we can hide them afterwards, or, at least, cover them up so they're not easily visible. Is that possible?' Chris asks. The three men look to each other, thinking, until George takes a small step forward, nominating himself as the unofficial spokesman.

'It depends on how deep and how wide?' George replies. 'The grass is long enough out there to cut some down and lay the cuttings across the top, that would cover it and blend in somewhat, but only if it's not too wide or deep.'

'We want it roughly two yards wide, so it's not easy to step over or jump, and deep enough to put either some spikes in or some flammable material,' Howie replies.

'Oh, I get it, like a trap for the zombie army,' Martin cuts in. 'Yeah, that can be done ... for spikes you would want a decent drop in there, for the body to be impaled though.'

'Yeah, a few inches wouldn't do it, unless they were razor sharp that is, otherwise you'd need a couple of feet at least,' Mark adds.

'I reckon we could dig 'em out about three feet deep and a couple yards wide and be able to cover them over; it won't be pretty, but I reckon we know what you want and we'll do the best we can,' George says earnestly, as Martin and Mark both nod.

'Good, we'll have some guards go out with you to give you some protection; we need to do this now, though. The most important thing is that you do not mention a word of this between here and getting outside the gate – that is vitally important, is that clear?'

'Sir, we won't say anything, but could you let our families know we'll be back a bit later? They'll only worry otherwise,' Martin replies.

'Of course we will. Chris will show you on the map exactly what we need and I'll be back in a minute,' Howie says, ushering the men over to the table.

Chris indicates the area of flatland immediately in front of the row of houses.

'We need it all the way across the entire width of the spit. Will three of you be enough to do this?' Chris asks.

'Yes, sir, the digging won't take long, cutting the grass and laying it across will take the longest part ... err, may I ask how you are going to fix the spikes in?' George asks.

'We're going to speak to engineers next and ask them to arrange it,' Chris replies, looking at the experienced man.

'That's a long strip you're planning sir, right across the width of the spit, and the spikes will need to be driven in quite a way to hold fast, but done without blunting the ends, especially if you're using metal. Also, where will you get the spikes from?'

'There's a workshop here; we'll find some engineers and mechanics to try and sort them out. You think spikes will be hard to do then?' Chris asks, openly taking their advice.

'Not impossible, but certainly difficult. We've got enough people here to do it, but if you're concerned of some of them being infected, then it will be bloody hard for you to trust that many to go outside,' George says.

'Okay, good point, we'll see if it can be done. Where are the diggers?'

'Over on the west side, stacked up between the two walls. We managed to get quite a few vehicles in the gap.'

'That's good thinking, keeps them safe,' Chris says.

'I've got runners telling your families you're busy for a little while, they can go to Sergeant Hopewell next door if they've got any concerns, and I've jacked up some guards to go with you. I've had to use some of your people, Chris, mine are all tucked up, but I've briefed them to what's needed,' Howie says, coming back into the room. 'Whenever you're ready, gentlemen.'

Howie leads the men out of the planning room and down towards the gate, stopping to speak to Blowers and Cookey, who are leaning against a post, smoking cigarettes and drinking coffee. Their assault rifles are strapped across their shoulders, allowing the rifles to rest at the front.

'Lads, how's it going?' Howie asks, as they walk closer.

'Mr. Howie, we're just having a coffee,' Cookey replies guiltily.

'No worries, lads, you don't have to apologise, I know you'll stay alert. Has anyone tried to get in or out?'

'Nope, we've had a lot of people come and ask us questions,' Blowers says, stubbing his cigarette out.

'How do they seem when they're speaking to you?' Howie asks.

'Nervous and pumped up, to be honest, sir, like they want to be doing something, rather just waiting,' Cookey replies.

'Okay. Just to let you know that we're taking these chaps out into the flatlands with some plant machinery, in case anyone questions the noise or anything,' Howie explains, as Cookey opens the small walk-through gate for them.

They step into the wide lane between the inner and outer wall. The concrete walkway is now covered with a cropped layer of grass. They turn left and walk down into the area that runs between the two walls, the plant machinery and other vehicles coming into view, as the lane bends to the left. Several armed guards are recognised by Howie, from back in the commune, and, already spoken to, follow at a discreet distance, their weapons gripped and ready.

Howie pauses to let the three men walk on to their vehicles:

'Okay, so you know what they're doing, keep a close eye on them and make sure they don't leave their vehicles and go into the estate. We've got a couple of our people already in the housing area, so be very careful if you have to venture in. In fact, I would say, don't go in there unless absolutely necessary, and make sure you let us know on the radio ... got it?' Howie says to the guards, who nod back, as the nearest of the diggers starts up with a noisy roar.

'We might be sending more people out , but I'll let you know if we do,' Howie says, leaving them to it and walking back to the gate. Once inside, he walks slowly back towards the south wall, thinking of the plans they have put in place, a visual image forming in his head.

We've got spotters out front, so we should get notified when they arrive. There could be undead already in the estate watching us, but we can't afford the time or people to sweep it clean, and Dave is in that area rigging some traps up. The zombie army has to come this way, so they have to go through the estate. Dave blows some of them up and slows them down. Then they push into the flatlands and into the trenches, with either spikes, or something else, to hurt and hamper them. After that, they have to negotiate the first bank and, hopefully, a load of vehicles set to explode; then the second bank and the deep ditch. After that, we're on our own. How many will they bring? Will they be armed? Fuck, what if they're armed? We'll be slaughtered. Nothing we can do about that. I suppose we can fall back into the Fort, if we have to, but it won't take long for them to get through. Mind you, we've got the Saxon up top with the GPMG; we can put more rifles and weapons up there and hopefully the cannon with grapeshot, if Dave can sort them out.

Thinking all this through, Howie realises how much they're relying on the quiet man – leaving him to rig the estate, which must be a hell of a task, then needing him to work out the cannon too. If they didn't have Dave, they would be at a loss. Howie knows he would have been dead a long time ago, if not for Dave. Thoughts race through his mind as he slowly paces back towards the south wall, oblivious to the many people who stop and stare at the man with the dark hair and dark features. There is something about his manner and appearance, the way he walks slowly, planting each foot in turn, the faraway look on his face, that puts them off from disturbing him. A few of the less sensitive ones step forward to interrupt his thoughts, only to find strong hands placed on their arms from the more astute people, holding them back with discreetly shaking heads.

Children go quiet as Howie walks through the camp, his mind racing with a thousand images and thoughts, but his face is stony and grave, eyes down and subconsciously avoiding trip hazards and guide ropes stretched out from the many tents. To Howie, it's like a movie in his mind: an image of grotesque decaying forms racing through the estate with sharpened, yellowing teeth. The traps fail to go off, then they leap over the pits and surge too quickly past the non-exploding cars, only to fall on the weak lines, devouring and wiping them out instantly.

Keep them coming, keep them running after them, until they eventually fall down and die again.

But then he has an overwhelming desire to fight them. To stand on that line and face them down. Howie thinks back to the feeling of battle, the horror and the fear, the blood and gore, the knowing that, at any point, he could be taken down and killed – only having his own strength and speed to rely on. The feeling of glory, the sense of doing something that is right; standing with his people and fighting with them, charging into almost certain death, but doing so knowing you're all in it together.

The pull of that feeling is hard to ignore, and Howie accepts that there is a big part of him wanting that final showdown.

Take as many down as you can Howie, and then fight them. They don't think of fairness or equal sides, so hurt them, cut them down and do what it takes, because that fight will be the end. Howie snaps back to reality, to find that he is in the middle of the camp. There is silence all around him. Howie lifts his head and nods once to the mass of people who stand and stare at him, before walking quickly towards the south wall and back to the reality of planning the impossible.

CHAPTER EIGHT

'You ... you ... and you two – come with me,' Dave points to several of the guards nearby, handpicking the ones he had seen fighting: serious men with calm expressions, fit and athletic. They get up and make ready, without question.

'Get some fluids and food, meet us at the gate,' Dave says, walking away towards the Saxon, Jamie following behind him.

They reach the Saxon, just as Curtis and the rest come out of the planning room. Dave opens the rear doors and climbs in, rummaging through the bench seat cupboards to pull two heavy, bulging canvas bags out. Dave then exits the Saxon, to see Jamie staring at the bags.

'Grenades,' Dave explains.

'Okay,' Jamie replies.

'Leave both of your rifles here, take this and put it on,' Dave says, handing Jamie a pistol pouch with belt loops at the rear, the black stock of the handgun poking out. Jamie hands over the two rifles; Dave slides them into the rear, as Curtis arrives at the vehicle.

'We're leaving our rifles here, take care of them,' Dave instructs Curtis.

'Yes, Dave,' Curtis replies, still making the name *Dave* sound like the word *Sarge*.

'Ammunition,' Dave says, handing Jamie spare clips for the handgun.

'I've never used a handgun before,' Jamie says.

'I'll show you,' Dave replies.

'Okay,' Jamie says, looping the heavy pouch onto his belt, to his right side.

'Ready?' Dave asks.

'Yes, Dave,' Jamie replies. They walk towards the gate in silence, each carrying a bag full of grenades over one shoulder; two quiet men with pistols strapped to their sides, walking silently through the camp. They reach the gate and wait in silence for the other guards to catch them up.

Ted appears, smiling.

'Going anywhere nice?' Ted asks.

'No,' Dave replies, flatly.

'Oh, right,' Ted pauses, the smile slowly disappearing.

'We need some vehicles,' Dave says.

'Okay, how many do you need?' Ted asks.

'Three,' Dave replies.

'Anything in particular?' Ted asks.

'No,' Dave answers.

Ted walks away into a nearby room, selecting keys from a key cupboard.

'Can you drive?' Dave asks Jamie.

'Yes,' Jamie replies.

'Good,' Dave says. Ted returns, handing the keys over as the four guards reach the gate, each of them with a rucksack on their backs.

'The vehicles are between the walls, to the left,' Ted says, as they step through the gate.

'Okay,' Dave answers.

'Funny bugger, that one,' Ted says to himself, closing the gate behind them.

They walk down the lane until they reach the vehicles, Dave stopping to look at the keys, then at the vehicles, trying to figure out which key fits which vehicle.

'You're going on point duty – you each get a radio. One of you has to go to the furthest point out that the radio will reach. Keep checking in on channel two until you lose signal, then come back. The other two, I want on the sides and out as far as the radios will reach. Got it?' The guards nod back as they take the radios and switch them to channel two, using the small dial at the top.

'The one furthest out takes one of the vehicles. The other two, out to the sides ... one gets a vehicle and you arrange where the other gets dropped off and the pick-up points, in case it goes bent – we keep the other vehicle. You will be there for some time. I will try and get relief for you, but that may not be possible. You are the advance contact points. Without you we will not have advance warning of when they come. Do not engage and give away your positions. Report back at the first sight, and pull back to the Fort. Got it?' Dave says. They each nod.

'Stay alert,' Dave says, handing all of the keys to one of the guards. The man sorts through them, then hands a set to Jamie.

'For that one,' the man points to the first vehicle.

'You get the vehicle ready,' Dave says to Jamie.

He nods in return and walks over to get into the driver's side, adjusting the seat and checking through the controls. Jamie glances out to see Dave speaking intently to the other men. Finally, they nod back, with very serious faces, and break away, heading for their vehicles.

'Okay,' Dave says, getting into the front passenger seat.

Jamie starts the engine and pulls away slowly. They get to the big vehicle gates on the outer wall, then Dave gets out and pushes the gates open, waiting for the vehicles to drive through. Jamie pulls over to allow the other two to drive on down the road.

Dave closes the gates and gets back into the vehicle.

'Where are we going?' Jamie asks as he pulls away.

'Into the estate; we're going to set some explosives,' Dave answers. 'We also need to sweep as we go.' Dave thinks of all that Mr. Howie and Chris have to contend with; he didn't need to ask if they wanted the area swept, they have enough to think about. Jamie drives down the long, straight road, past the banks and then through the flatlands, finally reaching the housing estate.

'Drive down to the right,' Dave instructs, as Jamie turns the wheel, going down the road between the two rows of houses – one row on the flatlands side.

'Park at the end,' Dave says. Jamie pulls the car up at the end of the cul-de-sac. They get out and walk around to the back of the vehicle. Dave pulls his pistol out and indicates for Jamie to do the same. Dave then shows Jamie how to load the ammunition clip and pull the sliding top back, to engage the first round.

'They kick quite a lot. Use a two-handed grip, same as the sniper rifle – squeeze and fire,' Dave says.

'Can I fire here?' Jamie asks.

'Yes, they won't hear from this distance,' Dave answers. Jamie raises the pistol and copies Dave, firing once – the loud retort sounding out into the quiet air.

'Good, you anticipated the kick without dropping or lifting the weapon. Two shots per target, like this,' Dave says, lifting his own pistol and walking towards the front door of the nearest house. As he steps onto the garden path, he fires two shots very close together. The rounds strike the door at mid-height, millimetres apart.

'Got it,' Jamie says, walking towards the same door and firing twice into the same height as Dave hit, both rounds hitting within millimetres.

'Good, we call it a *double tap.* Aim for the head, if you can, and be ready to reload quickly. Don't be afraid to put it away and go for bladed weapons, if you need to.'

'Okay,' Jamie answers.

'Show me a reload,' Dave instructs, and watches Jamie eject the clip, catch it with one hand, drop that same hand down and swap for a fresh full clip and slam it home, racking the top back – all within a second or two.

'Sorry, that was slow,' Jamie apologises.

'That's okay, you'll get faster the more you do it,' Dave answers. 'We'll do the first house together.'

'Okay,' Jamie replies. They move up the path until they reach the front door. Dave steps close to the front door and stares at Jamie.

'How many windows to the front?' Dave asks.

'Two on the ground level, two on the first floor,' Jamie replies, without breaking eye contact.

'Describe them,' Dave asks.

'The ground floor, far left, appears to be a lounge window; net curtains restrict the visibility, but the curtains are drawn back, which indicate the people are either not at home or were not home when the event happened. The other window looks similar, so it might be a dining room – it does not look like a kitchen,' Jamie replies.

'Upstairs?' Dave asks.

'The far left has partial net curtains with curtains drawn back, but there is no view of the inside from ground level. The right side is the same, but the curtains are half-drawn across.'

'Are the windows closed or are any of them open?' Dave asks.

'I think they are all closed,' Jamie replies.

'Okay, it's your first time, so I will allow for that, but, in future, remember this – we don't *think*, we know. Got it?'

'Yes, sorry,' Jamie replies.

'Good, now the door. Tell me about it?'

'Wooden, inward opening and hinged on the right,' Jamie replies, looking straight at Dave.

'Good, how many locks and where are they?'

'Central lock on the door handle to the left, letterbox is situated at standard height – I was unable to tell if there are any further locks.'

'Good, how can we tell if the door has further locks?' Dave asks.

'I don't know, pressure?'

'Yes, push against the door next to the door handle, does it yield?' Dave asks and watches Jamie push hard.

'No,' Jamie answers.

'Now, push at the top of the door, does it yield?'

'Yes, slightly,' Jamie answers, then pushes at the bottom.

'The base yields too; no locks on the top or bottom.'

'Good, so we know that to force entry we aim for the central lock ... now, do we use a shoulder or a foot?' Dave asks. Jamie considers for a split second.

'A shoulder will risk injury and I don't think people our size could generate enough force ... the foot?' he asks.

'Correct. Men the size of Clarence and Chris can use shoulders, as they have huge amounts of power and strength. Men our size do not, so we use our feet, but, before we do that, what should we do first?'

'Look for a key?' Jamie replies.

'Good, and also ...' Dave pushes the handle down and the door opens slightly. 'We check to see if it's actually locked first.'

'Got it.'

'Room clearance,' Dave says, as they step into the hallway. 'Working together we clear as we go; one remains at the door facing out, the other enters. We do not lean around corners with our weapons held out ready to be taken off us. Got it?'

'Got it.'

'Good. We walk in fast, with the weapon held ready to use; we face forward and sweep, like this,' Dave says, as he enters the first room on the right, pushing the door open with his foot and stepping in quickly.

He holds the pistol in the two-handed grip and sweeps the room rapidly, the gun rising and falling as he looks up and down, left to right.

'Got it,' Jamie says.

'You do that one,' Dave says, nodding towards the lounge door opposite them.

Jamie mimics Dave, pushing the door open with his foot and sweeping the room quickly, the weapon tracking his facial direction.

'Good, now, if we both proceed to the ground floor rear, we leave the stairs behind us and we do not know if upstairs is clear. So, one holds at the point of risk, while the other advances. I'll hold, while you clear the rest,' Dave says.

'Okay,' Jamie replies, stepping down the narrow hallway and entering the kitchen. He disappears from view and is gone for several seconds. He walks back out with the weapon slightly lowered, but still held correctly.

'Clear,' he reports.

'Good, stand behind me,' Dave asks, as Jamie walks to stand behind him.

Dave raises one hand and makes a fist.

'This means hold,' Dave says, then extends one finger.

'This means one target, two for two targets, three for three – all of the fingers extended means multiple targets.'

'Got it.'

'Good. If I point the finger like this, it means the target is that direction; if I point one way, then another, it means one target that way and one target the other.'

'Okay.'

'Good, we'll stick with that for a minute. Going upstairs, we keep the weapon raised to strike the target at the top, taking into account the height difference. Place your feet to the sides of each step, there is less chance of creaks that way.'

'Okay,' Jamie says, as Dave lifts his weapon and advances up the stairs quickly and surely, reaching the top and pausing to sweep down the hallway.

'Corridor ahead, loops back to the front bedroom, another room on the right, appears bathroom at the end, I'll hold, you clear the front,' Dave says quietly, stepping aside to allow Jamie to move along the few steps to the bedroom.

He walks inside and re-appears within seconds. 'Clear,' he

reports quietly, and moves on to the next bedroom. He repeats the action, then moves along to the bathroom.

'Clear.' He then returns back to Dave, weapon lowered.

'Good,' Dave replies.

They exit the house and move outside, to the next one, trying the door first, but finding it locked and no key to be found.

'Aim your strike next to the lock, do not expect it to burst open on the first hit,' Dave says, watching as Jamie steps back and powers his right foot into the door.

Jamie watches as the strike hits, then adjusts his stance and pauses for a second, appearing to draw power , then drives his foot forward again with lightning speed. The strike is perfect and the door pops open, causing the frame to splinter from the solid, brass lock being forced in.

'Good, now we move faster. Go, I'll hold,' Dave orders.

Jamie walks forward, kicking doors open and sweeping the house, room by room, reporting 'Clear' after each one.

Jamie takes the lead on the stairs, leaving Dave to hold at the top. The house is cleared within minutes and they walk back out.

'That was good, but we have a lot of houses and not much time, so do it faster,' Dave says.

'Okay,' Jamie replies.

The next house is cleared within two minutes and they exit again, moving across the lawns to the next one.

'My turn, you hold,' Dave says, as he kicks the door in and enters swiftly, striding from room to room, with quick, jerky, but controlled movements. He clears each room – then moves straight up the stairs and clears the rest. He is back outside in under a minute.

'Your movements are much faster than mine,' Jamie says, as they walk to the next house.

'Years of practise and drill, but you do not have that luxury – your turn,' Dave says, as they reach the door. Jamie quickly checks the door handle, locked. He pressures the top and bottom, steps back and kicks the door hard, forcing it open on the first kick. He enters as the door is still swinging open. Jamie strides into the first room, again mimicking Dave, as he quickly checks the four corners and moves back out, then moves on to the next room. They exit the house in just over a minute, again moving down to the next house.

'Better – keep that pace, but stay alert,' Dave says, testing the door handle and finding the door unlocked.

'You go again,' Dave says, as the door swings open.

Jamie strides into the lounge on the right, then back out and across the small hallway and into the dining room. He exits and clears the kitchen at the back, before moving back and climbing the stairs, pausing at the top, for a split second, to allow Dave to reach the top step.

Jamie advances towards the front bedroom, pausing at the door with his head cocked to one side. He raises a hand and makes a fist, then extends one finger and points to the door. Dave moves up close behind Jamie and listens; he taps Jamie on the shoulder once and waves his extended hand forward, then quickly about turns to watch the rear.

Jamie steps forward and pushes the door open with his foot. Walking into the room, he observes an undead standing on the other side of the double bed. The pistol already tracking with his eyes, he fires two rounds, very close together, into the forehead and is already moving to check the rest of the room as the zombie slumps to the ground, leaving a massive blood and brain spatter on the wall behind him.

'Clear,' Jamie says, exiting the room.

Dave enters the bedroom and moves across to look down at the body, then heads back out into the hallway.

'Good shots, the second was slightly off, though,' Dave says.

'I know. I started to turn away, to continue the sweep, too quickly,' Jamie replies.

'If you are satisfied that the first shot is enough, then you can start the move,' Dave says.

'Okay, I will keep to the double-tap for now, to practise, if that's okay,'

'Okay,' Dave replies.

Jamie clears the rest of the rooms and they move on, working house by house, clearing each one in under a minute, then crossing the road to start on the other side. They work back towards where they started.

'Now, we work alone – you start with this one and I do the next, you leapfrog and do the next one and I leapfrog after you, got it? Dave asks.

'Got it, same method?' Jamie says.

'Yes,' Dave answers.

'Okay.' Jamie walks to the front door and pauses until Dave has reached the front door of the next house. They nod to each other and, in unison, they check the door handle, the top and the bottom, then step back and kick the door open, entering, as the door swings open. They work from house to house, double-shots ringing out sporadically as they find undead in rooms. The street is cleared within ten minutes and they each exit their last house, both changing clips and re-holstering their weapons as they walk back to the vehicle.

'How many?' Dave asks.

'Three, you?'

'You know how many I had.'

'You had two.'

'Good.'

'What now?' Jamie asks.

'The next street behind this one,' Dave answers.

'Okay,' Jamie replies. They move down the central road until they reach the next junction; once again, two rows of houses run along on each side.

'You take that side, I'll do this side, meet back here,' Dave says.

'Okay.'

Ten minutes later, they meet back at the junction, Dave ahead of Jamie, but only having to wait for under a minute.

'How many rounds did I use?' Dave asks.

'Eight,' Jamie answers. 'Four targets.'

'Good.'

'Two more streets and we can start on the explosives,' Dave explains, as they walk further down the road.

'*Lead point to Dave,*' the radio crackles on Dave's belt.

'*Dave to lead point, go ahead.*'

'*Lead point to Dave, I am positioned approximately two miles away from your location, testing transmission strength.*'

'*Dave to lead point, transmission strong, can you move further?*'

'*Yes, will do so now, out.*'

'*Dave to East point, are you in position?*'

'*East point to Dave, Roger that, in position now. West point has retained the vehicle.*'

'*Dave to East point, received. Dave to West point, confirm you have retained the vehicle and are you in position?*'

'*West point to Dave, confirm I have retained the vehicle, confirm I am in position.*'

'*Dave to West point, Roger that. Dave to lead point, you are now North point, received?*'

'*North point to Dave, Roger that.*'

'*Dave to North point, switch to channel one and check signal strength to the Fort before you move any further.*'

'*North point to Dave, Roger that, doing now.*' Dave switches the dial on the radio back to channel one and listens for the transmission.

'*North point to Fort, radio check.*'

'*Fort to North point, are you forward observation point? Your signal is weak, but readable.*'

'*North point to Fort, answer yes, I am forward obs point, likewise your signal weak but readable. I will hold this position. North point to Dave, did you receive the last?*'

'*Dave to North point and Fort, Roger that, received the last. North, East, and West points will hold those positions and maintain channel one. Dave out.*'

Dave turns to Jamie:

'Explosives,' he says, simply.

'Did you hear that last transmission?' Chris asks, as Howie enters the planning room.

'Yeah, Dave's got the spotters in place?'

'Yep, at least we've got eyes on now, so we'll get an advance warning,' Chris replies. 'You okay, mate?' he asks, taking note of the expression on Howie's face.

'I'm fine mate, was just thinking it all through as I walked back,' Howie replies.

'There's a lot to think about,' Chris concedes. 'But all we can do is try, Howie.'

'I know, mate, any news on the engineers?'

'I spoke to Sergeant Hopewell and she's sent runners out ... did the digger drivers get away okay?'

Howie nods back, staring down at the plans on the table. 'Where do we put the soil that they dig out?' he says.

'They seem experienced men, Howie – I'm sure they will figure it out and put it somewhere ... out of sight,' Chris replies.

'Wouldn't they need dumper trucks to carry it away?'

'Hang on,' Chris says, reaching for his radio.

'Fort to guards with the digger units ... Fort to guards with the digger units,' Chris repeats several times.

'Digger guard to Fort, sorry, it's noisy here, go ahead,' a voice booms out, the sound of loud engines in the background.

'Fort to digger guards, make sure the soil taken out is disposed of, out of sight.'

'Digger guard to Fort, repeat your last please.'

'Fort to digger guard, MAKE SURE THE SOIL TAKEN OUT IS HIDDEN FROM SIGHT.'

'Digger guard to Fort, you want us to work all night?'

'Fort to digger guard, ANSWER NO – I WANT THE SOIL FROM THE HOLES HIDDEN.'

'Digger unit to Fort, Roger will do.'

'Bloody hell, they're going to wake the dead,' Chris says, shaking his head and putting the radio down on the table.

'Bit late for that, mate,' Howie jokes.

A knock and Terri enters, immediately smiling at Howie. 'There are some engineers here for you,' she says.

'Ah great,' Howie replies, stepping to the door and finding several men waiting outside.

'Come in, chaps,' Howie smiles at them, opening the door wide. They walk into the room, looking about with a keen interest at the interior and then head straight to the plans on the table.

'I'm Howie, this is Chris, nice to meet you all,' Howie says, politely shaking hands with the men, one by one.

'Sorry, is this the room for the engineers?' A middle-aged woman appears at the door, leaning in.

'Yeah, hi, I'm Howie, come in.'

'Hello, I'm Kelly,' the woman replies, shaking hands with Howie, then Chris.

'So ... are you all engineers?' Chris asks, once the handshaking has stopped.

They all nod at him.

'Good, forgive us for being blunt, but we need to get straight down to the point ... we need some sharp spikes to be made that can be embedded into the ground,' Chris says.

'Also, we want some very small sharp objects that can be hidden in the long grass, out in the flatlands,' Howie adds.

'You mean caltrops?' Kelly asks straight away, and leans forward to examine the plans on the table.

'Yeah, those,' Howie replies, surprised at her direct manner.

'What about the spikes? How many and how deep are they going in?'

'The spikes will be put into a hidden trench the width of the spit,' Howie explains.

'We can use sharpened wooden spikes for that, getting the material and fashioning them will be relatively easy. The hardest part will be getting them in, you'll need a lot of people for that, if you want it done quickly,' Kelly answers.

'We can get more people, that's not a problem. What about the caltrops?'

'Right, the first problem is materials. We'll need lots of metal, but then most metals can't just be bent into shape. They might be brittle and snap. We might have to heat them and then, of course, make them sharp – that will need power tools and you'll want them over a large area, so we need lots of them.' She finishes speaking, then looks expectantly at Chris, then to Howie.

'There's a workshop here. I'm sure we can rig some of the generators up for you,' Howie replies, impressed.

'Can we take metal from the fittings and fixtures if we need to?' one of the other engineers asks.

'Take what you need, do whatever you need to do – but get it done as fast as possible. We will have to put some guards with you, to make sure you don't go off and tell other people what you're doing,' Chris says, resting his hands on the desk and leaning forward to emphasise his point.

'Excuse me?' One of the engineers steps forward. 'What was that about guards and telling other people?' He is middle-aged with blond, swept-back hair.

'We cannot run the risk of anyone else knowing what our tactics are, so, for now, you will work alone,' Chris replies.

'Are you telling us or asking us?' the man asks, politely.

'Listen, I'm sorry it sounds harsh, but it's the way it has to be, I'm afraid,' Chris says to the man, equalling his polite tone.

'We were told we could come and go as we needed to, as long as we were checked when we come back in.'

'That was then. The situation has changed,' Chris says.

'So we can no longer come and go as we please?' the man asks.

'No, I'm afraid not.' Chris replies.

'Tell me, what will happen if we do?'

'Do *what* exactly?' Chris asks, still maintaining his polite tone.

'If we try to leave or if we try to tell other people of what we are doing?'

'You will be stopped,' Chris says, curtly.

'How?' the man asks, his cultured tones not slipping.

'By any means deemed necessary,' Chris responds.

'I'm sorry? You mean that if we try to leave or speak with the other people in the camp, we will be killed?' The man leans forward, staring intently at Chris.

'If that is necessary, yes,' Chris stares back.

'I thought this was a democracy, not a ...'

'I will stop you there,' Chris interrupts pointedly. 'This is *not* a democracy, and while I understand your concerns, I can only respond by saying there is no alternative. If those *things* coming here find out about our plans, we will lose the best chance we have of reducing their numbers before they get to us. We do not know if anyone in the camp is infected, so we cannot run the risk of people knowing what we are doing. It really is that simple.' Chris speaks calmly, looking at each of them in turn as his diplomatic skills shine through.

'Gentlemen, and lady, of course,' Chris inclines his head to Kelly. 'There is a huge zombie army coming for us, this is a fact. We have to do what it takes to cut their numbers before they get here. While Howie and I have the skills and knowledge and are prepared to meet them face-to-face, we need your skills and knowledge to try and even the sides. You are trained engineers. You have skills that we simply do not have, and we need your help. But it must be done in a controlled environment.' Chris explains, looking to each of them in turn.

'I agree,' Kelly responds immediately and with passion.

'We all heard what Howie said earlier, and we know the risks involved. We'll get on with it and do what we can to help.'

'Okay, I understand, but I'm a little uncomfortable with being treated like a slave or having some tyrannical despot ordering me about,' the man replies directly to Kelly.

The atmosphere becomes instantly charged and a silence follows his comments.

Chris is clearly struggling to contain his temper, and Howie has to bite his own anger down.

'I don't understand what your concerns are?' Kelly asks, slowly and clearly.

'My concern is being told this was a safe place and now finding out we are captives to be used as they see fit and without any form of redress – and being told who we can and cannot talk to,' the man replies.

'We can manage without this man. I think the rest of us understand your need for secrecy and we are happy to comply with that request, is that so?' Kelly asks the group in general.

'Yes, completely. I am amazed at you, Donald,' an older man with glasses responds, looking at the outspoken engineer.

'I have the right to question their motives,' Donald replies.

'You do, but we all know the situation and it would appear you are happy to accept the safety of this place without undertaking any of the risk involved in keeping it safe,' the older man says.

'That is not the case at all,' Donald responds, still maintaining a polite and calm manner.

'Donald, we are not on site now discussing the plans with the architect or planning officers. We are in the middle of an event of global proportions, and if we want to live, we have to accept that and deal with it,' Kelly says.

'I do accept it, but I still maintain the right to question the methods used. This could be one step away from some kind of communist regime where we are being controlled, and I simply will not accept it,' Donald replies.

Chris looks to Howie with a discreet shake of his head. Howie walks to the door and over to the police office.

'Debbie, we've got the engineers. We've told them what we need doing, but one of them is refusing to agree not to tell anyone else,' Howie says quickly.

Sergeant Hopewell looks up at him with a concerned expression, eyebrows raised.

'Look, we don't know if anyone else in the camp is infected, and we cannot risk people finding out what our defence tactics are, so we are controlling the access points ...'

'I know all of this, Howie,' Debbie interrupts him.

'I am concerned ...'

'Detain him,' Ted says firmly, from the back of the office.

'You have to Howie, you can't run the risk of him telling people or causing dissent,' Sarah adds.

'How would we detain him?' Howie asks.

'Leave it to me, there's a secure room back here that he can sit in for a few hours,' Ted replies, taking a thick black belt from a hook and fixing it around his waist, handcuffs and black pouches hanging from it.

He takes a police flat cap and puts it on, the peak low to his eyes, instantly transformed from genial Ted to official policeman.

'Where is he?' Ted asks.

'In the planning room, I think his name is Donald,' Howie answers.

'Lead the way then,' Ted says, with a voice full of authority. They walk quickly back to the planning room with Howie leading the way. Ted puts a hand out as they reach the door.

'Which one is he?' Ted asks, quietly.

'Err, middle-aged, with blond hair, sort of swept back,' Howie replies.

'Let me go first and do the talking, understand?' Ted says, not giving Howie a chance to reply as he steps into the room, pausing for dramatic effect as all eyes turn to him.

Ted keeps a stern, impassive face, eyes staring out from underneath the peaked hat. He looks at each person, taking them all in.

Years of experience in his manner and an aura of authority ooze off him. Ted nods and steps over to the blond man.

'Sir, are you Donald?' Ted asks, his eyes staring intently at the man.

'Yes, I am,' the man replies, clearly shocked at the arrival of a fully uniformed police officer.

'Sir, I need you to understand what I am going to say to you. We will remain calm and we will not react in an undue manner, is that clear?' Ted says.

'I'm sorry? What?' Donald replies.

'Sir, as far as we know, this Fort is the last safe place in the country. We have no knowledge of any other surviving colonies or places such as this. Therefore, this Fort may represent the country. Therefore, this Fort also represents the concern of the nation as a whole. I am led to believe that you are causing dissent and refusing to comply with the requests being made to you. I am therefore detaining you in the interests of national security. You will come with me where you will be held in a safe place, without fear of abuse or assault.'

'What? You can't do this!' Donald shouts with a horrified look on his face, and quickly steps away. Ted steps forward and takes a firm grip of the man's wrist, pulling it behind his back and fixing one end of a handcuff on.

'Sir, this *is* happening. These men are doing what is necessary for the protection and survival of all of us. They, and we, do not have time for inconsiderate and selfish people like you. Put your other hand behind your back, thank you. Now you will come with me and be quiet about it.' Ted spins the handcuffed man around and marches him towards the door.

'Once outside, you will not scream or shout and you will not cause distress or alarm to any other persons within this camp,' Ted says smoothly, and with such firm authority the man complies instantly.

Ted steps through with Donald and turns back to close the door, winking at Howie as he does so.

'Bloody hell,' Howie mutters.

'I'm sorry about that,' Chris starts to say, but is cut off by Kelly holding her hand up.

'Don't be,' she says. 'Extreme times call for extreme measures. I know he'll be looked after.'

'It did need to be done, I'm afraid. I've met Donald on a few jobs and he's always like that. Very contrary, which normally can be dealt with, but, as you say, extreme times and all that ...' the older man says calmly.

'To business, where is this workshop?' Kelly asks.

'Follow me, we'll find Roger and get him to lead the way,' Howie replies.

A few minutes later, they find Roger and follow him around the edge of the camp to the west wall and a set of large, wooden double doors.

Chris had found three guards from the dwindling numbers and briefed them fully, and Howie had grabbed a couple of runners and asked them to stay close.

Roger opens the doors up and steps aside as the group files in. Long, wooden workbenches run down the sides with old, battered metal cabinets filling spaces and gaps. Hand tools are pinned to walls with the black outline of their shape etched on, showing their intended space. The smell of grease, oil, and coffee is in the air.

'The power tools are in that room in the back, it's kept locked, but the key should be in the top of that set of drawers,' Roger explains, pointing to a metal filing unit in the corner.

One of the engineers opens the door and pulls out a single key on a large ring. The rest move slowly down the room, examining the various tools with professional interest.

The rear door is unlocked and the engineer doing the unlocking takes out a small flashlight from his pocket to illuminate the dark interior. The other engineers quickly join him, each taking out a small flashlight as they enter the dark room.

'Bloody engineers, always so practical,' Roger jokes.

'Is there a generator here?' a voice shouts from the back room.

'Yes, there's one here. We can get more for you if you need. We always had plenty of power as we're so isolated from the main power supply,' Roger says, walking forward and leaning into the dark room.

'Well, where is it then?' The voice calls out.

'You're the engineers, you figure it out,' Roger answers with mock indignation. 'This is not my usual environment,' he adds.

'Got it, hang on, we'll get some power going,' another voice calls out.

A few seconds later, a deep rumbling noise comes from the back room and the darkness is dispatched with illumination from the bright strip-lighting overhead. Murmurs of agreement and satisfaction reach them as the engineers mooch through the various tools and equipment.

'Have you seen up there, Howie?' Chris asks.

Howie follows his gaze to a suspended roof, adding extra storage to the room. Piles of long metal rods are stacked up in one end.

'Perfect, I love it when a plan comes together,' Howie jokes, and looks to see Chris staring blankly at him.

'What plan?' Chris asks. 'The whole plan or just this bit?'

'It's from *The A-Team*,' Howie says.

'What's *The A-Team*?' Chris asks with a puzzled expression.

'You are fucking joking right? Christ, you're worse than Dave,' Howie mutters.

'Of course I'm bloody joking,' Chris smiles. 'So, which one am I?' he asks.

'Hmmm ... I would say Hannibal, but with that beard, it's got to be BA,' Howie replies.

'No way, Clarence has got to be BA,' Chris responds.

'Yeah, fair one, well Dave is definitely Murdoch,' Howie says.

Chris chuckles.

'But you can't be Hannibal, as that would only leave Face, and I'm not being Face,' Howie says firmly.

'What? Face was great,' Chris says, shocked.

'In the movie or series?' Howie asks.

'Both,' Chris replies.

'Well, you be Face then, if you like him so much – I'll be Hannibal,' Howie says, as they start walking back to the planning room.

'No way, I can't be Face – you're much better looking than me,' Chris replies.

'You'll have to be Face, I'll be Hannibal.'

'Nope, shave your beard off and you'll make a great Face,' Howie says.

'I pity the crazy fool who tries to shave my beard,' Chris growls in a deep voice as Howie bursts out laughing.

'I pity the crazy fool who tries to make me be Face,' Howie growls back, as they reach the planning room door, entering to drink more coffee.

'What's next?' Chris asks.

'Clarence to the Fort,' the radio bursts to life with Clarence's deep voice booming out.

'That is, I guess,' Howie replies.

Chris smiles as he answers the radio,

'Chris to Clarence, go ahead BA.'

'I AIN'T GETTIN' ON NO PLANE,' Clarence's voice booms back, making both of them laugh.

'Clarence to Chris, we are on way back, will be with you in a few minutes.'

'Saxon to Howie or Chris, confirm we can see convoy of vehicles coming from the estate.'

'Chris to Clarence, Roger that. Hold at the gates, we'll come to you.' They down the now cold coffee and head back out of the door, walking through the camp, smiling at people as they walk past or stop to stare. Ted falls in and joins them.

'How's our man?' Howie asks Ted.

'He's all right, he's asking for a lawyer, so we told him your sister is a lawyer and he's trying to make a claim of unlawful arrest now,' Ted smiles.

'Fair one,' Howie replies.

They arrive at the gates to find Blowers and Cookey still there, joking with each other.

'Lads, how are you?' Howie asks.

'Yeah, we're good, Mr. Howie – how's the plans coming on? We've still got loads of people coming up asking if they can help,' Blowers says.

'Slowly getting there, it's seems to be taking ages though. You two okay down here?'

'Yeah fine, we've got coffee on constant flow and there's a toilet in there,' Cookey says, smiling.

'What more can a man need?' Howie says.

'Err, some women, some steak, no zombie army coming for us, maybe a television and an Xbox, some popcorn ...' Cookey replies.

'Oh, listen to him, *women,* he says ...You wouldn't know what to do with one, other than sit and talk about curtains and flower arranging,' Blowers cuts in.

'We could sit and chat with our legs folded up underneath us, wearing thick, woolly jumpers,' Cookey adds.

'What's wrong with woolly jumpers? I've got woolly jumpers,' Chris interrupts with a look of serious intent.

'Ha, nice one ...' Blowers laughs.

'Who's laughing?' Chris asks. 'I'm not.'

'Yeah, right, you got me like this before,' Blowers laughs, trailing off as Chris remains poker faced.

'You are joking, aren't you?'

'Do I look like the kind of man who wears woolly jumpers?' Chris replies as his face splits apart with a big grin.

'Well ... now that you come to mention it ...' Blowers jokes.

'You cheeky bugger,' Chris retorts. 'Have some respect and get that bloody gate opened up.'

CHAPTER NINE

Clarence steps out of the armoury and walks to the police office, thinking through all the items he needs to find.

'Hello,' he says, finding Sergeant Hopewell behind the desk. 'Howie and Chris said to speak to you, I'm taking a foraging party out.'

'What do you need?'

'Gunsmiths and hardware stores,' said Clarence.

'Hi, Clarence,' Sarah smiles, walking into the office with Terri.

Clarence starts to blush. 'Hello, Sarah,' he rumbles

'Hello ... Sarah,' Sarah mimics, trying to copy his deep voice.

'I don't sound like that,' Clarence chuckles.

'No, you're far worse ... I'm only joking,' Sarah says, putting her hand on his forearm and making him blush even more. 'What are you doing here?'

'I'm taking a foraging party out – Chris and Howie need some items,' he says, as a look of concern passes across her face.

'Are you taking many with you?'

'Yeah, there'll be a few of us.'

'Okay, well you take care and make sure you come back, I still need that knife training, remember?' she says.

'Um, okay, I will,' Clarence replies, aware of Terri and Sergeant Hopewell watching them.

'Here you go, there's a list and a map with them marked on,' Sergeant Hopewell says, handing him some papers and a map book.

'Thanks ... vehicles? Do you have any?' he asks.

'Check with Ted down at the gate, he's got all the keys.'

'Thank you, see you soon,' Clarence says, turning to walk out of the room.

Sarah quickly follows him out.

'Clarence,' she says, turning him back to face her and seeing his red, flushed face.

'You don't have to blush every time I talk to you.'

'I can't help it,' Clarence murmurs, looking down at his feet and then slowly back up at her face and her beautiful, dark eyes looking at him steadily.

'Well, just promise me you'll come back safely,' she says, looking up and holding his gaze.

'I will ...' Clarence starts to say, as Sarah quickly steps in close and stretches up on her toes to kiss him on the cheek.

'Come back,' she whispers with soft breath on his face, squeezing his arm. 'You'll catch flies again,' she laughs.

Clarence starts to walk away, his mind whirling and spinning from the kiss she gave him – still feeling the warmth on his skin and thinking he will never wash that bit of his face again.

After a few steps, he realises he's forgotten to get more men and turns back towards the planning office and the groups of guards resting outside.

'I need a few to come out with me,' Clarence says, stopping in the middle of them. They look at each other to see who will go. Two men and two women eventually step forward.

'Services or police?' Clarence asks, as they walk in a tight group towards the gate.

Two of them answer 'Services,' one Army, the other Navy. The other two explain they are police from the armed response teams, with one of them having previous military experience.

They chat amiably amongst themselves as they walk to the gate, meeting Ted and arranging to take four vehicles out.

Clarence rides shotgun in the first van and the others have one vehicle each. It takes a while to sort through keys and walk down to find vans that can be taken out from the clogged-in fleet, wedged into the alley between the inner and outer wall, but, eventually, they are out and driving down the road and through the estate. They stop at a large, multi-chain hardware superstore on the edge of a town; the streets and villages they pass through show signs of the devastation and decay of urban life. There are burnt-out houses and rotting corpses, vehicles abandoned and left at angles, and embedded into walls. Bloodstains and broken glass litter the ground. The superstore looks remarkably normal, almost surreal, like it's an early morning Bank Holiday.

'You two stay out front, you two with me,' Clarence says, taking the two armed police response officers with him, knowing they will be better trained in close quarters fire and manoeuvre tactics.

'What do we need?' the female officer asks him.

'Nuts, bolts, chains, and anything that can be fired from a cannon – also axes, hammers, scythes, and anything that can be used as a weapon,' he replies.

'Cannon? Are we using those old things in the Fort?' the male officer asks.

'We're going to try,' Clarence says. 'You two go for the nuts, bolts, and chains, and I'll do the weapons.'

'Roger,' the woman replies. The hardware store doors hang open, smashed and ruined from a previous looting; at least someone else has made the effort to gain entry and save them the time of having to do it. They find rows of trolleys inside the large entrance area and each take one and move off into the wide aisles, flanked on both sides with high shelving units. There is surprisingly little damage inside the store. Dried bloodstains and debris littered around the entrance area indicate that something happened here, but no bodies or corpses remain.

Clarence looks down the ends of the rows of aisles and looks at each of the large signs; he finds the one marked Hand Tools and heads that way. He aims for the section with the axes and quickly starts scooping them up and placing them into the trolley. He also finds sledgehammers, pick axes, scythes, and even long-bladed machetes.

Within a few minutes, the trolley is full. He wheels it outside and asks the guards to start loading, before heading back in and filling the trolley with more items.

He passes the two police officers heading outside with trolleys full of buckets and metal objects. They nod at one another, just like normal people mooching around the DIY store at the weekend.

Loaded up, they set off away from the store. The female police officer drives the lead van, with Clarence examining the map and giving directions to the closest gunsmith.

'I haven't seen any zombies at all,' the woman states quietly.

'Must be hiding,' Clarence rumbles and goes back to his map reading.

They keep on through the quiet, rural roads, passing fields and woodland and then head back into expensive residential areas of large, detached houses, eventually finding their way into a small market town.

'That's it, over there,' Clarence says, pointing towards the only shop that looks fortified and solid.

They drive closer and find a window display of air rifles and pistols, binoculars and hunter-style clothing.

'Someone had a go at getting in,' the woman driver says, looking at the half-smashed-in door.

Despite the quaint appearance, the shop had been well secured against such raids, and the door appeared to have withstood a half-concerted effort to get in.

'There's blood everywhere out the front, something happened here,' Clarence says.

'Turn the van 'round and back in close to the door,' he adds, getting out to examine the door closely.

He walks over to the next van.

'Did you get any big chains?' he asks. A few minutes later, and the van is revving loudly with a thick chain stretched from the tow bar back to the door handles.

'NOW,' Clarence shouts and the van accelerates quickly, powering away from the shop.

The chain springs up as the pressure pulls it, and the door is out of the frame with a loud noise of wood and metal tearing.

'Easy when you know how,' Clarence mutters, stepping through the ragged hole and entering the small shop, seeing rows of shotguns and rifles chained to a display cabinet behind the long counter and boxes of ammunition stacked up in a glass display case.

'Bingo,' the ex-Army man says, walking in to see the goods on display and holding a set of bolt croppers. 'I came prepared,' the man adds, walking around the counter.

He grips the thick chain in the mouth of the bolt croppers and starts squeezing, then squeezing harder until his face goes red from the exertion.

'May I?' Clarence steps forward, taking the handles from the now sweating man.' Clarence takes a handle in each hand and gives a sudden overwhelming push on each, driving the handles back together and severing the chain quickly.

'Yeah, well, I weakened it for you,' the man jokes.

'And I thank you for doing so,' Clarence replies, smiling, long used to the never-ending comments about his strength and size.

He reaches up and starts selecting the shotguns and rifles, twisting at the waist to turn and lay them on the counter.

'There's some good weapons here,' the ex-solider remarks, checking through the various rifles.

'Hu-huh,' Clarence replies, distracted and thinking about Sarah, her dark hair and eyes, the way she speaks and laughs and that kiss, wow that kiss, she actually kissed him. He, the massive, bald-headed, freak of nature, being kissed by someone so beautiful and graceful.

Clarence pauses, holding the last shotgun and staring off into the middle distance.

'You all right, Clarence?' the woman asks from behind him, making him start back to reality.

'Yep, never better,' Clarence grins hugely to her as he turns back to the counter.

'So ... what's her name?' she adds.

'Her name?' Clarence replies.

'The only thing that can make a man smile like that, in the midst of all this chaos, is a woman, so what's her name?' she repeats.

'Sarah,' Clarence rumbles quietly.

'Oh, Mr. Howie's sister?' the woman says lightly. 'She's very pretty.'

'She is,' Clarence confirms, still smiling.

'We need bows and arrows too,' he adds, remembering why they are here. They prise open the ammunition case and unload all of the boxes into plastic bags found behind the counter.

One corner of the store is dedicated to archery and crossbows.

'There's loads here, Clarence, do you want them all?' the ex-soldier asks, examining the longbows, compound bows, and dozens of packets of arrows.

'Yeah, get everything,' Clarence replies.

'And the crossbows?'

'Yes, I don't know anything about archery, so take everything.'

And everything is taken – the only thing they leave are the air weapons, on the basis of firing small lead pellets at a massive army of undead zombies will not have that much of an effect.

Within an hour, they find the next gunsmiths; this one is located in a much bigger town and already plundered and looted extensively; zombie corpses are everywhere.

They drive on through the town, weaving past the debris, until they reach a supermarket fuel station on the town exit road.

'Stop,' Clarence calls out.

The van slows to a stop, causing the following vehicles to brake suddenly.

'Pull into the garage forecourt,' Clarence instructs, staring hard to the side of the fuel station.

The van turns slowly and heads into the fuel station.

'Look there,' Clarence points to a set of large wooden gates.

'Good spot, Clarence, very good,' the driver says admiringly, seeing the top of the fuel tanker just peeking out over the gates.

'Do you think it's full?' Clarence asks, as they get out and walk over.

'That's almost too much to ask for,' she replies.

They find the gate locked with another thick chain and padlock. Clarence turns to see the ex-soldier jogging towards them with the bolt croppers.

'Do you want me to weaken it for you first?' the man asks, light-heartedly. Clarence grunts back and snaps the chain through easily, wrenching the chain and lock off. The gates get pulled open to reveal the all-white fuel tanker. After checking it out, they are jubilant to discover it is, indeed, full.

'Does anyone know how to drive it?' Clarence asks.

'I can, I was in the traffic department and did my heavy goods vehicle training,' the woman police officer answers.

She walks in and steps up on the metal plate to open the driver's door; a body falls out on top of her, making her scream. The rest race forward to see the corpse rolling off to one side and the woman on her arse, having been pushed back.

'Is he dead?' the woman asks in shock.

'Dead or undead?' the ex-soldier jokes, moving forward to punt the head of the corpse with his boot. The body rolls over to reveal normal human features, dead but normal.

'Nah, he's normal dead,' the ex-soldier remarks.

The woman police officer gets up and climbs gingerly back into the cab.

'Check him for keys,' she says, going through the controls.

Clarence bends down and quickly pats his pockets to find a set of keys and passes them up to her.

She inserts the key and starts the engine; the fuel tanker rumbles to life, spewing out a cloud of black smoke, which quickly dissipates.

'I'll take the van, you drive this behind me,' Clarence shouts up.

They start back to their vehicles and all stop and wince as the gears are crunched painfully behind them. They turn back to see the woman police officer sticking her middle finger up at them and laughing.

After an hour of driving, they are parked up and standing around the front of a florist's window, dead and wilting flowers in the display.

'Well, this is the address,' Clarence says, examining the map book, the list provided by Sergeant Hopewell, and then looking up at the building.

'That's definitely not a gunsmith,' the ex-soldier remarks.

'Nope, must have changed it,' Clarence replied.

'Who would turn a gunsmiths into a florist?' the woman asks.

'Where's the next one?' the male police officer asks.

'Never mind that, where's all the zombies gone?' the ex-soldier asks nervously, looking about.

They all look up and around, becoming increasingly aware of the lack of undead.

'I don't know, they must be massing somewhere,' Clarence says quietly. 'You're right though, this is eerie.'

A feeling of being watched descends on the group.

'There's one more place we can try, it's not too far,' Clarence says, very aware of the uncomfortable feeling amongst them, hands gripping weapons tighter and the jokes now gone. They load back into their vehicles and drive on, again following Clarence as he handles the map on the steering wheel and works his route as he goes, treading through narrow cobbled streets and past the once-boutique shops of this southern English hamlet.

Clarence feels the creeping sensation growing up the back of his neck; *there should be signs of life by now. The zombies can't all have gone, or there are even other survivors, maybe. But then, being this close to the Fort would mean those able to, would have fled to them by now*. Movement in the fields to his right catches his eye, a break in the hedgerow and a flash of distant colour. He slows down, but keeps moving along the country lane, constantly looking to the right and waiting for the thick hedge to end. Finally, he sees a large gate further up and slows down to take advantage of the gap. He brings the van to a stop and stares hard into the fields. What he sees is staggering: a long, thick line of people all moving at the same speed, in the distance, across the top of the fields. The vehicles behind him stop, the drivers getting out to come forward and stare through the gate. Each of them stop and stare with shock at the thousands and thousands of zombies stretched out in a long line, moving from left to right.

'Which direction are they heading in?' one of the policeman asks.

'North,' Clarence replies. 'The main road into the area is that way. They must be going to meet the rest coming down.'

'Fucking hell, there's thousands just there,' the ex-soldier says quietly.

'Right there for the taking too,' Clarence replies.

'We can't get to them though, the vehicles will never make it across those fields, and the distance is too great for these things,' Clarence adds, raising his assault rifle for effect.

'Where are they feeding in from?' the woman asks.

'I don't know, over that way I guess,' Clarence inclines his head in the direction they're moving from.

'The same way we're going,' the woman police officer states quietly. They break away without further talk, heading back to their vehicles and moving off slowly down the lane, watching the horde slowly move across the top of the fields through the gaps in the high hedgerow.

The country lane twists and turns, following the ancient hedgerow for several miles. Signposts indicate an historic town further ahead, various smaller signs urging the travellers to stop at points of interest, eat a pub lunch, rest in a picnic area, walk around some monuments or spend money on the crap punted out to unsuspecting holiday makers.

Something about the signs makes Clarence think of Sarah again. In the Services he was always deployed overseas, fighting wars and battles in far-flung corners that meant nothing to him. Flown in, briefed, trained, deployed, mission executed and moved out again. A couple of weeks' rest and then another one. The various missions and countries blend into one long memory of deserts, jungles, and snow-covered terrain, inner city ghettos and months spent living out of bedsits, watching subjects from windows and building lifestyle profiles that meant nothing to him. The Services and the type of work he was involved in meant he could never talk about what he did or where he had been. Over time, the connections that once existed outside the Service slowly eroded until all that was left were the people he knew inside. But then, over the years, they too slowly fell away as younger, fitter, and leaner men came through the ranks, and men like Clarence, Chris, and Malcolm felt like dinosaurs.

They left the Services, but the skills they had harnessed and built simply did not transfer to civilian life, and like so many highly-skilled but older soldiers, they were drawn to the world of mercenary soldiering with the promise of action and high wages. They all said it was for the money, but, in reality, it was the only way of clinging onto the life they had built – working with people who knew those same deadly skills and being able to belong to something. Former officers started security companies back in the UK and quickly contacted their former men, offering them steady wages and a dedicated role. Clarence responded to that, after years of mercenary work left a nasty taste in his mouth; shady deals done in back street cafés were not his idea of honour. His mammoth size and appearance meant he was perfect for door work, often his mere presence prevented most incidents from escalating, but even then, the constant hours in the seedy nightlife full of cocky idiots with gelled hair and t-shirt muscles soon wore him down.

Managers and bar owners were obsessed with profit, reputation, health and safety, log sheets, toilet checks, and head counts. Clarence's size, appearance and deep voice made him a target for many women – women who loved the idea of being with a tough man with a tough reputation, but Clarence was a professional, not a steroid-addicted bouncer obsessed with image and wearing a shirt two sizes too small – and those drunken women repulsed him.

He had intelligence and knowledge that just did not correlate with his appearance, and after years of being seen to be a big tough idiot, he accepted the type of woman he was likely to be with. But now, something magical had happened. Something he had never known before. A beautiful, educated, and intelligent woman was interested in him.

The way she spoke to him, not patronisingly, but speaking to him as an equal – touching his arm or shoulder, leaning forward and staring into his eyes – left him almost breathless. The desperation of the world, and the utter violence and degradation of mankind just in the last seven days, the hopeless feeling that no matter how they fight back or what they do, it's all pointless – those feelings now mix with a warm tingling feeling, of something different he had not felt before. Light in the dark. A single rose amongst weeds. Hope where there was none. Something to survive for. Something to fight for.

The road sweeps around to a long, wide junction; from the left are streams of zombies pouring from the town and heading into the fields to shuffle and stagger along in dead silence: lines of rotting, walking corpses, drawn to a meeting place where they will gather and mass in readiness of war. The vehicles stop back from the junction, far enough back to be able to respond if they turn for the attack, but they don't turn, they don't pay any attention at all.

'We can't get through that lot without picking a fight,' the woman police officer says after jumping down and walking up to stand by Clarence.

'Yeah, you're probably right,' Clarence replies, wishing they had the Saxon with them and the GPMG.

'So, the motorway to the north is that way then?' she asks, looking down at the map.

'Yeah, that must be the gathering point. The main motorway running south from London, I guess; if all these get to the various junctions feeding into it, then the main group will scoop them up as they come.'

'Maybe they're heading somewhere else?' she suggests.

'That,' Clarence replies, 'is just wishful thinking. Come on, we'd better get back.'

'Err, slight problem – this is a narrow lane, and that is a big fuel truck and I'm not reversing it all the way back.'

'Good point, you'll be needing the junction then,' Clarence says, turning back to look at the fuel truck.

'Yep.'

'How will you do it?'

'Pull out to the right, reverse back to the left and swing back in to this road,' she replies quickly.

'Right ...'

'That's what I thought.' She bites her bottom lip, staring at the constant stream heading across the junction.

'Well, the fuel tanker is big and heavy, and as long as you keep motion, you should be all right, and we did say we wanted to take a few of them out,' Clarence rumbles quietly.

'No, you said *you* wanted to take them out.'

'Yeah, but I can't drive that thing, or can I? Is it hard?' he asks.

'Yes it is, bloody hard, you'll stall the engine before you get more than a few metres. Don't worry, I'll do it.' She turns and walks back to the fuel tanker, pausing as she climbs up into the cabin and looking at the junction.

She nods to herself and slowly pulls out from behind Clarence's van, moving slowly up to the wide junction. Clarence watches as she seems to slow down, almost stopping; then, at the last second, the fuel tanker surges ahead, pulling over to the extreme left and brushing against the hedgerow.

The tanker then pulls quickly to the right, moving out of the lane and into the junction. The front of the tanker impacts on the line of undead staggering across, striking them from behind and shunting them all forward. The collective ramming drives them into the backs of the zombies in front, acting as a giant scoop and propelling them forward. The momentum causes them to either fall out to either side or drop down onto the ground, to be dragged along by the front of the truck or squashed by the massive wheels, causing blood and guts to be pumped out onto the road surface. The zombies neither slow down nor speed up, and they take no avoiding action as the truck pummels them out of the way.

The fuel tanker pushes out into the right side of the junction, then brakes hard, forcing the zombies caught at the front to be propelled forward. A loud grinding of gears can be heard as the woman police officer quickly works to engage the reversing gears and start moving backwards. The rear of the truck lacks the solid wall of the front, and the zombies behind are simply crushed by the rounded edge of the tanker and the jutting-out metal ladder. The tanker reverses quickly, driving backwards further down to the left until the front goes past the entrance to the lane. Once again, the tanker brakes hard and the gears crunch as she selects a forward-driving gear and pulls away quickly, swinging the front around and back into the lane, ploughing through more zombies as they blindly shuffle back across the junction. As the front of the tanker draws level with Clarence, he steps out and applauds with respect, smiling broadly at the excellent driving skills shown. She smiles back and salutes as she drives onwards past the waiting vehicles. Clarence gets back in his van and tries to do a three-point turn in the road, but the narrow width of the lane and the length of the van make it a seven-point turn – eventually he succeeds and moves out of the way for the other vehicles. They move closer to the wider section of the junction to complete their manoeuvre and, within minutes, the vehicles are driving back down the lane behind the fuel tanker.

CHAPTER TEN

Dave and Jamie move quickly to the edge of the estate, jogging in silence with fluid movements, neither showing signs of exertion. They stop at the country lane leading into the estate.

'The estate is here with one lane leading in, but they could use the fields on either side,' Dave says, examining the area.

'The fields have high hedgerows, and they're thick with brambles which will we be hard to push through,' Jamie replies.

'The natural path will be this lane. We can't do anything about the fields, but we do have a choke point here – the hedges on both sides are very high and the lane ends abruptly as it enters the estate. They will come down the lane and fan out into the estate and sweep through, but most of them will keep going straight down the centre main road,' Dave explains.

'The first trap should be here on the central road about halfway down; we then work back, setting more traps as we go. They will be crammed into the lane so they will naturally spill out to the sides and move down through the estate, using all available space. So we set one here and then more further out to the sides. That way there will be the maximum number of them in the area when the traps go off.'

Jamie listens in silence and watches Dave with keen interest, tracking his view to look at the same places.

Dave moves down the central road, going just past the halfway mark, looking at the parked cars nose to tail on both sides of the road.

'They'll come down the lane and have to go through the gap between the vehicles on either side,' Dave explains.

He takes two grenades from one of the canvas bags and walks back to the closest row of vehicles. Dropping down onto the ground, he positions the grenade snug against the inside of the rear tyre, then crosses the road to place another grenade against the inside of the tyre on the opposite vehicle.

'When the time is right, we tie wire onto both pins and wedge them in firmly. Pressure applied to the wire pulls the pins, which activates the detonation,' Dave explains, pulling a roll of very thin fishing wire from a pocket to show Jamie.

'Will these two be enough to detonate the rest of the vehicles?' Jamie asks.

'In theory, yes, but there will be a delay. These grenades will detonate the fuel tanks, but we need to speed the progress up so we get maximum effect.' Dave shrugs his rucksack off and takes out a container. He unscrews the lid and starts pouring a thin trail of black powder from the first grenade, working back to the next vehicle, and ending the thin trail underneath the fuel tank. Dave takes another grenade and rests it in a small pool of the powder.

'I see,' Jamie says.

Dave takes out another container and hands it to Jamie.

'You do the other side,' Dave says and returns to move on, trailing black powder over to the next vehicle. Jamie moves across and repeats the action, pouring a thin trail of black powder from fuel tank to fuel tank and leaving a grenade nestled in the black powder underneath each one.

'Good,' Dave says. 'Now we do the rest of the estate.' They go back into the estate, moving from road to road, and house to house, finding alleys and paths that work through the small streets. They place trip-wired grenades at various points of access, then get to the side roads connected to the central main road and stop to look at the cars and vehicles left in situ.

'We'll do all of these too; you do the far side,' Dave says.

They split up and Jamie crosses the central lane to work the other side, positioning trip wire grenades between the gaps of the vehicles and more thin trails of black powder stretched from fuel tank to fuel tank. They meet back in the central road.

'Now, go from house to house and turn the gas on; close the doors to trap the gas.'

'Got it.' They move off again from dwelling to dwelling, going into kitchens and turning the gas jets on low and letting the poisonous vapour seep out to fill the rooms. They continue to work throughout the day, moving into the side streets and laying traps with grenades, wires, and black powder – then going into the houses and turning the gas supply to hiss out as they move back out, closing the doors behind them. After several hours, they stand at the exit point of the lane where it stretches out into the flatlands and the diggers moving along, slowly churning the earth up.

'Clarence is still out with his foraging party; we'll wait for him to return and then put the wires across the centre path,' Dave says.

'What about the men out front on the observation points? They won't be able to get back through,' Jamie replies.

'I spoke to them. I left a clear path for them to run through on the side I worked on,' Dave replies.

'Okay,' Jamie nods back at him.

'Get our vehicle and leave it on the edge of the estate on the road. Meet me back at the entrance point,' Dave says, turning to walk back up the central road.

'Okay,' Jamie replies. A few minutes later, they stand in silence at the entrance to the estate.

'You did well today,' Dave says.

'Thank you,' Jamie replies.

Eventually, they hear engine noises coming towards them.

'How many?' Dave asks.

'Engines? Err ...' Jamie cocks his head and listens intently for a few seconds. 'I have no idea,' he finally admits, feeling ashamed that he is unable to work out the different sounds of the engines.

'Me neither,' Dave replies, and Jamie gives a rare and awkward smile.

The front vehicle comes into view, Clarence's distinct bald-headed profile clear through the windscreen. The lead vehicle slows to a stop a few metres back from the entrance.

'Everything okay?' Clarence asks, getting out and walking towards them with his assault rifle held like a toy gun in his massive hand.

'Yes,' Dave replies.

'Did you rig the estate okay?' Clarence asks.

'Waiting for you to go through so we can finish off,' Dave answers.

'Okay mate, we found a few things to bring back with us – we've got loads of nuts, bolts, and chains for the cannon,' Clarence smiles at the two quiet men.

'Good, is that a fuel tanker?' Dave asks, looking over at the large vehicle with the engine idling.

'Yep, and it's full too – thought we might make use of it.'

Dave nods, staring at the tanker.

'If they don't need it down there, we can use it here.'

'Roger, I'll pass that on,' Clarence replies.

'Let them know the estate is rigged and to be avoided,' Dave adds, as Clarence walks back to his vehicle.

The convoy stops on the single-track road leading to the Fort as Howie and Chris step out of the gates, accompanied by Blowers and Cookey. All of them look at the fuel tanker.

'Where on earth did you find that?' Chris calls out as they walk towards each other; Clarence turns to glance at the fuel tanker.

'We found it behind some gates next to a petrol station, couldn't believe it was still there. We've got loads of stuff from the hardware store and the first gunsmiths, but the next one was looted. The one after that was a florists and not much use ...'

'A florists?' Howie interrupts. 'Who would turn a gunsmiths into a florists?'

'That's what we said, so then we went for the last one ... and saw shitloads of zombies marching out of a town, heading north.'

'North?' Chris asks quickly, all of them focussing hard on Clarence's words.

'Yeah, it looks like they're going towards the motorway but moving as the crow flies, going across land and fields.'

'How many?' Howie asks.

'Thousands, just a solid line of them. They're moving slowly and they didn't pay us any attention, not even when we mowed a few down with the fuel tanker.'

'You reckon they're heading for the motorway?' Chris asks.

'Must be, it makes the most sense. They get to the junctions on the motorway and then tag onto the main bulk as they pass through. The most obvious theory is that they're massing, just like they did in London,' Clarence says, looking to Chris, then Howie.

'Well, we knew it was coming, this is just a dose of reality,' Howie says grimly.

'It changes nothing, we've got spotters out and Dave is rigging the estate now ...'

'He's done it, him and that other quiet one,' Clarence says.

'Jamie. They've done it already?' Howie replies.

'He wants the fuel tanker up there, if you don't need it.'

'I bet he bloody does, I bet his eyes lit up at that thing,' Howie laughs. 'Is it full?'

'With petrol,' Clarence nods.

'The last point of defence before they get to us is the deep ditch after the last bank; if we pour petrol in, we'll lose loads being soaked into the ground before it starts to fill ...' Howie muses.

'I see what you mean, Howie ... some pipes filled with petrol spraying out, maybe?' Chris adds, rubbing his beard as he thinks.

‘Flame throwers?’ Howie asks.

‘Big, fucking flame throwers, now that would be cool,’ Chris smiles. ‘But it will take too long to sort out.’

‘Maybe not,’ Ted interrupts. ‘We’ve got plenty of plumbers here, let me have a word with them and see what we can do.

‘You happy with that, Howie?’ Chris asks, looking at him.

‘Yeah, we’ve got no choice really. We know they’re massing or getting ready, so we need to pick the pace up, it’s already getting late.
‘

Chris, find out how the diggers are getting on, then how long before we can start putting the spikes and caltrops in.

‘We need Dave back here to sort those cannon out and see if they can be used. Ted, find those plumbers, and work out if we can rig something up with the petrol going through pipes in the ditch.

‘Clarence, you take the weapons and materials you found to Malcolm, and then get the lists of people that have weapons experience and start drilling or training or distributing the weapons. Use the top of the inner wall for the long-range weapons and get people up there ready. There’s some archers here too, find out where they need to be positioned. Ideally, we want them on the top of the inner wall too, firing high, so they get the best range.

‘Blowers and Cookey, stay on that gate and do not let anyone out that shouldn’t be going out, got it?’ Howie speaks firmly and quickly, looking to each man as he issues orders and instructions.

They nod back at each request.

‘Good, we need to move and get this done quickly, let’s go.’

CHAPTER ELEVEN

The afternoon rolls on, with the long hours flying by as those few men tasked with the responsibility work like demons without rest. Strong coffee, adrenalin, and the knowledge of what's coming their way keep them working at a pace that would leave most reeling from exhaustion.

Chris stalks the Fort, radio in hand, speaking to the guards with the digger drivers, urging them to move quickly and finding out the pits are nearly finished.

He locates Sergeant Hopewell in the office, already surrounded by people clamouring for her attention. Chris pushes through, using his bulk to force a path, and then instructs Sergeant Hopewell to find people to send out and cut weeds and long grass down and be ready to assist the engineers. Then he works his way to the workshops, to find Kelly and the rest hard at work and more people already drafted in to sort wooden shafts, posts, and metal poles into piles that are waiting to be sharpened into spikes – or to be cut and bent into the deadly foot traps. Several generators sourced from non-essential parts of the Fort chug and roar as the power tools scream out.

Sparks from metal cutters cascade out onto the workshop floor, and every space is dominated by small groups hard at work.

Chris pauses at the door, watching Kelly move from group to group, correcting and offering advice.

'Kelly, how's it going?' Chris asks, finally getting her attention.

'Good, the spikes are almost ready, they were the easiest. The foot traps are taking a bit longer though,' she replies, wiping sweat from her brow with an old cloth and smearing black grease over her forehead.

'Can we start getting them in then?'

'The spikes? Err, yeah I think we can.'

'Good, find someone to send out to supervise it if you can't be spared,' Chris replies firmly.

'No, I'll go myself, are there guards out there?' she asks.

'Several of them. No one is to go near the edge of the estate. The guards will shoot them if they do. Get out there as quick as possible,' Chris responds and walks out of the room.

Back on the radio, he informs the gate that engineers will be coming through shortly and then talks to the guards with the digger drivers. He tells them to get the pits finished and then use the drivers to help with whatever else is needed. Finally, he establishes that Dave is on his way back to the Fort with Jamie.

Ted moves away from the small gathering outside the Fort, moving quickly and with purpose back inside.

He walks quickly to the police office to find Sarah and Terri helping Sergeant Hopewell deal with the many enquiries – people now coming in to ask questions about all the activity taking place – and trying to find more people to help the engineers.

Ted finds the stack of lists and works his way through the pile until he finds names of plumbers and the sections within the camp they are allocated to. Striding back outside, he looks for runners to send out, only to find the supply of runners now exhausted.

'Where are all the runners?' he calls out, stepping back into the office and having to shout over the clamour of voices.

'All busy, Ted,' Sarah replies. Ted steps back out and casts his experienced eye around to see Tom and Steven strolling along in the camp, still bickering.

'You two, come here,' Ted bellows.

Tom and Steven both spin around, recognising his voice instantly, and move quickly over to him.

'We need plumbers, they're on these lists ...' Ted starts to explain.

'Have we sprung a leak?' Steven jokes.

'Shut up and focus, young man,' Ted snaps at him, and notices they both visibly straighten up at his tone of voice.

'Take these,' Ted hands the lists to Steven. 'And get them over to me as soon as possible, and I mean as soon as possible.'

'Okay, Ted.'

'Right Tom, Ted gave me the lists so I'll be in charge of this project, seeing as Mr. Howie said we're both the same now ...' Steven starts to gloat.

'I SAID NOW,' Ted booms at them; they both turn quickly and start heading back into the camp as Ted heads back towards the police office with a wry smile and a shake of his head.

As the small gathering listens to Howie, Clarence watches him closely. This untrained man, a supermarket manager, gives orders to trained and experienced soldiers. There's something about him, though, the passion he exudes and the absolute certainty with which he speaks. Even Big Chris defers to Howie, and Clarence thinks back to the many missions when Chris was in charge, but Chris was always a man's soldier, never an officer. Howie is like an officer, the type of officer the men all respect and trust, the officer always leading from the front. The officer that can see all the facets of the mission, not just the one bit he is doing. Clarence had met great strategists in his time, but none of them had the human touch that Howie possesses. His ability to look a man in the eye and say with certainty that this needs to be done and it needs to be done now. Clarence watches Big Chris and the way he listens to Howie. Chris had always been that rare thing in a soldier, a good diplomat as well as a good fighter. However, Chris had never taken to idiot officers very well and had been outspoken if he felt they were doing the wrong thing, often to the detriment of his own career.

Clarence breaks away and heads back to his vehicle; Blowers and Cookey drag the big vehicle gates open, then pull the huge gates of the inner wall open too, allowing the vehicles to be driven inside the safety of the Fort. The fuel tanker is directed into the gap between the walls; the other vehicles, headed by Clarence, drive slowly through the compound to the armoury and over to Malcolm waiting outside.

'Big man, did you get anything nice for me?' Malcolm greets his long-time comrade with a massive smile and a warm handshake.

'Well, we got a few bits: rifles, shotguns, and loads of ammunition. First time I've loaded up with bows and arrows though,' Clarence replies, going around to the back and opening the rear doors.

'Strange times, my friend,' Malcolm muses as he starts going through the various items. 'What the bloody hell are we going to do with shotguns?'

'Yeah, I know, but Chris and Howie said to get everything,' Clarence says.

'I suppose they'll be usable if they breech the walls and get inside – we'll use them for defence only. Some of these rifles are good, Clarence.'

'I suppose so, but a few dozen heavy calibre, general purpose assault rifles would be better.'

'Ha, and if we were in America we'd be able to pick them up in a supermarket too. Fuck me those blokes had some decent ordnance.' Malcolm reminisces back to conflicts he had fought alongside the U.S. Marine Corps and their never-ending supply of decent weapons.

'I bet there's some secure places over there,' the ex-soldier that went with Clarence interrupts as he helps them to unload the vans and carry the items into the large armoury room.

'Mate, I don't know your name,' Clarence suddenly realises, as the ex-soldier walks by the side of him with armloads of shotguns.

'Brian, nice to meet you,' Brian grunts as he lifts the heavy load onto a workbench.

'You too. Listen, I'll have to leave you to it, I've got some tasks to finish,' Clarence says, walking back out of the armoury and up to the police office.

He enters to find the inside even more frantic: radios blaring out with chatter, people talking loudly, and Sergeant Hopewell trying to do a hundred things at the same time. Clarence frowns as he looks at the bedlam in front of him, trying to figure out the best way of getting her attention without simply pushing everyone else out of the way.

A cool hand touches his arm and he glances down to see Sarah smiling broadly at him, her clean white teeth framed by those soft pink lips.

'You're back,' she says simply.

'I said I would be,' Clarence replies.

'I'm glad. I was worried,' Sarah says.

Clarence doesn't reply but stares for long seconds, losing himself in her dark eyes.

He gently puts his hand over hers, his giant mitt dwarfing her small, delicate hand. A tingling sensation prickles through him from the contact, a simple action, yet so endearing, that she steps forward involuntary until they are standing with bodies touching. In the chaos of the office, with voices shouting and people surging around them, they stand staring into each other's eyes and slowly move forward, until their lips are but a tiny distance apart.

'Did you need something, mate?' Ted's voice snaps them back to reality as he bustles into the office and heads over to the stacks of paper on the desk.

'Err, I, err, yeah I think so,' Clarence stammers, feeling a strange sense of loss at being so close to kissing her.

'You think so?' Ted asks with a puzzled frown.

'I'll see you in a while. I'm glad you're back, come and find me, if you get any spare time,' Sarah says quietly and slips away, back into the furore going on around them.

'Sorry Ted, I need lists of anyone with weapons training or experience – and the archers too.'

'Yep okay, how are you going to do it?' Ted replies, starting to leaf through a big pile of papers.

'Can you get them all down to the front, near the gates?' Clarence asks.

'It'll take a bit of time, Clarence, it's bedlam here, as you can see – and we've got no runners left,' Ted replies.

'The Saxon's got a loudhailer, use the radio and get one of them to put it out so everyone can hear it,' Clarence says.

'Good idea, now why didn't I think of that,' Ted mutters as he hunts round for the radio.

'*Police office to the Saxon,*' Ted speaks into it.

'*Saxon to police office, go ahead.*'

'*Police office to Saxon, can you use the loudspeaker and ask the people that registered their firearms experience to report to the front of the Fort?*'

'*Roger, confirm you want anyone with firearms experience to report to the front?*'

'*Answer yes, also anyone with archery experience.*'

'*Roger that, will do it now.*'

'Thanks Ted,' Clarence rumbles in his deep voice; he walks out of the office and down to the armoury, reaching the door as the amplified voice of Nick Hewitt suddenly fills the air. Nick's loud message creates a general buzz and a sense of excitement within the camp.

People start moving about quickly, talking loudly. Those people with weapons knowledge find their families or partners and hastily kiss and hold them before heading off with grim faces, meeting others along the way and walking together while talking. Clarence enters the armoury to see Malcolm, Brian, and a few others, still bringing in the items from the vehicles.

'I'm going down the front to start sorting out the people with weapons knowledge,' Clarence informs them.

'Do you need a hand, mate?' Brian says. 'I did an instructor course a few years back ...'

'Definitely. Malc, can you spare Brian?'

'Yep, crack on, we've got enough people here. Are you bringing them back here for weapons allocation?' Malcolm asks.

'Yeah, I'll take a few with me and can you send more down, as soon as you get the chance?'

'Roger, give me a few minutes to see what I've got,' Malcolm replies.

'Bloody quartermasters ... All the same,' Clarence jokes, as he leaves.

Cookey and Blowers disperse from the briefing, now long used to the sudden ferocious intensity of Howie. They both listen with awe as he gives clear instructions to the rest, giving them tasks, but leaving it to them how they get it completed.

They then stroll back and open the gates wide, to allow Clarence and the rest of the vehicles to get through into the Fort. The gates are closed after them and they once again resume their static guard on the front walk-through gate, watching as the men dart about with a renewed sense of pace and urgency.

'Kind of feels weird standing here, while everyone else is running about,' Cookey remarks after a few minutes.

'Yeah, I know what you mean, but Nick and Curtis are doing the same up top with the Saxon,' Blowers says.

'What about Tucker, where's he?' Cookey asks.

'Mr. Howie asked him to sort out the food situation.'

'He'll be in his element then,' Cookey says.

'I expect so, talking of which, I am bloody starving,' Blowers says.

'Aye, me too,' Cookey replies.

'Aye?' Blowers asks, picking up on the strange comment.

'What?'

'You said 'aye'.'

'Yeah, and?'

'Nothing ...'

'What?' Cookey asks.

'No mate, nothing ... it's just that sailors say *aye*.'

'Oh, for fucks sake, Blowers, don't start.'

'What? I never said anything, you can be a sailor if you like.'

'Why would I want to be a sailor?' Cookey asks.

'So, you can say aye ... and, of course, there's all the sea-men.'

'Oh, fuck off.'

'You like sea-men, don't you Cookey ...?'

'Piss off, Blowers.' They eventually stop talking and lean back against the gate to rest.

'Did you hear what Clarence said about them heading north?' Cookey says.

'Yes mate, there's going to be fucking shitloads of them coming for us.'

'Yeah, does it bother you?' Cookey asks quietly.

'I don't know. If I think about it then, yeah, I guess it does, but I keep thinking of the other scraps we've had and we've done all right so far,' Blowers replies.

'There's gonna be a lot more this time,' Cookey says.

'How can it be worse than London? There were thousands of them then, and besides, they can't all attack at the same time, can they?'

'Eh?'

'Well, like in London, we formed a circle and it's only the first row that could actually attack us, the rest just waited and stepped in when the first lot got knocked down.'

'Yeah, but we ain't gonna be in a circle this time, are we? We're gonna be stood in a big line.'

'Yes, but it's still only the first row that can actually attack us, the others are behind them.'

'I see what you mean. I'm sort of anxious about it, a bit scared and also kind of looking forward to it, like I want it to happen,' Cookey says plainly.

Blowers glances over at his friend speaking from the heart.

'Do you know what I mean, Blowers? I'm scared and terrified, but also excited and ready for it – all at the same time,' Cookey repeats.

'I know what you mean, mate, I feel the same. I think we all do, otherwise we'd have bottled long before now.'

'That was a bit deep for you, Blowers.'

'You like it deep.'

'Oh, for fucks sake.'

'We tie the wire onto the pin like this, then we have to make sure the grenade is firmly placed, otherwise the pressure on the wire will simply pull the grenade along the ground and not pull the pin out. Then we feed the wire over to the other side and position the second grenade, making sure the wire is taut.' Dave gently pulls the wire until it stretches across the road.

'Then we tie it off and again make sure the grenade is firmly placed, got it?'

'Got it,' Jamie replies.

They step back and move a few feet away; already the thin fishing wire is hard to see. Nodding with satisfaction, they move back down through the estate, heading towards the vehicle they left on the road to the Fort.

'Where will we put the tanker if we get it?' Jamie asks.

'Either in the middle so we get the full effect of the blast and the shrapnel it creates, or closer to the exit onto the Fort road.'

'Okay.'

The inside of the car is uncomfortably hot with warm, stale air; they both wind their windows down quickly as Jamie pulls away, driving towards the Fort.

The ditches on both sides are almost finished, with the diggers now working at the far ends, the freshly churned brown earth looking stark against the green flat lands. People from the Fort walk out over the flatlands carrying hand tools and heading towards the big patches of long grass. Clarence and one of the guards from the commune stand in front of the Fort talking to a large group of people, each of them holding a collection of rifles. A large group of archers are placed off to one side, some of them holding great bows the size of a man, others with smaller modern bows with pulleys and contraptions attached to them. They stand talking, pointing out to the flatlands and then back up at the walls behind them. Others in the group sort through the large boxes and packets of arrows. Dave turns back to take in the diggers and the men working with them, then back at the rows of workers coming from the Fort towards the long grass, Clarence speaking to the large groups and showing them the weapons, the archers making ready. Now, more people are filing out from the gates, carrying long, sharpened spikes and loading them into the backs of vehicles waiting nearby. Dave recognises the engineers carrying buckets of small, sharp, twisted metal foot traps and loading them into the vehicles. Jamie stops the car near the front. They climb out, and Dave walks straight over to Howie.

'Mr. Howie,' Dave says.

'Dave,' Howie greets him back with a genuine smile. 'How did you get on?'

'Good, the estate is all set.'

'Is Jamie okay?'

'Very good, Mr. Howie, very capable.'

'Takes after you, mate.'

'They must be the spikes for the ditches.'

'Yep, they've worked bloody hard getting them done so quickly, just got to get them driven in now. We've had to get a lot more people involved, which I didn't want to do, but we don't really have a choice if we want all these things to happen. The first load of caltrops are ready too, Clarence and that chap ... Brian, have got the lists of all the people with weapons experience, and they are checking to make sure they won't shoot themselves in the foot, or someone else for that matter ... then we've got the archers over there. Clarence found some good supplies and some of them had their own kit with them. I don't know if they'll be any good, but it gives them hope and something to do.'

'You've got a lot done,' Dave remarks.

'Yes, we have,' Howie admits.

'Ted is rounding up some plumbers too. We'll find out if we can rig some pipes up in the deep ditch after the last bank, for flame throwers.'

'Is that for the fuel tanker?' Dave asks.

'Yes, well, the petrol from the fuel tanker anyway, I heard you had plans for the tanker?'

'You can have the fuel first, I just want the vehicle.'

'Don't you need fuel in it to make this blow up?' Howie asks.

'No, the fumes trapped inside the pressured container will be enough.'

'Oh, so we can use all the fuel then?'

'Well, maybe just leave a little bit in there, if that's okay, Mr. Howie.'

'No worries, mate – I don't know if the flame throwing idea will work. Surely we'll need to store the fuel, then pump it into the pipes, and then if we put holes in the pipes for the flames to come out off, won't the fuel just leak out? Also, how does it get ignited? And wouldn't the flame just shoot back inside the pipe and blow the whole thing up?'

'Yes, yes, yes and yes, and you would need ignition from a distance, otherwise the person doing the igniting would get blown up and yes, it would all blow up,' Dave replies.

'Oh, I see,' Howie says, with a frown.

'But, you could just lay hoses down in the ditch and fill them with petrol. Put containers or buckets and other things filled with fuel: grenades, bits of metal, nails, screws – anything sharp, and ignite it from a distance. The whole thing will go then and the steep sides of the ditch will force the pressure wave and explosion straight up and not out to the sides.'

'Bloody hell, Dave – you really like blowing things up, don't you.'

'Yes, Mr. Howie,' Dave replies, flatly.

'We'll do that then – how about the cannon? Do you think you can get them working?'

'They already work, it's just a matter of knowing *how* they work, having the right mix of powder, charge, and then what we use to fire at them. I'll start looking at them now.'

'I'll get some coffee up to you,' Howie says.

'Okay, thanks, Mr. Howie.' Dave heads into the Fort and finds Jamie talking with Cookey and Blowers.

'What's next?' Jamie asks him.

'Cannon,' Dave replies.

'Like two peas in a pod, them two,' Blowers remarks as they watch Dave and Jamie walk off towards the steps.

CHAPTER TWELVE

Howie stands watching the activity unfolding in front of him, a deep look of concentration on his face. So far so good, he thinks, but the news of the zombies leading across the fields leave his mind unsettled. Howie knows the reality of the situation, probably better than anyone else, other than Dave – but for one of them to have actually seen them preparing brings it home. Two armies – one vastly outnumbering the other, getting ready to meet. He turns and heads back towards the Fort, deep in thought; Cookey and Blowers both remain quiet and let him pass without interruption.

The noise of the camp fills the air; the recent movement of people going outside to help with spikes, caltrops, cutting grass, weapons training, and archery have rapidly increased the air of excitement and charged the atmosphere.

Howie watches people moving quickly between sections. He notices that many of them are now armed with whatever they can find: sticks, metal poles, knives, hand axes, and hammers. The change is palpable and positive. The charged atmosphere has rubbed off on everyone and, for the first time, Howie takes note of the children in the camp. Small children are running between the tents, chasing each other and laughing. Bigger boys walk in groups and hold small sticks in their hands, ready to fight and kill all the zombies.

Howie notices the traditional roles of male and female have suddenly come back; the boys are carrying the weapons and the girls are working with the women to prepare food and clean the area, and helping to feed babies. The sound of children's laughter fills his ears and the gleeful, uncorrupted sound is like music; their innocence and utter faith that these adults will protect them from everything touches him deeply.

The resilience of their young minds have almost certainly faced untold horrors already, but here they are, running and playing like children have always done.

The thought of the undead army sweeping through them and getting into the Fort to savage these children fills Howie with a sickening feeling, and a thought process quickly enters his head. There's a problem here: if they do get in and there is every chance they will, then these children have nowhere to go. The mothers will fight like tigers, of that there is no doubt, but they too will fall. *They must be protected; at all costs they must be made safe and kept safe. Without them there is no purpose for all of this. We can stand and fight and show them how brave we are,* Howie thinks, *but for what reason? To give ourselves freedom to live so our race can continue. The thought of there now being two races of people on the Earth hits Howie hard. An evil race intent on killing every last human – and those small humans who are now running about and playing, and must survive in order to make more humans. There is nowhere else to run though; beyond that wall is the sea. There aren't enough boats to take them all away, and nowhere to go if they did find enough. But maybe ... just maybe ...*

Howie makes his way quickly through the camp, his mind whirling. *Why did he leave this so late*? He reaches the police office and is stunned for a second to see the almighty clamour going on. People are shouting and pushing forward to speak to a very harassed-looking Sergeant Hopewell and Terri,

'Sarah, Terri, I need to speak with you both now.' Howie speaks firmly and his voice cuts across the room, as the people realise Mr. Howie is here.

The three of them step outside and move away from the door to a quiet spot.

'Listen, I don't know why I didn't think of this sooner, but we are right on the sea here, so there must be harbours or mooring points 'round here. I want you to find boats and get them back here.'

'Why? What for?' Sarah asks quickly.

'When they come, I want the children loaded onto boats and moved out and away from the Fort. If they get in, we'll all be killed. We must do whatever we can to keep them safe, find some people that can handle boats and navigation and have them ready to report to a set place when the action starts. Get the mothers too, be ready to get them out,' Howie says intensely.

'Good idea, very good idea,' Sarah replies, nodding her head.

'There is one boat out there already, I saw it when we arrived,' Terri says.

'Good, get them to use that to go out and find more and bring them back. Work out how many children and mothers we have, and make sure they bring enough back with them.'

'Err, this is a horrible question, Howie – but what age child do we go up to? Sixteen, Eighteen?'

'Eighteen, they'll be old enough to offer some protection and care for the younger ones.'

'Some of the eighteen-year-olds won't want to go,' Terri says. 'They'll want to stay and fight with their fathers or brothers.'

'That's natural, but just do what you can. It's already getting late, so do it quickly, and I will want to speak to the boat people before they go. Send them to the planning office.'

Breaking apart to move off to their respective offices, they each feel the sense of pace increasing. Knowing that, with each passing hour, the zombie army build in numbers and draw ever closer.

Terri rushes into the office, ignoring the people moving towards her with questions – she pulls the stacks of lists from the desk and moves down to Sarah at the back of the office, purposefully putting her back to the rest of the room.

'How do we do this?' Terri asks, scanning through the lists of skills.

'I don't know if we even recorded people with boat skills.' She glances back to see Sergeant Hopewell still frantically struggling to cope at the main desk.

'Sarge, did we record people with boating skills?' Terri shouts across and gets a quick glance from Sergeant Hopewell, before she returns to dealing with the people in front of her.

'It's here, under occupations,' Sarah says. 'We've got Royal Navy sailors and commercial sailors in the camp, I guess being this close to the coast there would be.'

'Let me see,' Terri asks, leafing through the papers.

'There's a Royal Navy Reserves Captain here, Henry Marshall; he's retired and getting on a bit in age, but we recorded him having commercial experience, too.'

'Let's find him,' Sarah stands up, ready to go.

'Hang on; let me check something, yes, he's also on the list of people with weapons experience. He'll be down with Clarence at the front.'

'Clarence has a radio, can we call him and get him sent back?' Sarah asks.

Terri fights back through the crowds at the desk to reach the radio, then pushes back out to find some clear ground.

'Police office to Clarence.'

'Clarence to police office, go ahead.'

'Police office to Clarence, have you got a Henry Marshall with you?'

'Confirm Henry Marshall. Stand by.'

'Answer yes, Henry Marshall.' A few minutes go by, with Sarah and Terri staring intently at the radio.

'Clarence to police office, yes we have Henry Marshall with us.'

'Police office to Clarence, send him back to us immediately. His services are required urgently.'

'Clarence to police office, Roger that, he's on his way to the police office.'

'Police office to Clarence, thank you and out.'

'Good, now I don't know about you, but I need coffee,' Sarah says, heading to the back room and the kettle that has been running non-stop for several hours.

Howie moves back into the planning office after leaving Terri and Sarah. Big Chris is inside with several men, all looking over the plans on the table.

'Yes, these are the ditches here, we want pipes running with fuel that we can ignite from a distance and create a wall of flame,' Chris explains to the men.

'Cancel that Chris, change of plan,' Howie says quickly, then runs through the idea given by Dave.

'Much better,' Chris nods back.

'Sorry, you must be the plumbers, seeing as most of you have pencils behind your ears. I'm Howie,' Howie says, smiling and shaking hands with them in turn.

'Howie, leave this with me. I'll take these chaps down and get started,' Chris says, quickly leading the men outside. Howie pauses for a second in the sudden quietness of the room, the noise from the camp reduced as Chris closes the door behind him.

Rubbing his hands through his hair, he walks around the desk to the large flask and presses his hand against the side. Still warm. He finds a half-filled cup and moves back over to the door and throws the cold empty contents out onto the ground. He then closes the door and moves back inside. He takes a teaspoon and loads it up with sugar from a ragged bag left on the table, then pours the hot black coffee into the mug. The aroma hits him instantly and the simple act of making a coffee calms him immeasurably. Mug in hand, he feels his body relaxing for the first time in days. Staring into nothingness, he raises the mug slowly to his lips and takes the first mouthful, just as the door pops open with Terri leaning in.

'Howie, this is Henry Marshall, retired Navy Captain. Mr. Marshall, this is Howie.' Terri moves back and closes the door after a small built man with white hair and a white beard enters.

'Mr. Howie, good to meet you sir,' the man moves forward as Howie scrabbles up from his now seated position to shake his hand.

'Mr. Marshall, thank you for coming, please take a seat,' Howie offers.

'Please ... Henry is fine,' the man replies, smiling and taking a seat opposite Howie.

'Okay, and I'm just Howie, everyone seems to be calling me Mr. Howie lately.'

'Comes with the job, young man, people like to know who is in charge.' Henry smiles warmly, his voice rich with a deep baritone.

'Forgive me firing questions at you, has anyone said why you're here?' Howie asks.

'Not yet, I was with the others, going through weapons drill, when they said to come here.'

'Okay, may I ask, what's your experience with ships and boats?' Howie asks.

'Well, where do I start, young man,' Henry smiles.

'I was a commercial skipper on cargo ships, fuel tankers, then did a stint in the cruise liners, and I was also Captain in the Royal Navy Reserves. I've been around boats and ships all of my life.'

'Do you know these waters very well?' Howie asks.

'Like the back of my hand, young man. May I ask why?'

'Sir, as you know, there is a huge army of those things coming for us. We've got lots of children here, and we have to do what we can to protect them.'

'I was thinking of this when I first got here. Yes, it is an option, and yes, there are several small harbours around here that would have numerous pleasure craft moored up.'

'Could you take the small boat that's out the back and bring more boats back? Enough for the children and their mothers?'

'I can try. We'll definitely get some back, whether there's enough is a different matter, and do we know how long we've got?'

'We know they are massing now a few miles out, so it could be any time. The night would be the best time for them to attack, as they become faster, but they've been changing so much in the last few days that anything is possible,' Howie explains.

'Right, we'd best get moving then. I'll need some people with me. I know a few here that will be suitable to take with me.'

'Speak to Terri and Sarah next door, they'll help you find them. One more thing, do you have a safe destination to take them all?' Howie asks.

'There's two places: across the water to the Isle of Wight, or to one of the Forts in the sea,' Henry replies.

'Henry, this is absolutely vital. Do not tell anyone else where you plan to take them. Not one other person must know. If those things find out where you are going, they will hunt you down and kill you all, I cannot make that clear enough,' Howie presses on the older man.

'Yes of course,' Henry says, looking Howie in the eye.

'Now, please hurry and be as quick as you can,' Howie says, standing up.

Henry follows his lead and extends his hand to Howie.

'I won't let you down,' Henry says firmly before leaving the room.

Howie sinks back down on his chair, raises his feet to rest on the desk and once more takes a sip of his coffee.

'Typical, it's gone cold,' Howie mutters, staring down at the inky black liquid sloshing in the cup. His brow furrows as he thinks of something he was meant to do ... something with coffee.

'Shit, Dave ...'

'These rooms are very secure,' Roger explains to Dave, as he unlocks the solid metal padlock before inserting keys to the several locks on the door.

'They're alarmed too,' Roger adds as he pushes the door open to hear a loud urgent bleeping sound. He moves over to an alarm panel and keys in a number of digits.

'That's better, now do you know what you need?' Roger asks. Dave steps into the room to look at the wrought iron fence bolted across the width of the room and the small gate set into them.

'That's locked too, now let me see, it must be one of these,' Roger thumbs the keys on the big loop, trying several until, with a satisfying click, the gate swings open.

Entering the cage, Dave heads straight to the rear. Powder bags are already made up and stacked carefully on shelves above the ground. There are large signs telling people not to smoke.

'Is this where you got the powder from earlier?' Dave asks.

'Yes David, there are containers on the shelving unit that I think they use for the muskets,' Roger answers as Dave winces at the use of his full name.

'It's Dave, I need all of these powder bags to be brought up, plus all of that wadding, and I need lots of water, and all of those ramrods ...' Dave says, pointing to each item in turn.

'Anything else?' Roger asks.

'Yes, all of the black powder that's here and the empty powder bags too, get them all up to the top and leave them by the Saxon.' Dave turns and leaves, walking straight out of the door without another word and leaving Roger standing, bemused.

Dave walks across the compound and through the camp, ignoring everyone else, his mind entirely on the task at hand. Reaching the armoury, he enters to find Malcolm still sorting the weapons and ammunition.

'I need all of the cannon ammunition,' Dave says, flatly.

'Hello Dave, how are you?' Malcolm asks, irritated by his instant demand.

'I'm fine, where is the cannon ammunition?' Dave answers, not registering Malcolm's tone.

'We've got buckets of the stuff, tons of it. Clarence got a load on his forage and we went 'round to find more stuff.'

'Where is it?'

'We moved it all into one of the back rooms.'

'Why?'

'Because it was taking up so much bloody space, that's why,' Malcolm snaps back.

'I need it all up top,' Dave says, still devoid of emotion.

'Right, you need it up top, okay well, let's drop everything and get that done for you, is there anything else we can do while we're here?' Malcolm says sarcastically.

'No, just that. Thank you,' Dave replies and leaves the room to head back up to the top of the north wall.

'Fucking Special Forces, always the fucking same ...' Malcolm mutters.

He heads outside to find one of the guards, and instructs him to go into the police office and find people to form a chain to pass the cannon ammunition up to the south wall.

The guard nods and strolls into the police room to join the queue of people already waiting for Sergeant Hopewell's attention.

Thinking that his request is probably more urgent, he gently pushes through the throng until he reaches the desk and stands, dominating the view of the harassed sergeant.

'We need a chain of people to pass items up to the top of the north wall,' the guard says simply.

'How the hell am I supposed to do that?' Sergeant Hopewell snaps angrily. 'You've got a mouth, go and find people yourself.'

'Why can't you do it?' the guard asks defensively.

'Because I'm bloody busy, that's why,' Sergeant Hopewell shouts, ignoring the man and turning back to the person she was talking to before. The guard pushes back away from the desk and heads further into the room to see Sarah and Terri examining sheets of paper and talking quietly.

'We need a chain of people to pass items up to the top of the north wall,' the guard repeats.

'And I need more coffee and some sleep, and a bloody computer would help, rather than working in the dark ages with sheets of bloody paper,' Terri retorts.

'Yeah, but this is important,' the guard says, looking with distaste at the stacks of paper.

'Important is it? Because what we're doing clearly isn't important, then,' Terri shouts at the guard before going back to speaking with Sarah.

After a few minutes, the guard coughs and interrupts:

'So, can you get the people or not?' he asks.

'No, we bloody can't, we've got no runners left and a million other things to do.'

'Yeah but ...'

'Do not 'yeah but' me, find someone else,' Terri snaps, turning her back on the man. The guard walks away from the office scratching his head; he walks back into the armoury and finds Malcolm putting piles of shotguns together.

'That was quick, are they ready?' Malcolm asks.

'No, I couldn't find anyone,' the guard announces.

'Fucking what?' Malcolm shouts. 'There's seven thousand people out there, sitting around, doing nothing.'

'I asked in the police office, but they were too busy,' the guard starts to explain.

'Too busy? Doing what may I ask? Filing missing person reports for the forty million fucking zombies roaming around eating fucking brains? Get out there and find some people to get that shit up to the south wall,' Malcolm roars at the poor man.

He turns once again and heads back outside. A lifetime of Infantry experience in the Army taught him he is the lowest on the food chain, and to argue would most likely either invoke a beating or cleaning the toilets for the next month, or probably both.

He stands staring at the impenetrable mass of people in the camp. His lack of creative flair or ability to think outside of orders stumps him. Scratching his head, he wanders through the camp, looking for someone to ask but they all look so busy: talking, flitting between tents, or moving quickly between places.

His wandering brings him close to the front gate where Cookey and Blowers are still leaning and drinking coffee.

'What's up, mate?' Blowers asks, seeing the lost look on the bewildered guard's face.

'They need a chain of people to get the cannon ammunition up to the top of the north wall. I asked in the police office and they told me to piss off; I went back to Malcolm and he told me to piss off, now I don't know who to ask ...' the man explains.

'Ah, that's easy, me and Cookey will get it sorted,' Blowers says, relieved at the prospect of being away from his position.

'Yeah, definitely, are you sure?' the guard asks, sensing a sudden light at the end of the tunnel. Standing guard duty is easy, compared to having to actually speak to people.

'Yeah, of course. Now ... no one goes in or out without checking with Mr. Howie or Chris first, got it?' Blowers asks.

'Got it,' the man responds, happily taking up position by the side of the gate.

Blowers and Cookey walk away, stretching and feeling pleasure at being able to walk about for the first time in hours.

They walk over to the armoury to find Malcolm still wound up and muttering to himself.

'Hi Malc, that guard said you needed people to carry some stuff?' Blowers asks.

'Didn't he do it? Bloody people can't just get things done, can they?' Malcolm starts off. Blowers quickly holds his hands up.

'No worries mate, we'll get it sorted, where is it?'

'All of that stuff in that back room,' Malcolm points to the door at the rear.

'Got it, leave it with us. Have you still got the radio, Cookey? Get hold of Nick and ask him to do one of his supermarket announcements again,' Blowers says as they move back outside.

Cookey speaks into the radio, telling Nick what he needs.

'Listen to this,' Cookey says, smiling at Blowers.

'*ATTENTION PLEASE, ATTENTION PLEASE, CLEAN UP ON AISLE EIGHT,*' Nick's voice booms out over the camp, as Cookey and Blowers both burst out laughing.

'*ATTENTION PLEASE, WE NEED VOLUNTEERS TO FORM A CHAIN FROM THE SOUTH WALL TO THE NORTH WALL. PLEASE REPORT TO THE TWO UGLY-LOOKING MEN IN UNIFORM.*' The camp freezes at the announcement, some of the people smiling and laughing at the comments, some clearly not understanding. Within minutes, Blowers and Cookey have a long chain of people stretching from the armoury, going through the camp and up to the vehicle ramp onto the north wall.

More people than they need join in, but the action of doing something, anything, propels them to try and join in and the line quickly becomes overcrowded.

'Cookey, get Nick to ask them to separate into two lines,' Blowers calls out.

'*ATTENTION PLEASE, ATTENTION PLEASE, THERE ARE TOO MANY PEOPLE IN THE LINE. CAN WE HAVE ALL THE MEN IN ONE LINE AND ALL THE WOMEN IN ANOTHER LINE. COME ON, MEN VERSUS WOMEN, LET'S SEE WHO CAN GET THEIR LOAD DONE FIRST.*' Nick carries on, urging the camp into two lines, until, after a few minutes, the men and women stand facing each other, shouting with good-natured banter.

The noise slowly draws the people out of the police office. Sergeant Hopewell, Sarah, and Terri all come out to see the fuss and stand, watching the two lines slowly forming as Nick stands on the top of the Saxon directing them.

'RIGHT, AT THE FRONT YOU WILL SEE BLOWERS, THAT'S HIM WITH HIS ARM UP, HE'S ON THE MEN'S SIDE. THE OTHER ONE, COOKEY, THAT'S HIM WAVING NOW, HE'S ON THE WOMEN'S SIDE. THEY WILL PASS EACH CHAIN THE ITEM TO BE MOVED UP. THE CHAIN LEFT WITH THE LAST ITEM STILL BEING PASSED UP IS THE LOSER. NOW, ARE YOU READY?' A chorus of replies sounds out.

'I CAN'T HEAR YOU, I SAID ... ARE YOU READY?' Nick booms out over the loudspeaker; the two lines roar and cheer as Blowers and Cookey position themselves at the end of the two chains, pretending to jump up and down and get ready.

Malcolm walks out of the armoury and stands bemused at the sight; realising what's about to happen, he moves a few steps away and lights a much needed cigarette.

'THREE ... TWO ... ONE ... GO!' Laughing like children, Blowers and Cookey burst away into the armoury and race into the back room; they each grab a bucket of metal scraps and run back to the chain.

'HERE COME THE FIRST TWO, IT'S ALL EVEN AT THE MOMENT, OH! AND THE FIRST BUCKETS ARE INTO THE CHAINS AND BEING PASSED UP,' Nick commentates as Blowers and Cookey run back inside to get the next ones.

Blowers grabs two buckets as Cookey quickly grabs one and starts back.

'That's cheating, you wanker,' Cookey yells, as he goes back for another one and runs behind his friend to pass them on to the chain. The two lines roar and cheer as they see the two lads bursting out, each carrying two buckets.

Sarah starts smiling at the sight and looks to Terri, laughing, as the two lads push against each other to reach the lines first.

'COME ON, COOKEY,' Terri yells.

'That's bloody Tom and Steven in that line,' Sergeant Hopewell laughs, at seeing the two lads joining in with passing the items up.

'I'm joining in,' Terri laughs and runs across to the front of the line.

'I'm not having that,' Ted remarks from behind them, and jogs over to stand opposite Terri on the men's line. Blowers and Cookey keep running back into the armoury and grabbing buckets of metal to race back outside, waiting until they are in front of the people before they start barging into each other, both of them red in the face but laughing hard. Malcolm smiles as he quietly smokes, amazed at what's taking place in front of him. These people have suffered such loss but here they are, joking and playing, doing anything to break the tension, and all it took was three young mischievous soldiers pissing about. His smile widens as he thinks back to the escapades that he, Chris, and Clarence got up to early in their service. Nick continues with the commentary as people twist and turn, passing the items up, pointing out mistakes and making the others laugh and cheer. Dave, Jamie, and Curtis stand next to the Saxon and watch the growing piles of buckets being quickly passed up. The inside area of the main gate quickly fills up as those closest to the front first hear Nick booming out on the loudspeaker and then the sounds of cheering; they pause in their training and drill to move back inside and stand smiling at the spectacle.

Howie stands outside the police office, quietly drinking coffee and taking the scene in.

He watches Terri smiling and laughing as she reaches out to take a bucket from Cookey before he turns to run back inside, pushing and shoving against Blowers by his side. He watches as Tom and Steven grasp their bucket in turn and laugh as it's passed on, shouting and urging the men to move faster.

How can they all be taken? Fifty or so million people in Britain and every one of them has had their life changed forever. The rich and powerful may have been whisked to safety inside bunkers, but even their lives are changed. The thought process leads Howie to think of the populations of different countries. This started in Eastern Europe somewhere, so that means the whole of Europe, and if it spread to an island like Britain so quickly, it must have gone everywhere. Every man, woman, and child on the planet has had their life changed and for what? For another species to develop? For another race to take over? Or just an infection that courses through their systems without realising the futility of it all – that eventually it will infect everyone and have nothing left to feed on. He thinks of how McKinney would love this now, and would be laughing and joking up top with Nick and Curtis. Then he remembers Darren and the conversation they had on the bridge; with a jolt, he realises it was only this morning, only a few hours ago. It feels like days or weeks have gone by just in this one day. He thinks back to Friday night and being at home in his flat, watching television. That feels like years ago. He was a night manager in a supermarket then, now he is a leader of men and making ready to fight an army of dead people.

He shakes his head slowly in wonder. If only his father could see him now, how proud he would be. His thoughts darken once again as he thinks of his parents now part of that army coming for them, and of Darren's words on the bridge. *Lord, give me the grace to have five minutes with Darren when we meet, just him and me alone for five minutes.* Howie sips his coffee, visualising the moment he would take him down and make him pay for all the bad things that have happened; he cocks his head to one side and adds a final request to his prayer: *And can I have my axe with me, please?*

The race finishes with Cookey and Blowers both running out of the armoury with their last bucket each, using their free hands to push and pull the other one back. They grapple with red, panting faces, still laughing as they stagger and slip over, somehow managing to keep their buckets upright. Finally, they separate and make it to their lines at the same time, passing their buckets over and then racing along with them as they get passed from man to man and woman to woman. Nick's voice grows hoarse with excitement.

The ends of the lines disperse as the men and women race to

keep up with the buckets. The buckets reach the last few people as the view is entirely blocked by everyone crowding round to watch. With a roar, the buckets reach the top in unison, both being placed at the top at the same time.

'IT'S A DRAW, OH YES, A DRAW! THE AGE-OLD BATTLE OF MEN VERSUS WOMEN HAS FINALLY BEEN LAID TO REST HERE IN FORT SPITBANK WITH A DRAW!' Nick ends his commentary as the crowds all mingle into one, cheering and laughing and slapping each other on the back.

The day draws on, and slowly the camp returns to order as people file back down and continue with the tasks they had been doing.

Clarence leads his group back outside and resumes the weapons drills. Howie watches as Dave and Jamie, now joined by several others on the top wall, all start moving the buckets to the cannon sites. Howie heads over towards the vehicle ramp leading to the top of the north wall, passing the engineers workshop as he goes. He pauses to see Kelly inside, still moving between the various small groups of people and the growing pile of sharpened foot traps on the floor. She smiles and nods as he passes by; he continues on, passing smiling people moving back down to the camp.

'That was a good effort, Nick,' Howie says, as he reaches the Saxon.

'Thanks, Mr. Howie, it was a good laugh for a few minutes,' Nick replies, now back on the GPMG and staring out to the flatlands through a pair of binoculars.

'How are they getting on out there, mate?' Howie asks.

'Have a look.' Nick passes the binoculars over; Howie lifts them to his eyes and starts scanning over the flatlands to the estate.

The diggers have now finished and are moving back down to the Fort, having moved all of the earth taken from the ditches over to the far sides.

The long grass is now cut and being carried over to be stacked by the side of the freshly dug ditches. Men and women are working in the ditches to drive the sharpened stakes through, followed by more people covering the sections they have completed with the long grass. Howie sweeps over to see a van being driven slowly across the large area of land between the first ditch and the embankments, throwing the sharpened foot traps out onto the ground. Then he looks down to the first bank to see a group of archers firing into the bank; he watches them practise with firing high, and people moving amongst them giving tips and offering advice. He sweeps the binocs down to the deep ditch after the last bank and sees the fuel tanker parked on the road in the middle. Pipes connected to the fuel tanker are pumping fuel into the heavyweight hoses they found in the Fort. More people are filling containers and big drums with fuel, and then rolling them along the ground to be pushed into the ditch. Yet more people are wrapping metal shrapnel into bags and placing them on top of the drums and hoses. After the deep ditch, there is a wide open flatland to the Fort, now covered with lots of people who stand listening to Clarence and Brian. The people issued with firearms have laid them down in piles; now many of them hold the hand weapons foraged and brought back by Clarence, found within the compound or brought with them as they fled their homes.

He knows Clarence and Brian are doing their best to give some simple instruction on how to hold the weapons, and show them basic techniques of swipe, lunge, and hack. As Howie lowers the binoculars, he realises that nearly everyone in the Fort must now be involved in the defence and preparation. So much for his plans of keeping everything secret.

'Fuck it, Donald ...' Howie remembers the man he had locked up in the police office.

Suddenly the action he took rests uncomfortably on his mind. At the time, his decision seemed reasonable; the man was delaying what needed to be done.

'Tell Dave I'll be straight back,' Howie yells, as he starts jogging back down the vehicle ramp and across the camp.

The sudden thought that they have done something wrong, so very wrong, plagues his mind and it must be put right.

'Where's that man we locked up?' Howie asks as he bursts into the police office.

'That's what I want to bloody know,' a distressed-looking woman standing in front of Sergeant Hopewell's desk yells out.

'Are you his wife?' Howie asks.

'Yes I am, they won't let me see him, they said he's been arrested.' The woman sobs, eyes red and tears streaming down her face; she holds the hand of a small, scared-looking child.

'Where is he?' Howie asks Sergeant Hopewell.

'In the back room, Ted's with him,' she replies.

Howie pushes his way forward and opens the door at the rear, entering a small corridor.

'Ted?' Howie calls out.

'In here,' Ted answers and steps out of an open door at the end.

'Is that man in there?' Howie asks.

'Yes, he's right here,' Ted answers, puzzled.

Howie moves around Ted and enters the room to see Donald sitting on a chair in the corner of the room; his eyes are also red from crying.

'Donald, I am so very sorry for locking you in here, it was unforgivable ...' Howie blurts out.

'I'm sorry, I shouldn't have questioned you, please can I just go? My wife and daughter are alone and they must be terrified,' Donald pleads.

'No, you should have questioned us, I was completely wrong to have you detained like this.'

'I didn't mean anything bad, Mr. Howie, I was uncomfortable with what you were asking, but I shouldn't have made an issue out of it. You're right, there are thousands of people here relying on you and I won't question you again ...' Donald stands up slowly, clearly unsure of the change of events, looking at Howie, then at the open door and Ted standing there with a frown.

'So ... I can really go?' he asks, tentatively.

'Mate, your wife and daughter are out in the office ...'

'Donald! You're all right ...' the woman from the office bursts in to hold Donald tight, crying and sobbing.

The little girl holds back for a second until Donald drops down to draw her in close.

'Yes, I'm fine, darling, it was all a misunderstanding, really it's all fine,' Donald says softly, holding them both.

'Look ... Mr. Howie,' Donald's wife says. 'My husband Donald is an argumentative man, and he picks the wrong moments to say things and has often caused a lot of offence, so I can understand where you're coming from. But for him to be taken away like that and with no one telling me why or for how long, that was awful.'

'Yes, you're right. It was the wrong thing to do,' Howie accepts quietly.

'Mr. Howie, I do apologise to you for putting you in that position. Is there anything I can do to help now?' Donald asks, holding his head up and staring directly at Howie.

'The engineers are still hard at it in the workshops, I'm sure they could do with some help.'

'Right, in which case we should be leaving,' Donald steps forward, holding a hand out to Howie. 'I understand why it happened the way it did, and for my part I can see you are a genuine man and I'm glad this Fort has you on our side,' Donald says, as they shake hands.

'Thank you, that's a very kind thing to say,' Howie replies.

'And, as soon as society has been re-built, I will be contacting one of those *no win no fee* lawyers for compensation,' Donald smiles.

'Ha, good idea, I'll say it was Ted.'

'You won't be the first, that's for sure,' Ted responds good-naturedly. The family leave the room, still holding each other tightly, leaving Ted staring hard at Howie and nodding gently.

'That took some balls, Howie, well done,' Ted says quietly.

'Don't give me credit, Ted, it shouldn't have happened in the first place,' Howie replies.

'You did what you thought was right at the time, he wasn't injured or hurt, and he's been well taken care of,' Ted says firmly.

'Yeah, I guess, but the road to hell is paved with good intentions, Ted.'

CHAPTER THIRTEEN

At the top of the north wall, two teams of people left over from the bucket chain, and chosen by Dave, move ammunition and powder bags to each of the cannon.

Long hoses stretch along the top and down to the ground level and the outside taps found in each corner of the base of the wall. On further request, women bring piles of sheets, blankets, and material up, to be left with the ammunition. Dave crouches and draws his knife to cut a square of bed sheet, then takes a few double handfuls of bolts, nails, and screws to put them in the centre of the sheet. He wraps the sheet over, securing the metal fragments inside. He then takes the small bundle and shoves it into the black opening of the cannon mouth.

'Too small,' he mutters, and goes back to unwrap the sheet and add another double handful of the metal pieces. He wraps it back up and goes back to the cannon mouth, placing the bundle inside.

'Perfect. I need more of these made. The same size as this one, they must not be bigger than this, otherwise they will not fit,' Dave says to a group of people watching him.

'You get them made and I'll start showing this lot the cannon drill,' he adds, turning to the two distinct teams nearby.

'Right, one group will be on this cannon, the other on the second one. Watch and listen carefully, as we do not have a lot of time before night falls, and as soon as that area is clear,' Dave indicates the flatlands, '... we will be having some practise shots to get range, distance, and aim, got it?' The groups nod back, listening intently to the small, strange man.

'These are the fuses.' Dave holds up some lengths of fuse wire to show the groups. 'They go into this hole at the back of the cannon. We do not have lighted material or naked flame anywhere near the fuse at any point other than when we are lighting it. You two are the flame holders,' Dave indicates two men, one from each group.

'You keep the flame lit and away from the cannon until the teams are ready for you to light the fuse. Now we take a powder bag. This is full of gunpowder, and we place it into the cannon. That is your job,' Dave indicates another man from each group.

'The powder bag is then rammed down to the bottom of the cannon, like this.' Dave takes a ramrod and pushes it into the cannon, driving the bag down to the bottom and tapping it hard a few times. 'It must be at the bottom, so it pushes against the fuse wire sticking in through the hole. Next we take some wadding, and again we push it down,' Dave takes some papers from a pile near the cannon and rams it down with the ramrod.

'Next we take the ammunition, in this case the wrapped metal, and again we push it down the cannon. The metal is wrapped simply to keep it together. When the fuse is lit, it burns down and ignites the powder bag. The powder bags explode instantly with a lot of force. The energy of the exploding matter cannot escape from the back or sides so it is forced to move up the cannon, thereby driving our round, missile, or projectile out of this end at great speed. The wrapping material will be burnt away and the metal ejected. As it leaves, it will start to spread, at the same time as becoming incredibly hot. Not only do the enemy suffer from the impact of the projectiles, they also suffer from the heat of the projectiles. Do you understand?' He gets more nods from the people watching.

'Now, before the cannon be used again, water is put in and swept through, to make sure there are no burning materials left; otherwise, as soon as you put the powder bags in, they will explode and kill everyone. Now, these cannon are made from iron. They are strong, but they are very old, and we cannot tell if they have stress fractures. Iron cannon can sometimes just explode from the force of the repeated firing. If that happens you will all die, got it?'

The men look to each other with alarm.

'We cannot fire at the moment because of the people out there, but we can practise and we will practise. Any questions?'

'Will you be with us?' one man asks, straight away.

'For the practise, yes, of course I will be.'

'No, I mean when we actually fire them for real.'

'I don't know.'

'How likely are they to explode?' another asks, with genuine fear on his face.

'I don't know.'

'Err, have you ever fired one of these before?' the same man asks.

'No, now any other questions, before we start? No? Good.'

For the next hour the two groups are drilled incessantly and without rest, Dave making each group go through the motions. He pushes them again and again, giving clear instructions and correcting where necessary.

As the afternoon gives way to evening, Dave rests the groups, walks over to the Saxon positioned midway between the two cannon, and takes the radio from the front of the vehicle.

'Saxon to Mr. Howie or Chris.'

'Chris to Saxon, go ahead.'

'Saxon to Chris, we need to start live fire drills on the cannon. How long until the grounds are clear?'

'Chris to Saxon, we are almost finished and will clear very soon. I will give you an update once we are clear.'

'Saxon to Chris, Roger that, Saxon out.'
'Chris to Howie.'
'Howie here, go ahead Chris.'
'Did you get the last? We are almost finished at the front.'
'Yeah, I got that mate, I'll come down and meet you at the gate.'
'Chris to Howie, Roger and out.'

Howie steps through the gate after finding a different guard happily on duty, and wondering what mischief Blowers and Cookey might be causing elsewhere.

He crosses the gap between the two walls, marvelling at how the two high, thick walls deaden the sound from both sides.

'We're just about done,' Clarence calls out, leading his now large group of people back inside with Brian.

Some of them are armed with rifles, and there is a much larger group armed with a collection of hand weapons.

'I think that Chris is bringing the others back in now, too,' Howie replies.

'Are they all done then?' Clarence asks, moving back to Howie and watching the rest pass through the gate and back into the Fort.

'I think so. How did you get on with the training?' Howie asks.

'The firearms were fine, some of them were a bit rusty, but there's enough good ones amongst them to keep the rest up to standard. Mind you, all they've got to do is point and shoot.'

'What about the others with the hand weapons?'

'To be honest,' Clarence lowers his voice. 'That was a fucking nightmare. We'll be lucky if they don't all stab themselves before we even start. But what choice have they got?'

'Not much we can do mate, just hope we whittle the numbers down before they get here, I guess – here's Chris now.' Howie nods at the line of vehicles coming down the road towards them.

'It'll be dark soon, couple of hours to go,' Clarence remarks, looking up at the sky.

'I wonder how soon they'll come,' Howie says quietly, as the people head back into the Fort, nodding at him and Clarence as they pass.

'Mr. Howie?' a voice calls out.

Howie turns to see a man at the head of a procession of archers.

'You are Mr. Howie, aren't you?' the man asks, as he gets closer.

'Howie, yes ...'

'We're the archers – we need to know range, and where we will be firing from. If we're back here we've got no view ...'

'I was thinking we'd all be on the top of the inner wall to start with,' Howie politely interrupts him.

The man steps back to look up, but the outer wall blocks his view.

'It will reduce our range yes, but we can fire from there, if that's where you want us.'

'How far will you be able to fire to, from the top of the inner wall?' Howie asks.

'Hmmm, now that obviously depends on the type of bow. We've got a few different ones here, but I won't bore you with all that. I'd say most of us will be able to reach just past the first embankment.'

'That's great,' Howie remarks, looking at Clarence, who nods back sincerely.

'There won't be any degree of aiming from that distance though, we're working on the principle of there being a mass target and just firing into them, really.'

'I think you're probably right, but would you be able to get a fire arrow into that ditch from the inner wall?' Howie asks, pointing out towards the last embankment.

'Ah now, fire arrows have far less range and they're a bugger to aim over any distance. But if you just want it into the ditch that will be easy enough.'

'Good, can you make sure that you all have the ability to do that, when the time is right?' Howie asks.

'Okay, we can do that. We saw them being filled up with explosive material, are you relying on us to ignite them?'

'I think we will be, is that okay?'

'Yes, of course, is it okay to go up now and work out the best position?'

'No problem,' Howie replies. 'Nick and Curtis are with our vehicle, speak to them and let them know what you're doing.'

The man nods and joins the line of others walking back into the Fort.

Howie and Clarence turn to see the vehicles have now stopped, and Chris is walking towards them, looking tired and drawn.

'You look like shit, Chris,' Clarence rumbles.

'You too,' Chris smiles back at him. 'Mr. Howie still looks fresh as a daisy though.'

'It's the easy living I had before all this,' Howie jokes. 'Honestly though, I am fucking knackered.'

'We all are, Howie, we'll need to rest when we can – otherwise we'll all be falling asleep mid-battle,' Chris replies, rubbing his beard.

'So how is it?' Howie asks, now yawning after the mention of being tired.

'It's all done,' Chris replies. 'First ditch filled with spikes and covered with the grass. You can still see it, but it's quite well covered. The ... flatlands are completely covered with the caltrops ...' He trails off, seemingly losing his chain of thought.

'I saw the deep ditch being filled,' Howie takes up where Chris leaves off, and nods to the area of the ditch. 'We've got the archers ready to fire into it.'

'Let's get inside ...' Chris says, as the radio clipped to his belt comes to life with a hushed transmission:

'*Point North, Point North, contact, I have contact.*' The voice is quiet but clear, the speaker obviously holding his mouth close to the radio.

Chris scrabbles for his radio, pressing the button and speaking quietly in return:

'Fort to Point North, receiving you, what do you see.'

'Zombies, lots of zombies, all coming our way.'

'How far out is he?' Clarence asks, turning to look back up the road to the estate.

'A few miles, I think Dave said,' Howie answers.

'Fort to Point North, how far out are you?'

Silence follows Chris's transmission.

'Fort to Point North, how far out are you, I repeat how far out are you?'

Silence, then a sound of movement comes through.

'Maybe he can't transmit if they're too close,' Howie says, as they all stare at the radio.

'Fort to Point North, hold down your transmit button twice if you cannot speak,' Chris says quietly. The radio remains silent, then bursts to life with the sounds of struggling and the raised voice of a man shouting in desperation.

They all stare at the radio in silence, listening to the struggle and the shouts coming through, then the sound of growling, followed by a sickening, tearing noise and a scream.

'Fuck,' Howie mutters in horror, then the radio goes silent.

'Point West to Fort, I heard that, I'm bugging out.'

'Fort to Points West and East, Roger that, come back, I repeat come back.'

The radio bursts to life with the sound of static and a high pitched squealing; they stand listening, unsure who is transmitting.

The static and squealing fade but the line remains open.

One word is transmitted by a voice that only sounds part human.

'HOWIEEEEEE ...'

'Fucking hell,' Chris says in shock at the awful stretched out sound, looking at Howie.

'HOWIEEEEEE ...' The same voice, again.

Howie stares at the radio, his heart beating faster and faster and his stomach dropping.

'WE'RE COMING HOWIEEEEEE.' The goading tones are loud and clear.

Chris and Clarence both stare at Howie.

'Let's go,' Chris says, all signs of tiredness gone and his voice full of authority again. His voice springs them to action and they turn as one. Chris runs ahead and pulls the gates wide open to get the vehicles back inside.

Clarence and Howie go straight through into the Fort, as Howie grabs his radio and holds it close to his mouth as he marches through the gates.

'Howie to Dave, did you hear the last.'

'Dave to Howie, Roger, we heard the last, making ready now.'

'Howie to all personnel, switch to the predesignated channel; security breach on channel one.' He pauses and switches to the channel himself.

'Howie to Dave, I want all the people with weapons on the top of the inner wall, archers too. Get Nick on the loudspeaker.'

'Dave to Howie, Roger that, on it now.'

'Howie to Malcolm.'

'Malcolm receiving, go ahead Howie.'

'Malcolm, can you get all the ammunition to the top of the inner wall and let the triage and hospital points know what's going on.'

'Roger that Howie.'

'Clarence,' Howie shouts across to the big man. 'We need that fuel tanker in the estate. Find the driver and get it taken in; use a car to bring the driver back.'

'Roger,' Clarence replies before darting off into the camp.

'Howie to Dave, where do you want the fuel tanker placed?'

'Dave to Howie, on the central road close to the edge of the estate, by the flatlands.'

'Howie to Clarence, did you receive that?'

'Clarence to Howie, Roger got it.'

'ATTENTION PLEASE, ATTENTION PLEASE,' Nick's voice booms out over the loudspeaker on the Saxon. 'CAN ALL

THE PEOPLE WITH FIREARMS REPORT TO THE TOP OF THE INNER WALL; CAN ALL ARCHERS REPORT TO THE TOP OF THE INNER WALL,' Nick repeats the message several times as Howie ploughs through the edge of the camp towards the police office.

The camp erupts with a sudden frenzy as the few closest to the radios hear the transmission, then they see Clarence and Howie running in and then the request made by Nick. People start running about, fearing the attack is taking place.

Parents grab children, as men and women alike grip their hand weapons – mayhem ensues and the volume inside the Fort is instantly raised. Howie makes it to the police office, bursting in to see the room now empty of people. The sergeant sits behind the desk, Terri and Sarah next to her – all of them staring at the radio.

'Oh, Howie,' Sarah says, putting her hand to her mouth. 'That was awful.'

'Yeah, not very nice, was it,' Howie replies. 'Any news on the boats?'

'Nothing yet,' Terri replies.

'Get the children at the back and ready to load as soon as they get back. Where's Ted?' Howie asks, looking around.

'He went to the front,' Sergeant Hopewell says.

'I was going to ask him to go with the children, and err, maybe you too, Debbie, they're going to need some strong people with them.'

'Me? With children? Are you joking?' Sergeant Hopewell blurts out.

'Oh, is that a bad idea then? Just look at what you did here in a couple of days, Terri and Sarah too,' Howie adds.

'Sending the women and children away, eh?' Terri flares up. 'Why can't we stay and fight too?'

'To be honest, because we'll probably lose, and yes, women and children need to be saved. Those kids will need strong people, and you're it at the moment,' Howie replies with a firm voice and fixed expression.

'As much as I hate to say this, I agree,' Sarah says, looking to the two other women. 'Howie's right, three more out there fighting is not going to make a difference, but being with the children and mothers does make a difference.'

'So, we run away while everyone else stays and dies?' Terri says indignantly.

'If nothing else, we buy you time to get away,' Howie says. 'It's up to you, but it makes sense to me. I've got to go.' Howie leaves the three women discussing the idea and marches back into the camp, heading towards the north wall.

'Tucker, where have you been all day, mate?' Howie says as he collides with the large recruit.

'Mr. Howie, I've got all the stores sorted; they were a bloody mess ...' Tucker replies.

'Bloody hell mate, have you been doing that all day?' Howie smiles at him.

'Well, they had the wrong food types mixed together, no regard for the dates or perishable items, and some were stacked on the floor! So, I took one look at and thought, Roy, this won't do. Even if that zombie army comes tonight I want them to find nice, clean stores,' Tucker explains with genuine zeal.

'Well done, mate, good for you. Talking of food, though,' Howie says, still walking towards the north wall and realising how hungry he is.

'Ah, now that is sorted, Mr. Howie. I knew you'd all be hungry ... so I've got some food already prepared.'

'Really? Wow Tucker, that's impressive mate,' Howie says, looking with admiration at him.

'It's nothing special though, Mr. Howie, just all the stuff we needed to use up. High energy food though, lots of carbs, you see I found loads of pasta and tinned meat and then there were vegetables that were going off, so I thought ...'

'Tucker, mate, it sounds great,' Howie stops him as they reach the top of the vehicle ramp and walk towards the Saxon.

'Clarence to Howie, we're on our way now,' Clarence's deep voice comes over the radio.

Howie moves to the edge of the inner wall and looks down to see the tanker being driven down the road followed by a small car.

'Howie to Clarence, yeah I can see you now, be quick mate. Howie to points West and East, we've got a vehicle going to the estate now, we'll be there for a few minutes only if you can make it back in time.'

'Point West,' a heavy panting voice says. *'I'm not far away, I should make it.'*

'Point East to the Fort, likewise, I'm running like a lunatic, no sign of the army from my position.'

'Howie to Points West and East, Roger that. Clarence, did you receive the last?'

'Yeah, I heard it, keep running gents, because we ain't stopping for long.'

Looking up, Howie sees Nick gripping the GPMG and staring hard towards the estate, and Curtis standing by the side of the vehicle, scanning with binoculars.

'See anything, Curtis?' Howie calls over.

'Nothing yet, Mr. Howie,' he replies with the binoculars stuck firmly to his face. Howie looks about to see men running towards the waist-high wall; they find positions and lean down to rest their rifles, then start scanning ahead.

The archers split into two groups, left and right, and concentrate on fixing strings to their bows and placing piles of arrows down at their feet. All along the line, men and women make ready, and Howie notices some of them shake and tremble as they work with their equipment. Their faces are pale and drawn; the tension is palpable. He moves along to see Dave at the far end, next to one of the cannon, and speaking to a group of people. As he walks closer, Howie notices the heavy-looking bundles stacked on the ground to one side, long ramrods being held by some of the men, and powder bags ready to be loaded.

Howie stops as the group break apart, chatting amongst themselves.

'Dave, how's it going, mate?' Howie asks as Dave steps over to him, the small man looking exactly the same as he did a week ago, with no sign of strain or tiredness.

'Good, Mr. Howie,' Dave replies, with his usual reserve.

'I think we're about as ready as we'll ever be,' Howie says, looking back at the long line of people standing along the top of the inner wall.

'Yes, Mr. Howie, I think so.'

'The cannon? Are they ready?' Howie asks, looking down at the bags and piles of equipment.

'Yes, although we don't know the distance yet. Single shot can go quite far, but cluster or grape shot like this reduces the distance significantly.'

'Like a shotgun then,' Howie says.

'Exactly like a shotgun, more spread but less range.'

'Well, I guess we'll find out in a bit.'

'Yes, I guess so – I'll try a test fire on each, when Clarence gets back in.'

'So that tanker? Do you think it will go up well?'

'Yes.'

'But aren't they designed to withstand heat and pressure?' Howie asks.

'Yes, but I put loads of grenades in it,' Dave says, still devoid of expression.

'Oh, well, that's good then. So have you ever fired cannons before?'

'No, well ... no, not really.'

'What do you mean?'

'I've not fired a proper cannon before, not an old one like this.'

'So what was it then?'

'Similar.'

'Similar? Similar how?'

'I made one,' Dave answers flatly.

'You made a cannon?' Howie asks incredulously.

'Yes, although it was a one-time use only.'

'Did it work?'

Dave looks directly at Howie as though the question need not be asked.

'Fair one,' Howie says. 'Tucker's getting some food up for us,' he adds.

'Good, we can eat, then sleep,' Dave says with a nod.

'Sleep? How can we sleep?' Howie asks.

'They won't come yet,' Dave answers firmly.

'We heard them on the radio, they said '... we're coming for you Howieeeee.' Howie tries to imitate the voice, making himself laugh as he does it, but trailing off when he looks at Dave's deadpan expression.

'They'll wait at least a few more hours yet,' Dave continues.

'How on earth can you possibly know that?'

'They've covered a long distance on foot, so they'll be weaker now, plus it's still light and we can see them coming. They know we know they're here, so they know we'll be ready for them,' Dave explains.

'So they will wait a few hours to rest and either attack during the night when we're at our lowest ebb, or first thing in the morning, when we're all tired.'

'Oh, yeah, I guess that makes sense,' Howie says reluctantly. 'I hate it when you're always right like that, in fact I want them to come now, just so you're wrong,' he goes on, smiling.

'Maybe they will, Mr. Howie,' Dave concedes.

'But you don't think they will?'

'No.'

'You're certain of that?'

'Yes, Mr. Howie.'

'How certain?'

'I don't understand.'

'If you're wrong, you have to sing a song on the Saxon loudspeaker,' Howie says, trying to keep a straight face.

'I have to what?' Dave asks.

'Sing a song on the Saxon loudspeaker, but only if you're wrong.'

Dave stares at him.

'Okay, Mr. Howie, I'll do that,' Dave says.

'Bloody hell ... You will?' a shocked Howie says.

'Yes, and you have to do it if *you're* wrong,' Dave answers with a very rare grin.

'No, hang on a minute ...'

'Yes, Mr. Howie?' Dave asks innocently.

'GRUB IS UP,' Tucker bellows from the Saxon, watching a line of people carrying metal trays covered with aluminium foil.

'Saved by the bell,' Dave says quietly, and starts off towards the food.

'Oh, you're changing, Dave,' Howie calls out. Trestle tables are carried up from the visitors centre and laid out in a row near the Saxon; metal trays covered with foil are laid on them, along with piles of plates and stacks of cutlery.

Howie walks over to the edge and looks down into the camp at the cooking points. People are gathered around and drifting over, holding their weapons under arms or clutched between knees, as they stand eating from paper plates with plastic forks. Tucker moves along the trestle table, fussing about like a hotel head chef, adjusting the trays and crimping the foil down firmer to keep the heat inside.

'Bloody hell lads, where did you come from?' Howie laughs at seeing Blowers and Cookey first in the queue.

'We were here all along, Mr. Howie,' Cookey says with a grin.

'Tucker, we wondered where you had been all day,' Blowers calls out.

'I've been doing proper work, not like you two standing about a gate all day and drinking coffee,' Tucker shouts, smiling. Chris appears, walking up the vehicle ramp and over to join Howie watching the queue of armed men and women walking along to get scoops of hot food piled onto their plates.

'You all right, mate?' Howie asks the tired-looking man.

'Yeah, I think we're all set, just got to wait for Clarence to get back,' he replies, as Dave stops to join them.

'Dave thinks they won't attack for a few hours,' Howie says quietly, trying to keep out of earshot of the people waiting for food.

'It would make sense,' Chris answers.

'Give them a chance to rest and get us all wound up and tired for a few hours, probably attack during the night or first thing in the morning.'

'Oh, for fuck's sake,' Howie mutters, as Dave gives another sly grin.

'What?' Chris asks, looking between them.

'Nothing,' Howie says, sighing.

'Clarence to Points East and West, where are you? We're ready to go,' Clarence's voice comes out in stereo from all the radios attached in the area.

'Point East, I'm almost there.' The man sounds exhausted.

'Point ... West, hang ... on.' The second voice sounds worse, the man struggling to speak as he runs. Minutes pass as everyone pauses, staring at the radios and waiting for an update; the food queue holds fast, the servers frozen with ladles in mid-air, as everyone waits with bated breath.

'The food's getting cold,' Tucker mutters quietly, fretting about his beloved creation and moving down the tables to discreetly tug the foil covers back on.

'Clarence to Fort, we have both points, repeat we have both men, on our way back now.' Cheering erupts from the top of the inner wall, knowing they've lost one man, but saved two more.

The eating resumes as the foil is quickly pulled back off and the serving carries on. Howie, Chris, and Dave are joined by Blowers and Cookey, both of them hungrily tucking into the food and shovelling it into their mouths quickly.

'There they are,' Chris nods at the small car speeding down the road towards them.

They watch as the car slows to enter the gates and hear as the gates are pulled closed, securing them inside.

'Thank fuck for that,' Howie says quietly. 'We'll wait for Clarence and Malcolm and eat together,' he adds.

Within a few minutes, Clarence walks up the vehicle ramp accompanied by Malcolm, both of them carrying heavy canvas bags filled with ammunition.

They dump the bags by the side of the Saxon and move over to join Howie and Chris, as Howie motions with his head for Nick to come and join them, mouthing for him to get Curtis and Jamie on the way.

Within a couple of minutes, they are all stood together for the first time that day: Howie, Dave, Blowers, Cookey, Curtis, Nick, Jamie, and Tucker, then Chris stood in the middle of his trusted comrades, Clarence and Malcolm.

'Well, we did it,' Howie says. 'In one day we got the traps laid, found more weapons, rigged the estate, got two cannon working, hopefully, and even cooked a gourmet meal; bloody impressive if you ask me.'

'And found time to play pass the bucket,' Nick adds, as they all smile.

'Let's get some food,' Howie says. They move towards the tables and head for the back of the queue, chatting and joking amongst themselves.

One of the people stood near the back, moves a few steps aside and motions for them to go ahead of him; it catches on and, within seconds, the waiting people have all stood back, quietly and respectfully.

'Thank you,' Howie speaks clearly, nodding to them; the others join in, showing gratitude and offering polite *thank you's* as they move to the table.

'Have you already eaten?' Clarence rumbles, looking at the dirty plate held by Blowers.

'Err ... no?' Blowers says slowly, looking to Cookey and his dirty plate, which he quickly tucks behind his back.

'Bloody greedy, if you ask me,' Cookey says, nodding at Clarence. 'I'd never go back for seconds, personally.'

They get plates of steaming meat and vegetables, giving Tucker compliments about the food, and Howie notices the look of pride on the young man's face. They have worked hard today, all of them. Fighting all day yesterday, then fleeing through the night to get here. Not one of them has moaned or complained, and this effort with the food now has lifted the spirits of everyone here. They move away from the table, juggling heaped plates and already eating as they head over to the wall and sit down in a wide circle.

The sight of Howie, Chris, Clarence and the others all sitting down, eating and joking amongst themselves, sends a ripple out along the top of the inner wall, taking the edge off the fraught tension felt by all the other armed men and women.

'Mind if we join you?' a voice asks; the group twist around to see Ted grinning while Sarah, Sergeant Hopewell, Terri, Tom, and Steven get plates of food from the trestle table.

A chorus of voices greets them as they shuffle around to make room. Sarah moves deftly to sit beside Clarence and smiles a big grin to Howie, who nods and smiles back at her. The conversations break into smaller chunks as they joke and banter amongst themselves, easy conversation in easy company. Those that haven't met yet introduce themselves and nod greetings at one another – before long they're exchanging war stories of the last week. Tom and Steven both, at the same time, try to recount the time when Dave disarmed Tom with the Taser. Howie glances around to see the top of the inner wall and the groups of people now stood or seated, chatting and talking quietly. Guns, rifles, and bows stand propped up against the wall as the folks mingle. Howie thinks back to watching the television and then seeing the horrors start outside his house – the blind panic and screaming as he threw the contents of his flat at the zombies as they attacked. He had forgotten the man leading them away with the armoured van and encouraging them into the town. Then the first hands-on attack as he killed his first zombie, that was the start right there. That feeling of anger and vengeance that surged through him. He thinks back to meeting up with Dave in the supermarket, and again he gives thanks that he found Dave. Today has been the longest period they've spent apart in a week, and having Dave back at his side now feels normal. Like the balance is restored.

'I was thinking back to the supermarket, Dave,' Howie says, between mouthfuls.

'Yes, Mr. Howie?' Dave replies.

'All those bodies you stacked up. I wonder if you would have stayed there, if I didn't come along.'

'Probably.'

'You think?'

'I didn't have anywhere else to go,' Dave answers matter-of-factly.

'Yeah maybe, do you remember that fat woman that got stuck in the door?' Howie says, bursting out laughing.

'Yes, and I remember you walking into the door and falling up the stairs too.'

'Oh yeah,' Howie chuckles. 'At least I didn't put the wrong fuel into that car.'

'I didn't fall over and shoot a car,' Dave quips back, but still devoid of expression.

'Yeah, but you got stripped off pretty quickly when Sergeant Hopewell was watching us,' Howie fires back.

'You broke my shotgun.'

'When?' Howie says.

'In Portsmouth, at the barricade.'

'You told me to,' Howie says with mock indignation.

'I said to draw him out.'

'Well, it was either that or my head, and I gave you another shotgun.'

'Yes, you did, thank you.'

'That was that bloody John Jones, nasty fucker, and his son too.'

'The one you kept punching,' Dave says.

'Yeah him, I wonder what happened to them.'

'I don't know, Mr. Howie.'

'It's been a long week, mate,' Howie says, after a pause.

'It has, Mr. Howie.'

'That bridge was good,' Howie says.

'Tower Bridge?' Dave asks.

'No, the first one in that village when we were turning it by hand and they kept falling off.'

'Yes,' Dave says, nodding.

'And that freaky one that caught my axe when I tried to chop his head off, that was horrible.'

'The chainsaw was good.'

'Ha, did you see the chainsaw? I thought you were busy on your side,' Howie laughs.

'I saw it, and the lump hammers, and the sledge hammer, and all the other tools you tried.'

'The chainsaw was the best though. I love the axe, mind you.'

'I like knives,' Dave says flatly.

'Do you? I'd never have noticed ... I wonder how our Tesco lorry is doing.'

'Those kids probably stole it.'

'Yeah, probably,' Howie pauses, taking another mouthful of food.

'Salisbury was good, I'm glad we went there,' Howie says. 'Apart from that bloody officer,' he adds.

'Charles Galloway-Gibbs,' Nick says, as Howie realises everyone else has gone quiet and is listening to him and Dave.

'Complete tool,' Blowers says.

'Now that was a hard night, getting that Saxon,' Cookey adds.

'We did it though,' Howie says.

'There must have been a thousand of them at least.'

'Thanks to Dave and the GPMG,' Blowers says.

'Another five minutes and I think we'd be staggering 'round now too.'

'BRAAIINNNS, I WANT COOOKEY BRAAAIINNS,' Howie says, to laughter from the recruits, remembering the jokes from before.

'So, which is better? The feast Tucker did in the barracks or this one?' Howie asks, seeing Tucker's face lights up.

'The one at Salisbury was fucking lovely,' Nick blurts. 'Sorry, I meant it was very nice,' he adds quickly with a glance at Sergeant Hopewell.

'This is nice, but that was a feast and a half,' Blowers agrees. The conversations carry on, of great meals eaten in faraway places, of dangerous missions undertaken by Chris, Malcolm, and Clarence. The officers jump in with stories of incidents and strange crimes they've dealt with, each of them sharing an experience and memories of a life now gone, thinking this may be the last time they get to share something, to tell another human of who they are and where they came from. The close feeling shared amongst them grows and matures as they listen to each other, laughing or nodding with understanding.

'It's getting dark,' Chris says, as the conversations start to trail off; they look up to the sky to see the beautiful swathes of red mixed with the golden rays of the dwindling light.

'Red sky at night, zombies delight,' Blowers mutters quietly.

'Right, so what's the plan?' Howie asks. 'We wait for them to come and hope our traps work, then throw what we can at them from up here, and when that ends we go down and meet them? That's what I think, anyway.'

'Sounds about right to me,' Chris nods back.

'Any other suggestions?' Howie asks.

'Keep it fluid,' Dave offers. 'We've planned as best we can, and now we just have to be able to react accordingly,' he adds, to nods and murmurs of agreement and stares of awe from Jamie, Tom, and Steven

'Okay, keep your hand weapons to ... err ... well to hand, I guess, and, in the meantime, let's try and rest,' Howie says.

They break apart slowly, lingering to have a few words with each other. Howie steps over to Sarah, drawing her away from the group.

'Any news on the boats?' Howie asks, quietly.

'Nothing yet, but we've spoken to the mothers and got the children ready to move.'

'And Ted? Did you speak to him?'

'He was reluctant, but said he would do it as it was you asking,' Sarah replies.

Howie looks over to see Ted looking back, giving a single, knowing nod.

'Good, let me know as soon as they're back.'

'Howie, I, well ...' Sarah says, hesitantly.

'What is it?' Howie asks with concern.

'Well, we've not really spoken since you got me, and ...'

'Yeah, I know, I'm sorry, it's been manic.'

'No, you don't have to apologise. I just wanted to spend some time with my brother before, well before ...'

'You can say it,' Howie smiles. 'Before they come for us.'

'Yes, before they come,' Sarah says softly. 'You seem so different now, it's only been a week and you've changed so much. I hardly recognised you. I couldn't believe it when I saw you fighting through those things in London.'

'It doesn't feel like a week,' Howie muses. 'It feels like a lifetime.'

'What happened? How did you get like this?'

'I don't know, I really don't. I was lucky, I guess. I was at home when it happened, and it was happening right outside my house. They were trying to get in to get me, I fought back, but there were so many, I thought I was done for. Then this van went past, leading them all away from me. I managed to get out and then the rest just sort of happened. I was heading home, to Mum and Dad's house. I found some crappy old bicycle and was going on the motorway. This car went past me and then hit the barrier and flipped over. There was a woman in the wreckage; she was still alive when I got to her. I tried to pull her out and save her but one of those things was in the car and bit her; she died as I was trying to save her,' Howie explains in a flat, emotionless voice.

'That's awful,' Sarah says.

'Yeah, but then, like I said, she died. I was crying and she came back and tried to bite my face off,' Howie says.

'What did you do?' Sarah asks.

'I kicked her to death,' Howie replies. 'And I guess that was the point when I decided they were all dirty, evil scum. Then I went through a village and more of them came for me so I set them on fire and probably burnt the village down in the process. Then I got to a shop and killed some more. I finally got home and found the note from Mum and Dad, saying they had gone to look for me. I went back home but couldn't find them, got attacked a few more times and killed some more of them. I went to work, met Dave, and figured Mum and Dad would have gone back to theirs. I went back again; they weren't there and I sort of snapped.'

'Snapped?' Sarah asks.

'I went back to Boroughfare. I went back knowing I wanted to kill them one by one. Fortunately Dave came with me, and we've been going ever since. I came up with this mad plan to get a tank to get through London to find you,' Howie laughs. 'So we went to Salisbury to steal something big and hard, and ended up hooking up with that lot,' he nods at the recruits nearby. 'Had more fights, killed more of them and they wanted to stay with us, so we came to London.'

'Howie, that's amazing,' Sarah says, staring at her brother with awe.

'Not really, you stayed alive and fought back too. I saw what you did in the back of that van,' Howie says.

'Howie, please don't get me wrong. You saved my life and many others, by what you've done with Dave, but well, I've never seen you so alive, so ... I don't know ...' She trails off, uncertain of how to say it.

'It seems like you're enjoying it, Howie,' she finally says, looking directly at him.

'Enjoying it? The end of the world and being surrounded by death and destruction?' Howie replies with an offended and puzzled tone.

'The fighting, Howie, I saw you fighting in London, you were more alive than I have ever seen you. You were possessed, I saw your face and the way you were. I know you better than all of these people ...'

'What about Clarence? Chris? Malcolm? Did they look like they were enjoying it too? Have you seen Dave fight?' Howie demands, with anger.

'Yes, I saw Dave,' Sarah replies softly.

'Well, did he look like he was enjoying it? What about Blowers and the rest?'

'Howie, I don't know them. I only know you, and it was shocking to see you like that,' Sarah says.

'So what would you prefer? That I stayed at home and hid under the blankets?'

'That's not what I meant, Howie ... I mean, you were enjoying it, it gave you pleasure, and that's wrong.'

'Why? Why is it wrong? How did it feel when you and that other woman killed them all in the van?'

'It felt awful, Howie, it was survival and it had to be done, but that was it.'

'No sense of victory? No feeling of righteousness?'

'No,' she says firmly.

Howie pauses and looks down at his feet, then slowly over to the flatlands and the estate in the distance, watching as the shadows lengthen and twilight takes over.

'Maybe it's wrong, maybe it is completely wrong,' Howie says eventually, still looking away from Sarah. 'But the way I see it, it doesn't matter what the motivation or reason is, as long as it gets done. As long as those things are put down and killed. But, I see your point ... it's okay for Chris and the others to have that violence but not your brother, is that it?'

'Something like that,' Sarah replies, in a soft voice.

'I don't know what to say,' Howie shrugs. 'It is what it is, they want to kill us, and we have to stop them.'

'I know.'

'Clarence seems a nice bloke,' Howie says, with a sudden smile.

'Ha, yes he does,' Sarah smiles back, glad of the break in tension.

'Well, I'm gonna try and sleep, you sticking around up here?' Howie says.

'I'll be about,' Sarah replies, as Howie starts walking towards the Saxon.

'And Howie,' she quickly adds. 'I know we weren't the type of brother and sister that said it, but I do love you,' she says. Howie smiles back, the darkness lifted from his face for a few seconds.

'You too, Sis.' He walks off towards the Saxon, smiling and nodding at the people he passes.

Clustering in and around the Saxon, they all try to rest and sleep. Although there are now hundreds of people at the top of the inner north wall, they take no chances and still keep one on the GPMG; Malcolm offers to take the first watch. Howie and Chris take the quiet interior of the Saxon, the rear doors closed, so they can have more peace. Howie beds down on a thick layer of army coats discarded in the warm weather, Chris on the cushioned bench seats; they make easy talk for a few seconds before Chris starts snoring loudly, leaving Howie alone to think about the words Sarah said to him; as his mind tries to think, the rhythmic sounds from Chris get to work and, within seconds, Howie drifts off.

'I'm going to test fire the cannon, Mr. Howie,' Dave says, opening a rear door and leaning in to the Saxon.

'Okay mate,' Howie answers, sleepily.

As Dave walks over, he notices the two cannon crews still in their groups, running through the drills he showed them earlier.

They look at him eagerly as he approaches and he notices the first crew moves discreetly into position, waiting for the chance to do a live fire. Dave gets to the cannon and walks around, checking everything is in place: the powder bags, the wadding, the mounds of wrapped ammunition, the ramrods, the fuses, and, finally, the holder of the flame standing a short distance away.

'Good idea,' Dave nods at the gas canister fitted with a welder's flame that stands a few metres away, a man standing next to it, holding a petrol lighter.

'We've got one on the other cannon too,' the man replies proudly.

Dave nods and completes his inspection. He walks around to the back of the cannon and looks down the length and out to the flatlands.

'We'll probably get maximum impact if we aim for them as they come out of the deep ditch after the second embankment,' Dave says. 'Let's try it and see.' He has one final look around to see the first crew all stood in their allocated positions, ready and waiting to go.

He looks to the man with the lengths of fuse wire and nods once, before stepping away to observe. The man steps forward and pushes the fuse into the cannon hole, feeling for the resistance as the bottom of the wire hits the inside base of the cannon.

'POWDER,' the man shouts and steps back.

The next man picks up a powder bag and moves smartly over to the mouth of the cannon, pushing the bag inside.

'RAMROD,' he shouts, as the man with the long stick steps forward and beats the powder bag down to the bottom of the cannon.

'WADDING,' the ramrod man shouts and steps back as the next man pushes wadding into the mouth of the cannon.

'RAMROD,' he shouts, and again the man with the stick steps up and pushes the wadding firmly down the cannon.

'AMMUNITION,' then a wrapped bundle of nuts, bolts, nails, and screws is pushed in.

'RAMROD.' The man with the stick pushes it down.

He steps back and checks everyone is clear before shouting:

'FUSE'.

The gas canister knob is already turned, and the welder's torch has a soft yellow flame at the end. The flame holder lifts the gas canister and steps over to the fuse, and once again checks everyone is standing well away. He presses the flame to the fuse and pauses for a second as the fuse takes light and starts burning down.

'FIRE,' he bellows and quickly steps back away from the expected recoil.

They all stand with bated breath and hands covering ears as a huge bang rips through the air. The cannon is shot backwards as a massive tongue of fire shoots out the end with a thick, black cloud.

Dave is at the wall upwind and watching as the second bank is clearly peppered with metal fragments striking the top and firing far beyond. He turns back to the crews waiting and the many people turned to watch; he gives a simple thumbs up and a rare smile as they cheer loudly.

'Good, make it ready and we'll test the other one,' Dave says, and watches as they burst into action and the hose man steps forward like a ceremonial guard to sluice any burning fragments from the inside of the cannon. At the next cannon, the first crew stands by and watch with the experienced eye of expert cannon firers, and the second crew position themselves and wait for Dave. Once again he checks everything is in place before nodding once and stepping away. The second crew prove just as good as the first and move quickly, shouting for the next man as they each complete their duty.

The holder of the flame steps forward and lights the fuse, shouting 'FIRE' as he quickly moves away. Once again the cannon roars to life and flies backwards as a long orange flame comes out of the mouth, followed within a split second by thick black smoke.

Dave is at the wall, watching as the spinning metal fragments fly over the bank and reach a good distance into the flatlands.

'Good, too high though,' Dave says, and moves over to remove a wedge used to raise the mouth of the cannon.

'That will be perfect, make it ready,' he adds, before moving off back to the Saxon amidst the cheering and applauding again. He walks around the Saxon, checking on each of his men. Howie and Chris lead them but Dave accepts them as his to be protected and watched.

Although his different mind doesn't allow for the same feeling of impending doom the others have, he does feel a very keen sense of trepidation.

Dave has worked alone on hundreds of missions, and has been outnumbered many times before. But his ability to plan, fight, and move quickly meant he was rarely in danger in the same way that others may perceive it. In order to have a fear of death, one must have a sense of life, and Dave simply does not tick that way. Complete the task in front of you while planning for the next one. Dave had worked alongside regular troops before, but his status always kept him aloof and away. But no matter how different he may be, this week has affected him. These men have become familiar to him, their voices, their jokes, and the way they fight. Blowers and Cookey always side by side joking, but when they fight they do so with complete ferocity, always watching each other and covering the gaps. Tucker is a big lad and not as fit as the others, but he uses his bulk and size and overcomes that fear to drive on. Nick, a witty man with a good head for computers and electrical things – and again, he fights with his heart, never holding back, and pushing on with savage intent. Curtis: he is competent, which may seem a lowly compliment, but a competent man is worth his weight in gold. He knows where to be at the right time and never complains, a good driver too. Then there's Jamie. Quiet like Dave, but still different – he is highly capable and willing to learn, and, importantly, he is able to work alone, but not for his own ends. Dave looks at each of them as he passes and thinks of McKinney, and how Howie reacted when he knew Dave was going to finish him. That was the deepest feeling Dave had ever felt, not for the loss of McKinney, but for the anger and betrayal he thought Howie must be holding towards him. Howie is a natural leader and has a rare ability to show error and mistakes but still command respect. Whatever may come from this battle, Dave knows one thing. Men like Howie must survive, they know right from wrong. They know what must be done, and then they work out how to do it. Men like these that make other men fight when otherwise they would be quivering in a corner and pissing themselves with fear. Dave positions himself at the back of the Saxon, quietly finding a spot that means anyone trying to enter the vehicle from the back must first go past him. The bodyguard. The watchman.

The night closes in, and, for the first time in a week, Howie does not hear the howling of the undead voices lifting to roar in unison. He sleeps deeply, exhausted both in mind and body. They all sleep. All through the camp there is quiet, men and woman strolling around chatting in muted tones. Couples clasping each other tightly, knowing it might be the last time. Families huddle together and whisper words of love and life. Men keep their weapons close and women hold their children, for tonight may be the last night of life. Past mistakes are forgotten and petty squabbles are laid aside, as they acknowledge the lives they have led and prepare for what may come.

CHAPTER FOURTEEN

I wake up quickly, bathed in sweat, and I find myself sat bolt upright, breathing hard. Looking over, I see that Chris has already left. I know I was dreaming, but the images have faded instantly. I feel hot, still tired and dirty, but above all else, I need the toilet.

I clamber out of the vehicle to find the others half asleep, drinking from mugs of hot coffee being handed around by Tucker and his new team of catering corps volunteers.

'Morning, Mr. Howie, fresh coffee for you.' Tucker approaches me, with a steaming mug.

'Not now mate, gotta go.' The cramping in my stomach signifies an urgent action is required.

I run off in just my socks, no time to go back for my boots left in the back of the vehicle. I start jogging down the vehicle ramp, desperately trying to remember where the closest toilet is. The jogging motion just makes it worse though, and I can feel a pressing sensation pushing inside my stomach.

'Too much bloody coffee,' I mutter as I speed up.

People pass by me, trying to stop and talk. I wave them off apologetically and keep going. There's no way I'm going to shit myself in front of all these people. This might be the last day of humanity but I'm not going out with Chris, Blowers, Cookey and the rest of them all ripping the piss out of me. The visitors centre. That must have toilets, it's across the camp, but there's no alternative. There must be some closer ones but I can't take the chance to stop and ask now. I run down the wide central path, veering around children and people stepping out to chat.

'Fuck it, fuck it,' I mutter under my breath as I run faster.

I can feel my face going red and the cramping sensation is bloody awful. I want to stop and drop my trousers here, but that might not be a good thing. The hero of Fort Spitbank leaving a big steaming poo on the floor. No that wouldn't go down very well. There it is, I can see it. There's lights on inside, making it glow in the still darkness of the night. I glance up quickly to see the sky is just starting to lift. I reach the door and see a queue of people stood holding toilet rolls in the wide reception area. After killing many zombies, using bad language, and now preparing for an invasion of the undead army, I commit the worst British crime of all. I jump the queue. There's no other choice, if I don't get to a toilet now I will void my pants.

'Sorry, I'm really sorry,' I yell out, as I run around the quiet men and women stood chatting. I see the door with the stick figure of a man on the front and burst through. Inside, the cubicles are all closed, with more people waiting patiently outside each one. I glance at the urinals, thinking for a split second of sitting on one of them instead.

I grab my stomach as the cramping sensation doubles from the urgent motion of the running. A door opens in front of me and a man steps out. I stare pleadingly at the man waiting to go in. There's something in my eyes; he stares back with a look of absolute forgiveness on his face.

'Do you want to go next?' he asks politely, as I close the door in his face.

'Sorry mate,' I say through gritted teeth, as I scrabble at my belt, cursing the stupid buckles.

'That's okay, when you've got to go ...' the man outside says, his speech leaves it open for me to finish, but I'm otherwise occupied, fighting the hardest battle yet with my trousers.

Finally, I yank them down, pull my underpants down to my ankles and sit down. My arse hits cold plastic and I jump instantly back up, as I realise I've sat on the closed toilet seat.

'Fucking stupid toilet seat,' I roar out, wrenching the blasted thing up to sit back down. My bowels explode with wretched venom as the bomb doors unleash a devastating payload on the poor porcelain toilet bowl beneath me.

'Oh, my fucking God ...' I can't help the words coming out. My arse sputters like a Spitfire machine gun rattling fire at the enemy. The feeling of relief is immense.

'Err, are you all right in there?' the same man asks with polite concern at the long, whimpering sounds coming from me.

'Yep, fine,' I reply with a casual politeness, the spattering noise almost drowning my voice out.

After several minutes, the cramping in my gut abates and I'm left in a state of absolute bliss – that is, until the smell of shit hits my nose and I become acutely aware of my surroundings.

I twist around to the toilet roll holder but it's empty. Everyone in the queue had their own rolls in hand.

'Err, sorry are you still there?' I call out.

'Yes?' the man replies.

'It appears I didn't bring any toilet roll with me, would you have any spare I could ... borrow?' I ask. A hand clutching a full toilet roll appears under the door, and I reach forward and take it gratefully.

'Thank you very much.'

'You're welcome.' After a double flushing of the toilet I'm all done, and open the door to see other men politely look away.

'Bet that's a shitload off your mind,' someone says, to a few sniggers.

'Thanks for the toilet roll, mate,' I hand it back and move over to the washbasin and scrub my hands clean.

At the least the water's still running. Eventually I'm done and stroll out of the toilet and into the reception area, nodding apologetically at the people still waiting in the queue. Outside I walk happily through the camp, heading back to the north wall and still feeling strangely warm and comforted.

Walking back up the vehicle ramp I notice they're all up and drinking coffee, stood around chatting as the first tendrils of daylight push into the night sky.

I see Blowers, Cookey, and Nick all smoking cigarettes.

I see the red ends glowing brightly as they suck in the tobacco and exhale the lazy smoke clouds.

The vapour wisps come from the coffee mugs.

Chris stood off to one side is laughing with Malcolm.

Clarence is talking quietly to Sarah.

Curtis up on the GPMG at the top of the Saxon, the machine gun pointing off to the right, and Curtis leaning forward on his elbows clutching a hot drink.

Off to both sides, I see people stretching lazily and talking in muted tones, nodding to each other. A man throws a cigarette onto the floor and brings his heavy boot down to grind it out. My heart starts beating faster, the scene slows down, and I feel like I'm wading through thick mud. Tucker strolls past me at the top of the ramp; he's looking at me and smiling. He holds a steaming mug of coffee out in front of him, ready for me to take it. It takes forever to reach him, my senses have become heightened and adrenalin is coursing through my system. I look past Tucker and see Dave stood by the wall looking out at the flatlands.

Something flashes far beyond him. A quick bright light in the distance.

Everything slows and I see Dave start to turn back towards us, his face strangely animated, and I watch as his mouth opens and his eyes are blazing. This is it. I know it.

'COVERRRR,' Dave's voice roars out into the quiet night and it brings me back to reality in a heartbeat. To their credit, my group react instantly. As one, they drop down and spin to face the flatlands. Hundreds of heads all along the top of the inner wall snap around to face us; many within the camp hear Dave's awesome voice and they too stop and turn to look up. I stand still and look out to the estate. The first bright flash is followed by a low dull thump that rolls over the ground to my ears. Another bright flash, then another, followed by a series of bright flashes spread all along the width of the estate. Soundless at first, the speed of light being far greater than the speed of sound. But the sound does reach us as the dull echoing thumps roll out like soft drumbeats. Then the estate goes up. The whole of the thing, from far left to far right and as far back as the eye can see, explodes as one.

The still dark sky is lit for many hundreds of miles around as a mammoth sheet wall of fire scorches high up into the air.

My mouth drops open as I have never seen such a thing before. The most expensive special effects movies ever made cannot compare to this sight: a whole housing estate erupting instantaneously and filling the sky with flames the size of skyscrapers. Within a split second the pressure wave and the sound hit us. As one, we are taken off our feet; not a single person remains standing on the top of the inner wall. Down below in the camp, many are knocked down or simply drop to hug the earth in absolute terror. The ground seems to heave, and the noise is more than words can describe; a thousand jet aircraft taking off at the same time while a thousand marching bands pound through my skull. I go flying off to the side, I could be screaming or silent, I have no concept. All I know is that my senses are overwhelmed with sight, sound, and sensation. If there is a hell, then surely it has come alive here in this place. I stagger to my feet, not knowing what I'm doing. Looking around, I see every other person is down on the ground burying their heads with their arms. All apart from Dave, who is stood side on to me, his face turned to watch his glorious work – his profile framed by the scorching flames behind him. How he remained standing is something I may never know, but he and I stand and watch with awe. The incredible sounds continue and I see the flames are shooting out over the flatlands too, eviscerating everything in reach. This is something amazing, something beautiful, created by one man who can barely hold a conversation. Dave suddenly looks up and tilts his head to one side, seemingly staring at something in the night sky.

'INCOMING,' he bellows with his huge voice, somehow drowning out the sounds of the explosions still reaching us. I look up, puzzled at what they could be firing at us from this distance, and especially after that explosion.

Then I see it. A car on fire, rolling over and over gently in the air as it sails hundreds of feet over the Fort to land far out in the sea.

I glance back up to see more fiery objects flying overhead, leaving long blazing trails of sparks and fire behind them like mini-comets. I hear a loud wet slapping sound nearby and turn my head slowly, finding it hard to drag my eyes away from the glorious blaze. I look over and see a charred and smouldering torso laying on the ground a few metres away. Just a torso with the arms still attached, no legs or head though. I watch it with curious detachment then feel my body being slammed to the ground. Dave is up and grabbing at my arm, trying to pull me to my feet. He's just knocked me down and now he wants me back up.

'GET UP, MR. HOWIE,' he shouts at me, and his voice penetrates enough to get me to my feet and staggering behind him as he pulls me around to the back of the Saxon. He wrenches the rear doors open and shoves me bodily into the back. I get to my senses and shuffle forward to look out of the windscreen. Flaming body parts are landing all along the inner wall and behind us in the camp. Burnt and scorched heads, legs, arms and torsos, torn apart and sent flying high into the sky to come tumbling back down upon us. Dave runs around the front of the vehicle and starts pulling at Sarah, yelling for her to get up. I run back and jump out of the Saxon, landing with both feet firm on the ground. I race round and lift Sarah to her feet by her shoulders, shoving her roughly towards the back of the vehicle. She looks dazed and confused and we dodge burning body parts landing all around us.

'DAVE, PROTECT THE CANNON,' I scream out.

Dave turns to face me with a sudden realisation.

'I CAN ONLY DO ONE,' he roars back and races off to the left.

I run forward, grabbing at bodies and pulling them up.

Someone screams and I look over to see an archer being squashed by a heavy zombie body landing on him, others scrabbling forward to try and pull the burning body away. I glance down into the camp and see chaos reigning, people running in all directions and screaming as the burning body parts come slamming down.

Tents are ablaze and brave men and women beat at the deadly flames with coats and blankets. Malcolm is up and staring around with a look of utter horror on his face. I run over and grab his arms to make him face me.

'MALCOLM, PROTECT THE OTHER CANNON. IF THOSE POWDER BAGS GO UP, WE'LL BE FUCKED!' I scream into his face several times, until he quickly comes to and nods back at me before running off. Within a few minutes my group are up and working, running up and down the top of the inner wall, stamping down on flaming body parts to beat them out. I run down to see Malcolm using the hose from the cannon, running about and spraying the water over any burning material.

I'd forgot about the hoses and give thanks once more for Dave's forward planning. Dave joins me back in the middle and together, with our band of brothers, we stare out to the flatlands. The sky is much lighter now and daylight is almost upon us.

'Thank fuck it didn't set the fuel off in the deep ditch,' Chris says. His feet are planted apart, his hands on his hips as he stares out to the blazing estate.

'Dave, I want everyone up here to make ready. We'll use the Saxon to fire first as it has the range. Everyone else holds until they get closer, so we don't waste ammunition,' I bark out the order as I stride forward to stare out over the flatlands.

I hear Dave take a sharp intake of breath and wait for his voice to come bellowing out.

'MAKE READY, YOU WILL MAKE READY AND WAIT. HOLD YOUR FIRE.' The inner wall springs to action as hundreds of people surge forward to take up their arms. Clips are pushed in with a multitude of loud clicks. Firing bolts are racked back. Men and women make ready their weapons. Ready to stand proud and fight. Silence falls amongst us. Even the camp seems quiet now as everyone prepares for the attack they know is coming.

'BLOWERS, GET OUR LOT FORMED UP HERE,' I indicate the area of the wall immediately in front of the Saxon and facing out down the road leading to the estate.

'NICK, YOU'RE ON THE GPMG. DAVE AND JAMIE, I WANT YOU BOTH SNIPING, TRY AND GET THAT FUCKER SMITH.' They react without hesitation.

Tucker runs up carrying my rifle and hands it over as he takes up position on the wall. I spare a glance to see my glorious men kneeling down and removing ammunition clips from their bags, placing them at their feet, ready for use. Their hands are steady and there is a steely look in their eyes.

'HOWIE, MY MEN ARE YOURS, USE THEM,' Chris shouts from the back of the Saxon.

'FORM UP ON THE WALL HERE,' I bellow out, pointing at the space being used by my recruits.

'WE FOCUS OUR FIRE ON THAT ROAD,' I shout out and watch as the guards from the commune jump in.

'GET YOUR CLIPS OUT AND READY. FOCUS YOUR FIRE. HOLD UNTIL TOLD!' I hear Blowers stepping smoothly into his corporal role.

He moves along our line, checking each is ready.

'COOKEY, I'LL DO THIS END, YOU DO THAT ONE,

MAKE SURE THEY'RE ALL READY,' Blowers yells over to his friend.

They split, with each one moving off down the line of the wall, checking each man and woman is ready with their ammunition and repeating for them to hold their fire until told. Tucker runs past me heading to the back of the Saxon. I pay little attention as I see Sarah running up the vehicle ramp towards us. I didn't see her go off anywhere so I'm puzzled to see her coming back.

'Howie, the boats are back,' she yells out.

'Get those children ready and get them loaded to go.' I turn to Chris as he steps away from the Saxon, holding an assault rifle.

'Chris, I've got boats to take the children away. I've got this here, can you go and make sure they move quickly.'

'Got it,' Chris replies and turns to jog after Sarah. I turn back to the wall as Tucker comes up beside me.

'Mr. Howie, sir,' he says.

I turn to see him holding a pair of boots. My boots. I look down to see I'm still wearing just my socks.

'Well done, mate,' I smile at him and walk over to the Saxon and start pulling them on.

I glance to the side to see Dave and Jamie both have rifles with scopes attached. No suppressors or silencers now. They take position front and middle, looking directly at the road. I step away and see Blowers and Cookey returning to their posts, both of them nodding at me as they take position. The estate is still well ablaze but I know it won't be long before they try and push through. I can imagine Darren is sending them in to find paths and routes safe enough to get through. I look up to see Nick standing calmly with the General Purpose Machine Gun in front of him; he looks down and smiles.

'You ready mate?' I call up.

'Yes, Mr. Howie,' he says, with a clear voice.

'EYES ON,' Jamie shouts, and every head snaps forward as the tension increases tenfold within a split second.

'COMING THROUGH NOW,' Dave shouts out, sweeping along the estate line with his scope.

'Mr. Howie,' Nick calls out and throws down a pair of binoculars.

I press them to my eyes and adjust the setting until the burning estate comes into focus. Most of the houses are gone. The sheer ferocity of the explosion has shredded everything on the estate. The fuel tanker and the open gas lines created such a powerful explosion that everything that could be burnt was burnt. Now, with very little left, the flames are dying down. Thick, black smoke billows up into the sky, but between the wreckage and blackened stumps I see the zombies pouring forward. A thick line of them comes into view through the smoke; several of them drop from heat or flames, but the mass just keeps rolling forward.

'THIS IS IT,' I bellow out.

'THEY'RE COMING THROUGH THE ESTATE NOW,' I report what I see.

The sight of them triggers an instant response inside of me. The anger is knocking to come in, but I bite it down. I'll need it later but, for now, I can do this myself.

'ALMOST AT THE EDGE. NICK, YOU'LL GET A VIEW OF THEM ANY SECOND.'

'ROGER,' Nick shouts out loudly and racks the bolt back noisily.

I glance up to see him tightly gripping the handles and staring ahead with ferocious concentration. I put the glasses back to my eyes and see them surging forward.

'HERE THEY COME,' I shout as they reach within metres of the edge of the estate.

I drop the binoculars down and watch with the naked eye. The edge of the estate suddenly comes alive as a solid, black, mass emerges.

'NICK,' I shout out.

'COME ON,' Nick roars, and the air is split apart by the heavy constant sound of the General Purpose Machine Gun coming to life.

Nick aims well and sweeps along the entire front row.

From far left to far right, I can see bodies falling down as Nick sweeps across them, then back again, as the awesome power of the weapon shows true. I lift the binoculars again and follow Nick's arc of fire, watching as the bodies are shredded apart and sent flying backwards into the pressed ranks behind them. The following hordes stumble over their fallen comrades. I sweep back and my heart sinks as I see a solid mass stretching back into the estate, and no sign of the end. I move my view down and watch with my breath held as they near the first obstacle we prepared. They move as one, keeping their lines smartly and presenting a solid wall. Not running, but not shuffling either. A steady pace as they advance.

'Go on, go on,' Cookey urges them on to the next trap.

'Come on you stupid fuckers,' another voice joins in, and is taken up as more shout out, urging and willing them to keep going. They reach the first ditch and I watch as the first few lines simply fall out of view, dropping into the ground.

Cheering erupts up and down the wall as the forward ranks of zombies drop down to be impaled on the sharpened spikes. The pressure from the oncoming hordes keep driving the undead forward to topple into the wide ditch.

'YES!' Cookey shouts with violence in his voice, 'HAVE SOME OF THAT.'

I spin around and look to the back of the Fort. Sarah and Sergeant Hopewell are by the opened rear doors, urging the women and children to move out quickly. I guess Chris and the others must be outside lifting them into boats. I turn back in time to see the next ranks of zombies dropping down as they reach the ditch, but not going out of sight. The bodies must have stacked up deep enough to bridge the gap, but it at least slows them, and many have already been vanquished from the estate going up and now the ditch. The GPMG roars with incessant noise as Nick continues to sweep from left to right in a steady motion. Then two more loud and distinct bangs join in as Dave and Jamie start firing with their high-powered rifles.

'READY,' I roar out and see a visible reaction as the men and women on the line seem to hunch forward, push their shoulders into their weapons and aim down the sights. I pause just for a second as I watch the front lines of the undead army start dropping down as they run over the foot traps.

'FIRE,' I drop the binoculars for a second and scream the word as loud as I can.

I see a devastating effect as many of the zombies are dropped instantly by the volley. I use the binoculars again and see, not only the firing from our weapons are dropping them, but the foot traps are working far greater than I had hoped.

A small smile forms on my mouth as I see zombies staggering forward and then suddenly dropping down as their feet are penetrated by the deadly sharp metal barbs. They might not feel pain, but the physical action of the metal driving through their skin and breaking the delicate small bones of the foot is enough to make them fall down. All along the lines I see zombies blown apart and shredded by the deadly hail of bullets from the GPMG. The rifles and assault weapons also prove very effective; not every shot is a headshot, but the simple action of being penetrated by a high-speed large calibre rifle is enough to blow them backwards and knock more down. Dave and Jamie's shots are, without question, perfect. Puffs of pink mist explode time and time again as they blow the skulls apart and send deadly bone fragments into the closely packed horde. I glance up and down the line, to see men and women using bolt-action rifles, rates of fire increasing as they aim, fire, rack the bolt – aim and fire. The movements are becoming faster and more fluid with each shot. Placing the binoculars down, I stride forward and take up position on the wall with my assault rifle. Selecting single shot and pulling the bolt back, I take aim, which is almost completely unnecessary as there are so bloody many of them, so just waving the gun in their general direction will surely hit something.

I pull aim for front centre, at the section of zombies coming down the central road. The better weapons being used by the recruits and guards in this section means those zombies are suffering high casualty rates and being withered as they advance. Each one dropped is instantly replaced, but still we pour fire into them and every shot counts as they are slowly reduced. My shots join the deafening noise as I fire into the oncoming mass. Working in concentrated silence, the minutes pass as the zombie army slowly but surely takes ground and moves ever closer to the Fort, rising and falling as they step on the fallen bodies in front of them.

The foot traps keep working and they keep dropping down, but still they keep coming until they are but metres away from the first embankment. With no sign of Darren – Dave and Jamie have taken up their assault rifles to increase the rate of fire sent from us. Nick brings the GPMG to focus the fire directly into the front centre line on the road. With the sustained firing of Nick and the recruits and the guards all using assault rifles, the zombies on the road are obliterated.

Large gaps start forming as the following horde are forced to weave around the broken and mangled bodies. The undead army reaches the first embankment and I watch as the first lines rise up and over the crest to pour down the other side. A huge boom sounds out off to my left, and I glance down just in time to see flames shooting out the end of the cannon, quickly followed by a cloud of thick black smoke. The results of the cannon fire are awesome, and a whole swathe of undead are eviscerated by the scorching metallic fragments. The second cannon off to my right then booms out. I keep my eyes on the horde this time, and realise that everyone else does too. The impact is simply staggering, and my mouth drops open as the grapeshot from the cannon spreads out, becoming superheated by the incredible power of the cannon, and rips through whole lines of zombies.

The projectiles go through the first rank like butter, and several lines back are instantly taken down. Each shot of the cannon destroys hundreds at a time. Again, large gaps form as the zombies can't move fast enough to fill the gaps and now the front line is not solid. But still they keep coming, and it takes moments to prepare the cannon for the next round of firing.

'That was fucking awesome,' Cookey says during the pause of firing, as we all watch the effect of the second cannon firing.

'EYES FRONT,' Dave bellows, and snaps us all back to the moment.

Stepping back, I look down the top of the inner wall to see the archers have split into two groups: one group on the left and the other on the right. Two archers from each group are standing next to the cannon flame holder, their bows dipped down with arrows resting against the wire in the rest position. The end of the arrows have been swathed in something, ready to be lit and fired into the deep ditch. As the zombies reach halfway between the two embankments, the archers are given an order to prepare. They move out into a long line stood well back from the wall. Each of them presses the arrow into wire as they lift their bows and pull back to stand braced. For a second, I'm transported to medieval England as I see long lines of archers holding their bows aimed high into the air.

'RELEASE,' someone shouts, and the bowmen and women release their arrows to fly high and straight. The arrows reach the arc of their trajectory and the strength of gravity takes over, pulling them back to earth, gathering speed as they plummet down. The arrows drive into the zombie army, many of them striking into the exposed skulls and taking zombies down with instant kills. Some of the arrows hit arms and legs, causing the zombies to be pushed down, only to rise back up and keep going with the long barbs stuck through their limbs; some of them crawl along the ground, only to be trampled down by more zombie feet already pierced and damaged by the foot traps. As the first volley of arrows hit home, the second volley is already in the air. The two cannon both fire with massive recoiling booms and again whole swathes of undead are killed outright. More large gaps form and their lines become more ragged. The GPMG, the assault rifles, the single shot rifles, the cannon and the archers, all pour deadly fire into the undead army, as we continue to cull their numbers.

'I SEE HIM,' Jamie drops his assault rifle to quickly pick up the scoped sniper rifle.

'Where?' I call out, ceasing fire to glare out at the army.

'Sir, he's on the road, about fifty metres back from the front line. There's a whole dense section clustered round him,' Jamie shouts back as he rests the rifle on the wall and looks down the scope.

Dave has already dropped his assault rifle and picked his rifle up to rest alongside Jamie and stare down the scope.

'I see the dense section,' Dave shouts out.

'NICK, FIRE INTO THE MIDDLE,' I turn and shout at Nick, waving my arm to show him where I want the fire aimed.

Nick nods once, grim-faced, and turns the heavy calibre weapon onto the front middle section.

'THEY'RE AT THE SECOND BANK,' Clarence's deep voice shouts.

I look across and see the zombies are now scaling the far side; they reach the crest of the embankment.

'FIRE ARCHERS MAKE READY,' I shout out, but the constant and sustained noise prevents my voice from reaching the archers further down the lines. I run back to the Saxon and pull the microphone out.

'FIRE ARCHERS MAKE READY,' I repeat, and my voice is amplified down the lines.

The fire archers move in to cluster round the cannon flame holder. He presses the flame against the ends of their arrows, which start burning with oily black smoke curling up.

The fire archers step forward to get a view from the wall and hold with their arrows pointing down to the ground. The zombies scale the bank and start pouring down the nearside, dropping down into the fuel-filled ditch.

I hesitate, to give more time, until the nearside bank is thick with undead staggering down.

I glance across to see the fire archers staring at me with pleading looks. I raise my right arm up high, signalling the archers, who pull their arrows back and take aim with their bows.

Clarence turns to stare at me, glaring at me to give the order to release, but I hold and wait for more undead to drop down.

The ditch is deep and I know they can't climb out, so they will have to use the bodies of their undead brethren to bridge the gap.

The risk is that the ditch will become too clogged with bodies and prevent the arrows from igniting the fuel. At the last second, when the guards and recruits are turning to look at me with desperate looks, I push the button down on the microphone and lift the mouthpiece.

'RELEASE FIRE ARROWS.'

The archers release and their arrows fly out, leaving a thin black trail hanging in the air behind them. The timing is perfect. The arrows strike home, and the flaming heads ignite the fuel held in the hoses and containers. They detonate within a split second as the ditches explode. Bodies are flung high up into the air and the pressure wave clears the nearside bank instantly as the bodies are pushed back up and go spinning off. The zombies still coming over the crest are then met with a boiling surge of flames and metal fragments. More and more of the undead are shredded and turned to carbon. The zombies on the road are being taken down in droves. The GPMG and the assault rifles held by the recruits and guards concentrate solely on them. The incredible sustained fire withers the lines and soon there is a very deep horseshoe shape forming. The undead react, and rather than just filling the gap from behind, they surge in from the left and right, seemingly desperate to keep that area protected. The undead keep surging up the second bank and down the nearside to be instantly incinerated by the wall of flames leaping up from the deep ditch.

With every gun now aimed at the road, we hold them at bay. We take many down and slowly, ever so slowly, we reduce their numbers. Dave and Jamie lean forward with their rifles resting on the wall, their breathing slow and controlled, looking intently down the scope and gently squeezing the trigger to send a bullet with Darren's name etched on it spinning to his evil, undead skull.

However, the zombies appear unwilling to give up their beloved leader, and they press into densely-packed ranks ahead of him, pouring in from the sides to present an undead shield.

'He keeps moving back,' Dave reports out loud, his voice matching his manner: calm and controlled.

A huge boom on my right and the cannon sends another deadly hail into the ranks of zombies still trying to come down the road.

The cannon crew take the initiative to adjust the aim and focus on the middle section. Once again, the effect is devastating; a large chunk of bodies is simply swept away. We keep pouring everything we have at them. Each man and woman is firing with precision and speed that depletes our ammunition as quickly as it cuts them down.

Glancing down the line, I see people scrabbling about and looking for fresh magazines. Chris runs back up the vehicle ramp and pauses at the side of the Saxon as Nick shouts down at him, and then runs to join me.

'Kids are loaded and away,' he pants. 'Nick said he's got one magazine left after this.'

'We're running out here too,' I shout back at him.

'But look, the end is in sight,' I point out to the flatlands and rear end of the zombie army now in view.

I run back to the Saxon and the sight of the camp below stops me in my tracks. Thousands of people are standing still and looking up at us, armed with whatever weapons they can find. They stand quietly, not one of them flinching or crying. Something about the visual image stops me in my tracks, and I look back to the flatlands and the army moving towards us. They still outnumber us massively, but at least I can see the end of them now. They are no longer infinite. They are *finite*. They are a set number, and that number is being reduced with each bullet, arrow, and cannon shot sent their way.

'Nick, wait until we run out of ammo, then open up with that last magazine. Keep your fire concentrated on the middle section so we can get out to meet them. You join us as soon as possible,' I say to Nick as he works with now well-practised hands to load up the last magazine.

'Got it, Mr. Howie, I'll be right behind you.'

'I'm out,' Clarence shouts, simply dropping his assault rifle and stepping away.

Within a few seconds, the last of the shots are being fired by Jamie and Dave, their rate of fire with the sniper rifles much slower than the assault rifles.

Here it is.

The time we all knew was coming.

With hard staring eyes and a nod, Clarence moves around to the back of the Saxon and starts drawing our hand weapons out.

'GPMG NOW,' Dave roars, as the undead start gaining ground on the road, slowly advancing towards the Fort.

Nick squeezes the trigger for the last time, as the glorious weapon roars to life, spewing its deadly rounds into the zombies; within seconds, they are being repelled back. Dave stands slowly, gently resting the sniper rifle against the wall. He gently rolls his head from side to side, stretching his neck and rolling his shoulder joints. I watch him open and close his hands, making tight fists and stretching the fingers out. He turns to stare at me, his eyes blazing. His hands move behind his back and slowly draw the long, straight-bladed knives out, then he stands motionless, with the knives turned up against his forearms. A chill runs down my spine and the hairs on the back of my neck stand on end. Clarence steps from the back of the Saxon clutching a load of long-handled axes, foraged and saved for us. One by one, my recruits and Chris's guards take an axe and stand, ready and waiting.

Clarence hands the last one out, then leans back into the Saxon and draws two more axes out – each one with a long handle and a double-bladed head. He hands one to me, which I take; a surge of adrenalin pulses through me as I grasp the weapon and feel the weight.

'Go down, I'll be right behind you,' I say to the group.

They nod and turn to start moving quickly down the vehicle ramp.

Dave joins me and we stand together, watching every man and woman walk past us holding a variety of weapons. The rifles and bows, now redundant, are left by the wall. The two cannons each give an almighty boom as they fire their last shots, decimating several ranks of zombies in the process.

The crews abandon their posts and run down the vehicle ramp.

Dave and I start after them, getting a firm nod from Nick as we go.

'Well, this is it, mate,' I say to Dave.

'It is, Mr. Howie.'

'Been a bloody long week, mate.'

'It has been, Mr. Howie.'

'Are you ever going to call me just Howie?'

'No, Mr. Howie.'

'You got your knives then?'

'Yes, you got your axe too?'

'Yeah, it's a good axe.'

'I like knives.'

'I know mate ... we did well.'

'We did, Mr. Howie.'

'We killed bloody loads of them.'

'We did,' Dave replies, as we reach the bottom and walk through the silent crowd to the front.

'Still a lot left though.'

'There is.'

'I was worried for a minute.'

'What about, Mr. Howie?'

'I thought we'd kill them all and not have any left ...' We reach the front and I look back at the thousands of people now crammed into the front of the Fort, all of them facing the now open gates and staring hard at the outer wall and the horror that lies on the other side.

'IS THERE A PLAN?' someone shouts, and every face turns to look at me with expectation.

'YEAH, WE KILL THEM ALL,' I shout back instantly, that familiar feeling just starting to pluck at my insides.

'WE GO OUT THERE AND WE FUCKING KILL EVERY ONE OF THEM. WE SLAUGHTER THEM AND WE KEEP GOING, UNTIL THE LAST MAN IS STANDING. WE DO NOT GIVE UP, WE DO NOT RETREAT, WE DO NOT BACK DOWN. WE ARE THE LIVING AND THEY ARE THE DEAD.' My voice roars out, as I feel the anger building inside me.

'DO NOT GIVE IN. WE HAVE KILLED MANY OF THEM ALREADY. YOU WILL SEE THOUSANDS UPON THOUSANDS OF THEM. BUT WE ARE THOUSANDS TOO AND THEY ARE WEAK AND DEAD. WE ARE ALIVE AND WE HAVE STRENGTH AND WE WILL STAND TOGETHER.'

The recruits, guards, and men of the front line stand with faces flushed, as they too allow their anger to course through their veins.

'STAY TOGETHER, AIM FOR THE HEAD, AND KEEP A TIGHT GRIP ON YOUR WEAPON.' I turn back to face the doors, two men standing ready, grasping the handles ready to pull the big gates open, and we wait for the GPMG to run out of bullets.

CHAPTER FIFTEEN

'Where are you?'

'I am here.'

'Are you coming?'

'Do you want me to come?'

'You know I do, bring your associates too.'

'No.'

'No?'

'I won't.'

'Why not?'

'Because you want me, that's why not.'

'I do want you. I need you.'

'An addict's words, Howie.'

'So?'

'Sarah was right, you're addicted and you're enjoying it.'

'No, I am not.'

'Then do it yourself, you've had lots of practise, and you're a big boy now.'

'I don't want to do it myself, I want you to help me.'

'No Howie, I told you there was a cost to using me.'

'I don't care about the cost.'

'You should care, Howie.'

'Why?'

'It will destroy you if you keep using me.'

'I will be destroyed if I don't, we all will.'

'What about after, what then, Howie?'

'There won't be an after without you.'

'Do it yourself. Do it without me.'

'No. I won't. It's not the same without you.'

'You want this fight Howie, you want it.'

'No, I don't, but it's here and I have to deal with it.'

'Run, hide, do something else, do anything else.'

'I won't run or hide.'

'Admit that you want it.'

'I don't want it.'

'Admit it Howie, admit it and tell me you want it.'

'No.'

'I want to hear you say it, Howie.'

'Okay.'

'Say it.'

'Will you help me if I say it?'

'Say it Howie.'

'I want it.'

'Louder.'

'I WANT IT.'

'Louder Howie, I can't hear you.'

'I FUCKING WANT IT. I WANT THIS FIGHT.'

'Come on Howie, snarl, scream, make me hear you.'

'I WANT THEM TO SUFFER. I WANT REVENGE. I WANT TO KILL THEM.'

'Good, Howie.'

'Will you come?'

'I'm already here. I always have been.'

My heart thumps strong in my chest. My rate of breathing increases as my system floods with oxygen and surges with adrenalin. The whites of my knuckles are stark from gripping the handle of the axe so tightly.

I wait for the thumping sound of the machine gun to end. Glancing to my sides, I see every man and woman on that front line has a grim and determined expression, and eyes full of rage. Lips twitch and snarl as we struggle to hold the anger in check. Eyes narrow and brows become furrowed in these few seconds. I take a step forward, wanting to be the first out, wanting that first kill. Dave takes a step forward and joins me, then the rest of the line follows – followed by the thousands of people behind us all moving forward.

I look left and right with a snarl on my face, unable to contain the growing fury. Snarling faces look back at me: wild animals, feral, untamed. I step forward again; so does Dave and the rest. In frustration, but too full of rage to voice my thought process, I growl deep in my throat and again take a step forward. Dave steps with me and then everyone else does too. Then there is silence. Sudden and unexpected. The two men holding the large gates lean forward and pull with all their might. The doors open inwards but it feels slow, so slow. I fear I will explode if I don't get out there now. I can feel myself inching forward, waiting for that gap to just open enough and I'll get through it. I feel a pressure across my waist, and I look down to see Dave holding his arm out across me.

'We go together,' he growls, but inches forward as he says it.

'Fine,' I growl back, and stretch my arm across his waist too, both of us pushing against the arm of the other, inching forward together. I feel another pressure and see Chris on my other side, his shoulder leaning into mine and trying to hold me back. A quick glance and everyone is holding everyone else back. Shoulders pressed tight, arms stretched out. Every one of us wants to be the first, so we hold each other back and, in doing so, our entire front line growls and snarls as we inch forward as one, leaning forward. The big gates are old, and they are very heavy. The hinges are tight and the gates just brush the ground as they open, causing friction and resistance to the men pulling them.

As the gap widens to a man-sized width, they come free and the friction ends. The gates are pulled wide open within a second or two ... and there they are. The zombie army is in front of us, in all their decaying, decomposing, and fetid glory.

'Ready, Dave?' I snarl.

'Yes, Mr. Howie,' he snarls back at me.

'READY LADS,' I roar, as loud as my cracking voice will allow.

'YES!' Thousands of voices filled with fear and rage roar back at me. Dave's arm drops from my waist, I drop my arm from his and we break free, charging at the wide entrance. There's a guttural, animalistic roar as I am finally allowed to unleash the pure fury inside.

Dave's voice joins mine, along with Chris, Clarence, Blowers, Cookey, and Curtis, Tucker, Jamie, and Malcolm. Our voices become many and the sound of it drives us on. The gates are only wide enough for a few at a time and we are the first out and heading for the road in the middle.

The deep ditches are now crawling with smoking zombies climbing out onto our side. The army of the living faces the army of the dead.

We spread out as we pour through the gate. The undead army speed up coming at us. We speed up and charge at them. They charge at us. The gap between the ditches is our meeting point and we both know it.

As we take the last few paces towards each other, I lift my axe high out to the right, pulling my shoulder back and preparing for the impact. An image of Sarah suddenly fills my mind, safe and protected out on the boats with the children and their mothers. My parents are gone but at least she is safe, and the more of these we take down now, the better chance for survival they have.

We go to meet death and we all know it. The power of hope keeps a glimmer alive that maybe we'll walk away from this, but a conflicting dose of reality makes it known that we stand very little chance.

Ah, Hope says, but there is a chance.

For Sarah I will go to meet my death. For those children and the hope for mankind I will go to meet my death. For that slim chance that we can destroy this evil spawn, I will go to meet my death.

My name is Howie. I was named after my father Howard, but it became too confusing to have two Howards, so I became Howie.

I am twenty-seven years old, and I am the leader of the Living Army.

I bring death to you.

The undead stretches forward at me; his upper body leans forward and his lips pull back to reveal a row of uneven and dirty yellow teeth.

His movement exposes his neck and I slam the axe blade into it, slicing through cleanly, and the head simply drops from view. The first drops of blood are spilled and, if nothing else, I will know that I did that. I drew first blood in this battle. The axe drives on in the powerful arc as the blade bites into the face of the next undead, cleaving through the cheekbone and taking half the face off. I twist around and use my momentum to ram my right shoulder into the next one. He gets propelled backwards and I uppercut the axe into his groin, almost cutting him in half. I glimpse Dave dropping low and driving forward to plough through the first few lines to rise up deep within their ranks.

For one glorious second he pauses, a mighty look of concentrated fury on his face, and he gives a small smile. Then he sets to work, and the amazing ability of his body bursts with life as he starts spinning, dropping, turning, twisting and, with each poetic movement, an undead body drops with a cut throat.

For a split second I feel guilty, guilty that we've brought an army to fight them when all we ever needed was Dave and two knives.

Back to reality and I swipe the axe out wide – slicing through shoulders, arms, and faces as I create space around me. For a minute, we gain ground as the first few lines drop easily from the weapons used, but then the sheer numbers on their side compress against the backs of the line in front of us and now we hold, neither gaining nor losing ground.

We hold our lines and kill them as they step and lunge forward. I have no idea how the rest of the line is working, whether the undead army have burst through the deep ditches, if our line is too spread out or too tightly packed. All I can do now is fight and kill the thing in front of me. The first, wild sweeps clear a space around me, but then I settle down to practised strikes and lunges – conserving energy and strength. My axe bites into skull after skull as I sweep back and forth, lunging forward and driving the axe overhead to destroy, kill, maim, and end the undead lives of these foul abominations. The fury surges through me and I work faster and harder than ever before. Each killing blow drives me on.

'STEP BACK,' a voice roars nearby and, for a second, I'm confused as to why we are giving ground, but then I realise we are fighting and tripping over the bodies on the ground.

We step back and allow the undead lines to stumble and clamber over their dead comrades; we take advantage of the obstacles and cut them down in droves, adding more and more broken bodies to growing piles. The glory of battle is within me as I swing my axe, cleaving, smashing, pulping, and destroying. I take two down with a massive swing and catch another fleeting glimpse of Dave, still deep within the ranks.

He leaps high into the air, his arms rising above his head as he dives back down. Bright arcs of blood spurt into the air to show the path he weaves. Clarence simply uses his awesome strength, gripping the axe at the base of the shaft. He swings left and takes several down at once, then pauses for the next row to step forward and then swings right, taking them down and repeating the action over and again.

The undead are simply too stupid to learn from his tactic. Chris and Malcolm work like I do, taking small choppy lunges and sweeps to target each victim and take them down with the smallest expenditure of energy. Blowers and Cookey stand side-by-side, fighting like demons. Tucker has that look of terrified rage on his face, and uses his bulk to swing out and take them down. Jamie, small and lithe like Dave, holds knives in each hand and attacks one zombie at a time with clinical precision, never over-extending and always aware of the next target.

Zombie after zombie, axe swing after axe swing, and we go on fighting and battling. Strike and move, strike and move. Heads keep lunging at me and I strike across to smash the things apart. Skulls cleaved open like ripe melons, shower me in greying brain matter. One appears in front of me, the skin on his face already falling off, exposing dirty white bone underneath. The remains of his lips pull back and his mouth opens, strands of saliva drool and hang down as he comes in close for the bite. I lash out hard and the axe takes the top of his head off. Another one steps to my right, a fat female undead; how she kept up with the mass marching is beyond me. I keep the swing going and drive into her neck, severing through the spinal column and she goes down.

Stepping forward to meet the next one, I drop him with an overhead smash, then step forward as I uppercut, wasting no energy in making use of each swing of the heavy axe. I sense someone fighting right behind me and I catch a quick glimpse of Clarence ploughing away. I move forward again and Clarence steps up to my right side. Exchanging a quick look, we both step and swing forward.

Suddenly, Chris is on my left and the three of us fight together, side-by-side. Then Malcolm joins our line on the other side of Chris and now we are four, synchronised and swinging the axes. Left to right, right to left. The effect is awesome and we make headway, stepping forward and tramping the broken and mashed-up bodies underneath us.

'WATCH THE SIDES,' Chris bellows as we drive in too deep

and the zombie army start curling round and attacking Malcolm and Clarence to the sides.

Blowers and Cookey move up and fight out to the sides, joined by Tucker, Curtis, and then Nick running in fresh with an axe he'd kept back in the Saxon.

Some of the guards join us and we form a circle, just as we did in London – fighting forward and presenting a solid wall on four sides. With my friends to my sides and behind me, I feel a fresh surge of energy and we fight on, the zombie army pressing in as we keep our shape and drive further and further into their ranks. Every time I glance up I see bodies being dropped by Dave just feet from me. I realise he's staying close, offering his never-ending protection. For every zombie I take down, Dave takes down two or three, and *his* kill rate alone must be destroying so many. The heat becomes unbearable and sweat pours off us, so many bodies all pushed into a tight space, and I become aware of their fetid and disgusting odour, the stench of their breath, the smell of decomposing and rotting flesh. They now truly are the living dead. They are corpses infected with evil, and something dark works inside of them and drives them with an insatiable hunger for human flesh. Their presence offends and disgusts me, the way they keep coming, wave after wave of zombie bodies being thrown against us. The rage threatens to burst me apart and I fight harder, faster, striking with more power than I have ever done. The fury within me is so powerful, yet it isn't enough, give me more, give me more rage and anger. Fill me with utter vengeance and make me stronger. With frustration and blind anger I roar out with animalistic rage, my voice guttural and wild. I hack and hack away, killing and destroying all within my range. Nothing matters now, my thirst for death will never be satiated. I want death and destruction. I want to bathe in their blood and tear their evil bodies apart with my bare hands. Darren is in there somewhere; I fight harder, for every step I take brings me closer to him. I told him to come after me, I told him to see what happens if he tried. Now he's here but he's hiding from me. I want him, more than anything I want him. He is the evil; he is the devil spawn that brought this plague to my people. He is the reason we have all suffered. *I am Death, Darren, I am Death and I am coming for you. I told you I would destroy you and I will.*

I fight and kill as I push on deeper and deeper into their ranks. I am the spearhead that drives through these ranks and my men fight with me. This isn't enough though; the power of the anger and rage is not enough. I want more, give me more. Give me all the fury of the world and channel it into my arms so I can fight on. Why isn't it enough? Why am I not strong enough to surge forward and sweep these things away? Frustration mixes in with the already powerful feelings pulsing through me and, for a few minutes, I have extra strength and more speed. I fight away from my circle; I plough deep into their lines. I hear Clarence and Chris shouting my name but I pay no heed. They are together and protected and I am already dead. I made that deal with myself when I came out here. I knew I would be coming to my death and I will do it on my own terms. I will not expose my friends to my reckless actions, but reckless as they are, they are my actions that I choose to take, and I take them willingly. I fight on and push harder, sweeping my beloved axe around and around, cleaving and hacking and killing. They cannot touch me, for the anger and fury is so great within me, but no, it isn't enough, and I feel my power abating. It ebbs away and I drive myself on, pushing myself and forcing the rage out. I can't see my men now, I'm too deep within their lines, but I keep going, for as long as this power is within me, I can kill them. My killing blows start to ease off, the power generated by each swing is less and less. I swing out and tears of frustration sting my eyes. I feel my power leaving me and there are so many crowding around me. I lash out again and stumble as my legs start to shake. I roar out but my voice feels weak. I lift the axe and smash a face in, but the power is so much weaker now. My men. I can see them, through my tear-filled eyes I see them fighting, but their power is weakening too. We are trapped with the evil undead crowding around us; my legs feel so heavy, and each step finds me faltering and staggering. I look over to my men and see their circle starting to give. Tucker swings out, his normally ruddy face now pale and drawn. He too can feel the power leaving, and I see his swings getting more and more feeble. I scream as they lunge forward and take him down, they drag Tucker to the floor and the undead bodies are on him, frenziedly biting and tearing at his flesh. I scream out loud, my beloved Tucker, that gentle lad who took care of us. I stumble forward and feel my legs give way; I go down onto my knees and stretch my hand out, so far away from Tucker but I can't help him. Curtis rushes to his side, beating the undead back and hacking away desperately, trying to save his friend. I try to shout a warning as I see zombies rushing Curtis from behind, but my voice is pathetic, weak, and dying.

Curtis is taken down, his body landing heavily in top of Tucker as they are both ravaged and killed. Malcolm twists back to run at the boys and is taken from the side, going down heavy and swamped by zombie bodies tearing into him.

Chris screams and fights back; they all give ground and the circle gets smaller, the zombies pressing in.

Pure looks of terror on Blowers' and Cookey's faces, Nick crying with shame, as he knows they will die. Not like this, please God, not like this. Don't let them take anymore. We were meant to win, we are the righteous and we came so far. These are just boys, brave boys that have fought and you are letting the evil take my beautiful, brave boys. I lash out with my fist and punch an undead's face; he drops away, and I know I'm only seconds away now.

I feel drained and weak and there's nothing left inside of me. Nothing left to use.

'Why did you do this to me?'

'I told you I would destroy you, Howie – I warned you.'

'You have to help me, you have to give me more anger and rage so I can fight.'

'There's nothing left, Howie, you've used it all up and it's left you weak and pathetic.'

'Oh God, dear God, please Lord give me the strength to do this, give me the strength to rise up and fight.'

'You wanted anger, Howie, you wanted rage and fury and power.'

'Then give me more.'

'It's gone, Howie, there is no more to give.'

With my head bowed I wait for them to take me.

'Our Father, who art in Heaven,' the words come to me and, in final prayer, I hold an image of Sarah in my mind.

'There it is, Howie.'

'What? There is what?'

'You fool, Howie, it's right there inside you. Take it.'

'Take what?'

'Sarah, that feeling for your family. What is that?'

'She's all I have left, she's my family.'

'What does she mean to you, Howie? What did you feel then when you thought of her and said those words, what was that?'

'That was love.'

'YES, HOWIE, that was love.'

'Our Father who art in Heaven ...'

'YES HOWIE, LOUDER, SAY IT LOUDER.'

'OUR FATHER WHO ART IN HEAVEN.' I feel something surging through me, a feeling starting so deep and coursing through my system.

'YES, HOWIE, LOVE IS THE MOST POWERFUL THING OF ALL.'

'OUR FATHER WHO ART IN HEAVEN ...' My voice, starting off weak and choked, quickly becomes strong and firm. I look up into the faces of the undead coming at me, teeth bared for the kill.

'OUR FATHER WHO ART IN HEAVEN.' I rise to my feet, the axe held in one hand. I stare about at the advancing faces as my voice booms out with strength. The men look to me and I hold their gaze, daring the undead to keep coming.

'HALLOWED BE THY NAME.' I feel it. I feel power unlike any before, surging through me. My heart beats faster and faster.

My mind is clear and the strength flows back into my arms and legs.

'THY KINGDOM COME, THY WILL BE DONE.' They are close now, so close. I can feel their breath upon my face. I stare ahead, eyes fixed on my men. The undead want me, I can sense it, but something holds them back, something makes them weary. The whole field pauses for that second, waiting with bated breath. Faces filled with fear and terror slowly become filled with hope.

'ON EARTH AS IT IS IN HEAVEN,' I roar, and my voice carries far as I explode with action and I am no longer weak and exhausted. I am strong, I have strength, and I whirl my axe around and take many down with one massive swing. My axe flies and spins as I chop down, chop left, chop right, and they keep dropping. Every step I take they wilt away from me. I slice and hack my way through to my men.

'GIVE US THIS DAY OUR DAILY BREAD,' I swing out and send two undead back to the hell from whence they came. The love flows through me with absolution, and each blow is precise, brutal, violent, but necessary. I no longer want them to suffer agonising pain. I want them stopped. To kill them swiftly and end this suffering.

'AND FORGIVE US OUR TRESPASSES,' I burst through the last line of undead that stood between me and my men. Chris and Clarence step aside and leave a gap for me to take up. I step in and hear as they take up voice with me, Blowers, Cookey, and Nick joining in, and our voices are strong.

'AS WE FORGIVE THOSE WHO TRESPASS AGAINST US.' Our combined voices carry and I hear more joining in. Men and women behind us, holding the line, raise their glorious voices and join as we pray loud – and with fresh hope we fight on.

'AND LEAD US NOT INTO TEMPTATION.' For McKinney we fight on and take them down, new strength flows into us. For the blessed love of Tucker, Curtis, and Malcolm, we fight and stand our ground.

'BUT DELIVER US FROM EVIL.' Our words taunt them. The

undead roar with defiance and attack with ferocity, snarling and growling, but we hold them back and cut them down – and they fall.

'FOR THINE IS THE KINGDOM.' They surge on against us and they fall as we cut them down. Thousands of voices cry out in exalted prayer as thousands of hands wield weapons and cut down thousands of zombies. The living are taken time and time again, but instead of despair we fight as humans have never fought before. This is not just about survival now; this is good versus evil. This is right versus wrong.

'AND THE POWER.' Our voices cry louder, carrying all across the battlefield. Little did we know the strength these words would carry and how they could combine our strength and resolution when we learnt them at school.

'AND THE GLORY.' Still we fight on, and the tide is turning; they know it because they attack with more violence and surge into us again and again.

'FOR EVER AND EVER,' we scream out in unison, us the living – shouting our defiance with glorious words of scripture against the vile foul things that try to kill us.

'A ... G ... A ... I ... N,' I hear Dave's voice roar out from somewhere deep within the ranks. I look to the direction and, as one, we turn and fight towards him, as we once more lift our voices and repeat the Lord's Prayer.

Dave battles through rank after rank of undead, his body twisting and flexing with incredible speed. The knives started off bright and metallic, flashing as they rip through the air to be tugged against throat after throat. He drops down and severs hamstrings, pausing for a second until the body drops down and then he digs into the jugular with a short, sharp stab. Pulling away, he leaps up to avoid the mouths lunging forward, arms ready and in position as he plummets back into the rank of filthy zombies.

Gallons of blood spill as artery after artery is opened. Mouth after mouth lunges at him, but he steps away with amazing grace. He kills without slowing and the more he does, the faster he gets. The muscles warm up and his heart increases the flow of oxygen and blood, causing him to shift a physical gear and generate more incredible speed and power. Then something is wrong, a shift in the equilibrium within his mind. He was powering forward, intent on finding Darren and destroying him quickly.

Something changes; his connection with Howie makes him pause and turn back. Dave fights with a ferocity that he has never shown before, his arms twirling and spinning, his body dropping and leaning as he searches through the gaps for a glimpse of Howie and the others. The sense of change is palpable and he knows something bad is happening, Howie is threatened and Dave curses himself for moving into the ranks too deeply.

With a low growl and a look of pure violence, he powers through zombie after zombie, killing and maiming, desperately fighting back towards his friend. The undead in front of him become dense, as though they are drawn to something. They block his view and he leaps high to catch a glimpse of Howie faltering and stumbling, his axe swings slow and weak. He pushes on with fear in his heart, his deadly blades becoming dull edged from repeated use. He discards them both and uses his arms to grab at zombie neck after zombie neck, twisting with a violent wrench to snap the spinal column. Dave catches another glimpse of Howie dropping down onto his knees and listens as Howie screams out. Dave twists around to see Tucker dead and Curtis being savaged.

The undead seem to know Dave is fighting to rescue Howie, and they push into him, blocking his path with body after body. In desperation, Dave draws the last set of knives tucked into his belt line and sets to work, slicing jugulars open with frenzied action. Then he hears it, Howie's voice, weak at first but then strong, and it carries across to him.

The Lord's Prayer is being bellowed out and Dave catches

another glimpse of Howie up on his feet, standing ready, his eyes blazing as the whole world seems to pause.

Dave's heart thrills as he watches Howie explode with power and his voice cries out, loud and true. As more voices take up the prayer, Dave pauses and quickly tries to decide which way. *Back to Howie? Or keep going for Darren?*

Darren has to be stopped; if he is controlling this lot then taking him down could end this far sooner. With an almost reluctant shrug, he once more turns and starts fighting deeper into the ranks. He listens to the words of the Lord's Prayer booming out in unison. He senses the change in the zombies and watches as they surge faster and quicker. The reaction causes the undead to become more fierce, but Dave notices something else – something that only someone with hundreds of hand-to-hand combat battles would pick up on: the harder they attack, the weaker they become.

Something is changing; they are attacking harder than ever before, but it feels easier to drop them now. Blows to the head and neck have always cut them down instantly, but body blows are also dropping them now. Deep cuts that would easily down a man, but would not affect the undead too greatly, are now causing them to fall. We should be getting beaten back now from the ferocity of their attack, but instead, we are not only holding our own – we are gaining ground. They growl and snarl and roar as they attack, driving into us time and again. They are being pushed; something is pushing them harder. They can sense the change in us. We were almost beaten, we were almost stopped, and they had the taste of flesh by taking Tucker, Curtis, and Malcolm. But now, now we rise up and fight so hard that they feel desperate and attack harder and faster. Whatever the thing is inside them, it cannot sustain their rate of energy expenditure for this long, it's simply too much for their decaying and already dead bodies.

'DAVE?' I bellow out between axe strikes, desperate to find him.

'HERE.' I hear his enormous voice, he is close now and we push on harder, swinging our axes and cutting down many undead as we plough through them trying to reach Dave.

Dave feels them weakening with each blow. Whereas he focussed on the neck and head for each killing move before, now he senses their weakening state and he takes the risk to use the knives as stabbing tools. He thrusts the blades into the chest cavities; it works, and they start dropping from stabbing thrusts that before would have had no effect. Now he works faster; no longer impeded by the necessity to angle himself to take the throat, he stabs out with increasing speed, puncturing chest after chest. His blows rain out until his arms are just a blur, each arm seemingly working independently, pistons driving the sharpened points of the knives into the soft, decaying flesh. They fall away from him in vast numbers. Each step he takes, he kills and kills.

'DARREN,' Dave's parade ground voice bellows out as he plunges into the horde. They close ranks and try to present a solid mass against him.

'I'M COMING DARREN, I AM COMING TO KILL YOU,' Dave roars out, as his arms spin and drive the knives deep into the chests and throats, puncturing lungs, hearts, and brains with each deadly thrust. As the last two drop down, Dave pauses.

He sees open ground in front of him, and another solid mass of undead ahead. Howie bursts through the undead lines to his left as his men cut down the final rows of zombies until they too, stand before the open ground and look to the solid mass of undead standing before them.

I hear Dave screaming for Darren and I know we must be close. We drive on, attacking and attacking, ploughing through them until we burst through their lines and I see open ground ahead of me. A quick glance and I see Dave stood to my right, holding his knives and staring at the solid massed horde. There, right in the middle, stands Darren. He has surrounded himself with the biggest and strongest undead. I can see they have been held back. The battle still rages behind us, the people from the Fort still reciting the Lord's Prayer, but they feel distant now. For here, in front of us, is the leader of the undead army.

'Dave,' I shout over, to alert him we are here.

'I see you Mr. Howie,' Dave replies.

The men behind me cut down the final few undead and then spread out into a line, facing the horde protecting Darren. We stand with chests heaving, dripping blood and gore from every inch of our bodies. Our faces are smeared with filth but we live, we breathe air, and our hearts pump living blood through our veins. I lock eyes with Darren Smith; he stands in the middle of his undead bodyguard, and he looks terrible, pale and drawn with a sickening pallor. Red, bloodshot eyes stare back at me. His brow drops, and the feeling of hatred he projects at me is tangible. My mind races with what to say – a smart comment, something witty and inspiring. This is not the time for words though, all that needed to be said, has been. The corner of my upper lip curls up and I feel a growl growing in my throat. My whole body pulses with energy. Living energy. I feel more alive in this second than all of the seconds in my life combined. That, I know, must be driving him crazy. His face twitches, and his whole body twitches. Whether this is from the utter rage within him, or the side effects of the filthy infection in his system, I do know not. They outnumber us, and they are big, mean-looking zombies. Every one of them stands motionless, staring back at us. Darren's gaze shifts to Dave and he stands, staring at the small man holding a knife in each hand, the blades turned up against his forearms. Several of the undead bodyguard suddenly detach themselves and move away towards Dave. They stop and reach their arms around to pull knives out. Each of them holds a deadly-looking blade. I count eight big nasty-looking zombies holding knives.

'Take him,' Darren growls softly, and they start moving towards Dave.

I turn towards him but Dave holds a hand up to stop me, his eyes never leaving the pack of knife-wielding zombies coming towards him.

I watch closely as Dave stands stock-still. He adjusts his position slowly. One foot moves back and he lowers his body a few inches. His left arm comes forward and he holds it across his chest. The right arm pulls back slightly. Then he does something that Dave rarely does, he smiles. A small wry smile that grows into a big grin that lights his face up. His eyes blaze.

'At last ... some decent competition,' Dave mutters quietly. The knife-carrying zombies spread out to form a rough circle around him. Dave, in turn, remains motionless, apart from his eyes shifting left and right and picking up their positions.

'TAKE HIM,' Darren spits the words out and they rush in as one.

Movement catches my eye off to my left, and I glimpse Jamie moving around to try and get behind the horde in front of us. Dave holds his static position until I fear he is just going to wait to be cut down. Then, at the very last second, he takes two steps and leaps high over the undead man in front of him, twisting his body so that he lands facing the undead man's back. The zombies rushing in all collide as their momentum drives them into each other.

Dave shakes his head once and stabs his knives forward into the zombie's neck, sawing viciously, and the first one goes down. Dave steps back as they recover and rush at him. After that, it's just a blur of arms spinning and twirling. I hear the clang of metal against metal a few times. Grunts and growls sound out as Dave punishes them without mercy. He is in the middle somewhere, and I know he is still alive, as every few seconds a knife-wielding zombie staggers away to fall to the ground with blood spurting out of his opened jugular.

'GO,' Dave roars out from the middle of his knife fight. The order clearly is intended for us and we respond instantly. Gripping our weapons tight, we charge forward.

'TAKE THEM,' Darren screams out and his bodyguard burst towards us.

The vain wanker should have given them weapons too – his belief that firstly, we'd never get this close to him, and secondly, that Dave was the only one that posed a threat to him – well, his vanity, or the vanity of whatever it is inside him will be his undoing. These undead coming at us are big, strong, and full of rage. A guttural roar sounds out and I see a long-handled, double-bladed weapon spinning through the air. It embeds deep in the chest of a zombie and he goes flying backwards. Clarence, still roaring, sprints ahead, his hands now empty, and, like Dave, he now has some fair competition so chooses to fight on equal terms.

'Fuck that,' I mutter as I charge in, gripping my axe tighter, in case I get a sudden urge to throw it at someone.

Clarence powers into them, his massive arms punching out left and right, his elbows flying back to smash the noses and cheekbones of undead zombies that are trying to bite him. He picks a zombie up bodily and throws it hard at two more coming at him. I snap forward and swing my axe out hard, biting into the neck of one running at me. His momentum drives me backwards and I fall to the floor as he staggers past me, my axe stuck in his neck. I jump up and clamber towards him, desperate to retrieve my weapon. Strong hands grip me and I get flung like a rag doll through the air, landing several metres away. The zombie that threw me comes on, his teeth bared and growling like a dog. I scamper backwards and get to my feet.

'Fuck it,' I growl back at him and charge.

We collide, but I scrabble around and jump onto his massive back, wrapping my arms round his thick neck and squeezing with every ounce of my strength. He staggers about, his arms flailing, but his sheer size prevents him from being able to reach around and pull me off. He slumps down onto his knees and throws himself backwards, trying to squash me under his enormous weight. I squeeze and squeeze with everything I've got, as I feel my breath being crushed out of me. My hand is across his face and I move it up slightly to avoid his gnashing teeth. I feel the soft pressure of an eye socket and drive my thumb in hard.

He squirms and howls as I drive my thumb in, pushing against the resistance of the pressured eyeball. It pops and I feel warm, sticky goo spurting out over my hand. I increase the pressure with my arms and hold on for dear life until eventually he goes limp. I push him off and wriggle out, running back to grab my axe. I wrench it free from the neck it's stuck in and run back to the fat nonce that tried to squash me. I lift the axe high over my head and drive it down into his skull, bursting it apart, and the dirty grey matter explodes out over the blood-soaked ground. I spin around and swing the axe into the next one coming at me, stepping to the side so I don't get mown down again. I cut deep into his shoulder and he goes down onto the ground. I pull the axe back and chop down at his still-moving body, taking his head off.

Another one coming from my right ... I grab a fistful of hair and lift the decapitated head and throw it hard. It hits the oncoming zombie square in the face, and I almost chuckle at the thought of the head-butt. It stalls him for just a second, but it's enough for me to step around and slice the axe into his leg, cutting through to the bone. He goes down and again I chop down viciously, taking his head off. I hear a scream and spin round to see Jamie launching himself at several undead still standing with Darren.

His knives do deadly work and drop several, but his skill isn't the same as Dave's, and suddenly he's gripped by an undead on either side. Jamie thrashes and kicks out but, like Dave, he is small and his blows go unnoticed.

Darren runs over and drives a knife deep into Jamie's stomach.

Jamie screams and thrashes.

Darren goes around behind him.

I roar out and start running, but Darren smiles at me as he pulls Jamie's head back and sinks his teeth deep into Jamie's neck. All of us see it: me, Dave, Blowers, Cookey, Nick, Chris, and Clarence, and we scream out and charge forward.

Darren laughs and steps away. The remainder of his bodyguard charge at us, as Darren turns to sprint. The bodyguards throw themselves at us with ferocious attacks, and it takes several minutes to finish them off. By which time, there is no sign of Darren. I look over and see Dave running to the limp form of Jamie. Gasping for breath, I rush over and slump down. Dave rolls Jamie onto his back, and I see the ragged wound in his neck, blood pumping out. Jamie is still alive, albeit barely. The rest join us, shouting to each other and asking where Darren went. One by one, they drop down and we form a kneeling circle round Jamie; each of us reach forward and place a hand on his body. Jamie grips Dave's hand as Dave stares down with an intense look. I reach up and push Jamie's hair away from his eyes. He looks at me and smiles – the young, quiet lad who followed Dave with heroic worship.

'Did you get him?' Jamie whispers at me.

'We will Jamie, I swear it, we will,' I whisper back.

Jamie looks at his hero, and I see tears falling down Dave's cheeks.

'Don't cry, Dave,' Jamie whispers, his breathing becoming shallower.

Dave leans down and places a hand on Jamie's forehead.

'You did good Jamie, very good. I'm proud of you,' Dave says in a voice so soft.

Jamie smiles once at Dave, his face lighting up with the praise from the man he worshipped. Then he's gone; the life drains from his eyes, and his face falls slack. Hot tears fall down my cheeks as I watch Dave gently reach out and close Jamie's eyes. I reach my hand out to Dave's shoulder, knowing what must be done. Dave looks at me and nods.

Chris's hand covers mine, and I hear him speak softly:

'He was one of yours, I'll do it.'

Dave and I lock eyes for a second; we both bow our heads.

'Bye, Jamie mate, see you on the other side,' I whisper, and move away.

Blowers and Cookey drop down and I hear them whisper their goodbyes.

Nick goes next, until Dave is left holding Jamie's hand. Then gently, so gently, Dave reaches down and softly kisses Jamie on the forehead.

A sob breaks out from Cookey and I see him drop down onto his knees. Blowers reaches a hand down to Cookey's shoulder and I move over to them. Nick stares back, for a second, before Dave joins us. We turn away as Chris does what needs to be done.

Without Darren, the dead army slow and become the normal daytime shuffling zombies. What's left of the men from the Fort make light work and, before long, the ground is filled with thousands and thousands of zombie bodies.

I look down towards the Fort and realise we have lost many during the battle. Of the several thousand that charged out of the gates, maybe a thousand remain. The losses are huge, but we knew what we faced and we did so as free men. Standing here now, in the midst of the carnage, I think back to the losses that we, as a group, have suffered: McKinney, Tucker, Curtis, and Jamie. Each of them so unique and so brave. Young men who survived something so truly terrible yet they laughed and joked and made that decision to fight back. I look over at Chris, Clarence standing by his side, just the way Dave is always at my side, and he too must be thinking of the people he has lost, and I know losing Malcolm will be hitting him hard.

For all our losses though, we have gained something special. Those brave men that laid their lives down did so knowing they were giving humanity another chance. For that, I am thankful. Darren has escaped, but I already know from the looks in the eyes of my men that we won't stop until we find him. Now though, there is much to do. Bodies need to be burnt, injuries need to be tended. We need to find the children and their mothers and bring them back to the safety of the Fort.

Most of all though, we can do something we have needed to do since this war began.

We can grieve.

ALSO BY RR HAYWOOD

EXTRACTED SERIES

EXTRACTED

EXECUTED

EXTINCT

International best-selling time-travel

#1 Amazon US

#1 Amazon UK

#1 Audible US & UK

Top 3 Amazon Australia

Washington Post Best-seller

In 2061, a young scientist invents a time machine to fix a tragedy in his past. But his good intentions turn catastrophic when an early test reveals something unexpected: the end of the world.

A desperate plan is formed. Recruit three heroes, ordinary humans capable of extraordinary things, and change the future.

Safa Patel is an elite police officer, on duty when Downing Street comes under terrorist attack. As armed men storm through the breach, she dispatches them all.

'Mad' Harry Madden is a legend of the Second World War.

Not only did he complete an impossible mission—to plant charges on a heavily defended submarine base—but he also escaped with his life.

Ben Ryder is just an insurance investigator. But as a young man he witnessed a gang assaulting a woman and her child. He went to their rescue, and killed all five.

Can these three heroes, extracted from their timelines at the point of death, save the world?

16159181R00140

Printed in Great Britain
by Amazon